TIMELESS
WESTERN
COLLECTION

Mercer's Belles

TIMELESS
WESTERN
COLLECTION

Mercer's Belles

HEATHER B. MOORE
TERI HARMAN
LINDA CARROLL-BRADD

Mirror Press

Copyright © 2019 Mirror Press
Print edition
All rights reserved

No part of this book may be reproduced in any form whatsoever without prior written permission of the publisher, except in the case of brief passages embodied in critical reviews and articles. These novels are works of fiction. The characters, names, incidents, places, and dialog are products of the authors' imaginations and are not to be construed as real.

Interior Design by Cora Johnson
Edited by Kristy Stewart and Lisa Shepherd
Cover design by Rachael Anderson
Cover Photo Credit:
Cover models: Period Images
Background with ship: Deposit Photos #33071381 by Elen Studio

Mercer's Belles is a Timeless Romance Anthology® book
Timeless Romance Anthology® is a registered trademark of Mirror Press, LLC
ISBN: 978-1-947152-70-0

Timeless Western Collections
Calico Ball
Big Sky
Mercer's Belles

Enjoy our Timeless Regency Collections
Autumn Masquerade
A Midwinter Ball
Spring in Hyde Park
Summer House Party
A Country Christmas
A Season in London
A Holiday in Bath
A Night in Grosvenor Square
Road to Gretna Green
Wedding Wagers
An Evening at Almack's
A Week in Brighton
To Love a Governess

And our Timeless Victorian Collections
Summer Holiday
A Grand Tour
The Orient Express
The Queen's Ball

INTRODUCTION TO MERCER'S BELLES

The first story in this collection, *One Dance* by Heather B. Moore, is based on the first voyage from the east coast to Seattle in which Mr. Asa Shinn Mercer, entrepreneur and former university president, guided eleven women in 1864. Two years later, he transported a larger group of single women and widows. The second two stories, *A Journey to Love* by Teri Harman and *A Faraway Life* by Linda Carroll-Bradd, are set during the second voyage. Mercer's stated purpose in convincing women to leave behind friends and family and travel to the Washington Territory was two-fold: for them to teach school and help populate the area with single women, with the goal of potential marriages. These voyages were quite controversial, received a lot of interesting press coverage, and included some wild and amazing events. Yet, many women from these voyages went on to play an important role in the society and history of what would become Washington State.

TABLE OF CONTENTS

One Dance 1
BY HEATHER B. MOORE

A Journey to Love 99
BY TERI HARMAN

A Faraway Life by 197
LINDA CARROLL-BRADD

TIMELESS WESTERN COLLECTION

One Dance

HEATHER B. MOORE

1864

"Harriet, you must come at once," Vivian said.

Harriet Silverton could barely move, let alone come *at once*. Since departing San Francisco, she'd been feeling rather ill. The fresh air didn't help, and lying down only made her feel more queasy. There was nothing Harriet could pinpoint her illness on. She'd been on the *S. S. Illinois* from New York to San Francisco, since boarding out of New York on March 14.

Nearly two months ago. And she'd been healthy.

"You're going to miss it," Vivian said.

Harriet rose from the rough-hewn deck chair, then made her way to where Vivian was leaning a bit too far over the railing of the *Torrant, the sailing vessel they were now on to make the final leg of the journey to Seattle. Because of a delay in the Panama Canal, they'd missed their steamer connection at San Francisco. So Mr. Mercer had booked this smaller lumber bark that was on its way to Puget Sound in the Washington Territory.*

"There," Vivian said, pointing with a proud finger.

1

Harriet leaned over the rail, tamping down the increased nausea, and peered into the dark, churning water below.

"Do you see it?" Vivian asked.

At first, Harriet only saw the endless water that she'd been seeing for weeks now. And then . . . a dorsal fin crested from one of the waves. She gasped. "A dolphin!"

"Yes," Vivian said in a triumphant voice. "Mr. Mercer told us we might see dolphins, but you were skeptical."

Harriet wasn't listening. She was utterly fascinated with the creature moving in and out of the water. The dark tumult of the water must be freezing. It was a true wonder of nature anything could actually live in the ocean. Beneath all that cold water.

The dolphin seemed to be following their vessel.

"What is it doing?" Harriet asked.

"I don't know," Vivian said. "I'm going to fetch the others. They'll be fascinated."

It wasn't long before they were surrounded by other spectators, exclaiming over the single dolphin. Harriet glanced over at Mr. Mercer, who was explaining in detail about the patterns and habits of sea life. He really was an impressive man, full of knowledge on all sorts of topics.

When Harriet had read an article about Mr. Mercer in the newspaper back home in Philadelphia, she'd been immediately intrigued. The wild West was no longer wild but in desperate need of teachers for its schoolhouses. Another sentence in the article had caught her attention: "The West, especially Seattle, is filled with young, hardworking men who are on the brink of settling down and starting families."

Mercer had made no secret of the fact that he was interested in aiding the young women joining the voyage in finding a suitable husband in Seattle. But, he'd also given the caveat that the women were perfectly free to determine their own future. This opportunity was not one of the mail-order bride ventures.

Harriet was twenty-six, past the typical age for marrying, and all of her friends had done just that. Married with babies, some with more than one. It didn't bother Harriet, not really. There were plenty of women who married later in life. Not that she knew any, but she'd read many books of older heroines... though she couldn't remember a single one at the moment.

The crowd that had gathered to watch the dolphin was now exclaiming about something else. Harriet looked toward the shoreline they'd been skimming for several hours. "We'll stop over in Teekalet," Mr. Mercer said to the women. "Then tomorrow we'll arrive in Seattle."

A place to settle down at last, and it couldn't be a moment too soon for Harriet. She would not miss a thing about Philadelphia. Not the dances, where only the men over fifty asked her to dance, not Mrs. Raphael, who asked her every time she came into the bakery if she was engaged yet. Not her twin brother Harry, who spent more time drinking than working nowadays.

Yes, the deaths of their parents five years ago had been impossibly hard. But Harry had inherited the house and property and their father's accounting business. She had inherited dependency. And she was tired of being dependent. She wanted to make her own way in the world, live her own life, make her own decisions.

They were nearly to the harbor now, and the women of the Mercer's Belles group had all left to finish packing their belongings.

Harriet was already packed, so she remained on deck, watching the bustle of the approaching harbor. Dock workers milled about, and several of them were unloading carts behind impatient horses. When the vessel docked, Harriet joined the others and walked down the gang plank.

A couple of men were at the end of the plank, giving a gentlemanly hand to the ladies stepping onto land. A nice gesture, especially since the women's skirts were long and heavy. Harriet took her turn behind Vivian, who was prattling on about something or other. It was hard to keep up with the woman's conversation.

The seagulls soared in the air about them, their screeches an odd, welcoming cadence. A child started to cry ahead of her. One of the passengers. He'd dropped the red ball he always carried around on deck, and now it bounced on the gangplank right before Harriet.

If it weren't for her long skirts and rather fitted shirtwaist, she might have been able to bend more gracefully and snatch the ball before it fell into the water. But that wasn't the case, and as Harriet attempted to rescue the ball, she missed.

And lost her balance.

Then fell.

Into the cold, dark water.

Two

IT WASN'T EVERY day that Caleb Munns saw a woman topple off a gangplank and land face first in the Pacific Ocean. Truth be told, he'd never witnessed such a sight. If he'd had time to analyze it all, the passengers disembarking from the sea vessel, walking the gangplank toward shore, the rather round boy dropping a red ball, the ball bouncing once, twice, then a third time precariously on the edge of the gangplank, the boy's displeased cry, the woman behind him reaching for the ball, tumbling toward the ocean . . .

Caleb had never taken off his thick fishing coat so fast in his life. There was no time to worry about his heavy boots or anything else on his person. His hat flew off when he jumped. He would miss that hat.

But a woman needed saving.

And fortunately, or unfortunately, Caleb had never been good about stopping his impulses. Which was why he now found himself swimming through fiercely cold water toward a very water-logged woman with the bluest eyes he'd ever seen.

She couldn't swim, that was quite obvious by the widened panic in her eyes and the way that her mouth gaped like a fish.

Although Caleb rather liked fish, now wasn't the time to notice physical features. The woman was making a valiant effort to stay afloat with her frantic splashing, but that wouldn't last long.

Even in May, the Pacific was cold enough to turn an innocent situation into a deadly one quickly.

"Ma'am," he said as he reached her and grasped one of her arms.

She was looking right at him but didn't seem to see him.

"I've got you," he said. "You can stop thrashing now."

But she pushed him away, likely in a panic. And Caleb would be darned if he was going to leave her here to drown. Besides, no one else had deigned to jump in, so it was up to him.

He hauled her toward him a bit roughly. "Hold onto my shoulders," he ordered.

She gasped, then choked on some water. Coughing, she pushed him away again.

"Come on, woman," he growled. "You're going to drown us both."

These words seemed to register with her, and she suddenly threw her arms around him, grabbing for his head.

He nearly went under. "Not like that," he sputtered, peeling her hands from his head. He turned her so that her back was toward him, then he wrapped his arm about her torso. "Lie back and relax. I'll pull us in. All you have to do is keep your chin up."

But she wasn't relaxing in the least. She was still kicking and gasping. Her elbow jabbed him in the gut.

"You infernal woman, pretend like you are dead," he said. "Don't move. I will pull you, do you hear?"

Inch by inch, she gave in, and by the time she did, his lungs were screaming with exhaustion. He couldn't feel his feet, and his legs were heavier than an ox.

But they were making progress. He swam on his back, clutching her against him, as he propelled them toward the dock. "This would have been much easier if you'd been unconscious." Perhaps it was the wrong thing to say, but holding his tongue was not one of his strong suits.

She didn't reply, not that he expected her to.

Plenty of men who hadn't wanted to get wet extended helping hands as he reached the dock. Within moments, Caleb and the woman had both been hauled onto the wood planks, and while Caleb spat out a mouthful of sea water, the woman was surrounded by a gaggle of other females.

They seemed to know each other—likely had all been on the boat together. It was just as well. She'd be taken care of.

Caleb didn't stand quite yet, because he needed to catch his breath. He was soaked through, freezing, and a bit pleased with himself. Although he'd not heard one word of thanks, he'd write that off to the woman's shock at nearly drowning. What had possessed her to go after a crummy child's ball while standing on a gangplank was beyond his understanding.

He scrubbed at his face, then shook the water droplets from his rather long hair. It had been months since he'd seen a barber, and that would be the first order of business once he reached Seattle. He'd spent a few weeks in Teekalet, helping a fishing franchise get off the ground. They'd paid him handsomely, and now he was on his way back to Seattle to his own little fishing outfit.

His gaze sought out the woman, but she was still being fretted over by her posse of females. Her hair was dark, her limbs slender, her cheeks red with cold, and her eyes . . . Yes. Still blue. Like the sky in Montana. A home he missed, but one he could not return to. Not if he valued his dignity.

Through the throng of pant legs and skirts, their gazes connected briefly before another woman moved between them.

Someone clapped a hand on his shoulder. "I must thank you, sir. On behalf of my entire company, you have our deepest gratitude."

Caleb turned and looked into the gaze of a distinguished gentleman. The sort who never got his hands dirty on a fishing boat. He wore a fine suit and well-placed hat. When he extended a hand, Caleb took it and stood.

"Your *company*?" Caleb asked.

The man smiled. "I'm Mr. Mercer, and I'm leading the charge of bringing education to the West. Seattle, specifically."

Still, Caleb didn't understand.

Plainly, this Mr. Mercer had encountered this type of confusion before. "Schoolteachers," he said, leaning a bit closer. "Each of these women is bound for a teaching position, either at a school or a private residence."

Caleb glanced over at the women, who'd now ushered the half-drowned one some distance away where their stacked trunks sat.

"And . . . they are all single, of course." Mr. Mercer leaned close and lowered his voice. "They are open to marriage prospects as well."

Caleb frowned. "You mean . . . they're coming to Washington Territory looking for husbands?" From his viewpoint, the women appeared to be nicely dressed, and if they were schoolteachers, they obviously were well educated. What were women like these doing in a place like this?

Mr. Mercer rocked back on his heels. "What about you, sir? Are you in need of a wife?"

Caleb snapped an incredulous gaze to Mr. Mercer. Was he propositioning him . . . offering up one of these traveling ladies to the first man he spoke to?

"Perhaps you'd be interested in Miss Silverton for yourself," Mr. Mercer said, a gleam in his eye. "You did rescue her. Lady in distress, and all that. Or we have Miss Cheney or Miss Gallagar. I could point them out to you if you'd like to be more discreet. Or I could invite a few over to meet you."

Caleb rubbed the back of his neck that was suddenly too hot. He was speechless. Well, not completely, because he had no trouble responding. "I'm afraid you have the wrong man, Mr. Mercer. With all due respect, I don't think a woman should ever be paraded in front of a man. And, I'll not marry again. Not ever."

Three

HARRIET COULD FEEL his gaze on her, and when she couldn't stand it a moment longer, she turned to confront him. But there was no one at the rail on the sloop they now traveled on called *Kidder*.

She spun to search for him. Where had he gone?

Perhaps the dip into the cold Pacific the day before had rattled her brain, and now she was imagining things. Like tall, copper-haired men with deep brown eyes following her around the deck of the boat. She'd seen him board today, but she hadn't spoken to him. And she should have. At least to thank him for saving her life.

Instead, she'd let the opportunity pass. The sun had already set, and the vast sky was a mixture of purples and deep blues.

She should find him before they reached Seattle.

Her pulse raced at the thought. Why, she didn't know. Just because he was a bit wild looking. Just because he'd effortlessly rescued her from a horrible fate. Just because he looked like he could defeat a grizzly bear with one blow. He was a man, that was all. She could do this.

She inhaled. Exhaled. Shored up her resolve and set off to find him. He couldn't have gone far.

She turned and ran straight into a post. Where one shouldn't be.

Strong hands reached out to steady her, because, yes, she nearly fell over.

"Easy there."

She'd heard his voice before, of course, but the deepness of it rumbled through her. Making her feel . . .

Looking up into his brown eyes, she saw that there was a bit of green in them too. "So very sorry," she managed to say.

"It happens," he said. "I wasn't exactly looking where I was going either." He wasn't smiling, but there was a bit of lightness to his tone.

Her heart skipped a beat. "I mean, I'm sorry about . . . yesterday," she said. "I didn't mean to fall into the water, and then you jumped in too. And got all wet."

He folded his arms.

She looked away from the gesture, away from the corded muscles in his forearms. Shouldn't he be wearing a coat or a jacket, or something, out here? The wind was rather brisk. And his windblown hair reached the top of his shoulders. She'd never been much for the wild type, but on this man, it seemed to fit.

"Did you fall into the ocean on purpose?" he asked.

Had his lips quirked?

"No, of course not."

"Then why are you apologizing?"

This question brought her up short. "Because . . . I inconvenienced you. And I didn't exactly make it easy for you to rescue me. I think I hit you more than once, possibly kicked you at least a dozen times."

He looked at her for a long moment. Had she annoyed him even more?

"If saving a drowning woman is an inconvenience," he said in a slow tone, "then I need to get my head checked."

Harriet stepped back, because she was standing much too close to him. "Well, I'm sorry all the same, and I'm grateful that you . . ." She waved a hand toward him. "Sacrificed your person to save me. I mean, you could have drowned."

Now he was smiling.

Her heart skipped two beats.

"I wasn't going to drown," he said matter-of-factly.

"But you said that I was about to drown us both," she said, heat rising in her neck.

"Not possible," he said, his lips twitching again. "I might have been overdramatic."

She stared at him.

"I mean," he started out slow. "I practically live on the sea. Swimming a dozen yards in the harbor water isn't all that treacherous, unless one doesn't know how to swim." He gave her a pointed look. "The only thing I regret, Miss Silverton, is losing my hat."

He knew her name? She didn't even know his. "Then I will replace your hat," she declared. "What type was it?"

It was his turn to stare at her, but then his expression shifted into another smile. "Don't worry about it. The hat's not replaceable."

She opened her mouth to question the truth of that statement when the boat suddenly powered down, and Harriet nearly lost her footing.

True to his rescue-habit ways, the man grasped her arm to steady her. For a long second, they were sharing breathing space again, and she had to pull her gaze away from his brown eyes.

"Do you get seasick?" he asked.

Her stomach did feel queasy, but she wasn't going to admit that to him. How unladylike. "No."

His scan of her face did nothing to ease the nerves tumbling in her belly. "You look pale."

"I am Caucasian."

He threw his head back and laughed.

His laugh was low, and deep, and unfettered. When he stopped, she had given up on holding back her smile.

"Lavender," he said. "It helps with the queasiness. But seeing that we're only a half hour from land, you'll have to save it for your next sea voyage."

She wrinkled her nose. "I don't think that's going to happen. Seattle will be a fine location to live out the rest of my life."

At this statement, he arched his brows. She felt a little surprised herself at her declaration.

"You're not homesick?" he asked.

"I'm only homesick for dry land, not Philadelphia."

He nodded, a thoughtful expression on his face.

Voices approached, and a couple of other passengers headed toward the nearest rail. Harriet's private conversation with this man was over.

His gaze cut to the newly arrived passengers. "Well, I'd love to hear your story of why you're not homesick, but I need to speak to the captain about a few things before we land."

He was leaving. Why did she want him to stay? "Do *you* live in Seattle?" she asked, feeling desperate to know something about him. Anything.

"I do." He stepped back and tapped an imaginary hat. "Nice to meet you, Miss Silverton."

"Harriet," she said quickly.

His easy smile was back. "Harriet."

Her cheeks heated at her presumptiveness. Did he notice her blush?

With a final nod, he turned.

"Wait," she said.

He paused in his step and looked back at her. Those brown eyes connected with hers, with that quirk of his mouth that was already familiar, and she almost lost her courage. "What's your name?"

"Caleb Munns."

Four

HARRIET BOTH WANTED to laugh and blush with embarrassment at the same time. Thankfully it was dark, since they'd arrived in Seattle after 11:00 p.m. All about the dock burning lanterns had been placed so that there was enough light to disembark. As Harriet walked with Mercer's group, Vivian stayed close behind her on the gangplank, acting as a protector. Mr. Mercer walked in front of her after saying, "If you slip, grab onto me."

Short of holding her hand like a small child, she was being coddled. In fact, he'd insisted she carry her parasol. "To act as a cane, if needed."

"I'll be fine," she'd said more than once, although the sight of the black water below the gangplank sent a shudder through her.

Adding to the whole occasion was Caleb Munns, standing on the dock, holding up a glowing lantern as he watched her making her way across the gangplank.

It was all ridiculous. Falling into the harbor at Teekalet was a one-time event, not a precursor to each and every time she sailed. And she'd been serious when she'd told Mr. Munns that she wasn't going to be sailing anytime soon, or for the rest of her life, for that matter.

She had no reason to return to Philadelphia, and she'd already determined that Seattle would be as fine a place to live as any other. By the time she stepped foot on the dock, Mr. Munns had disappeared into the crowd of passengers, dock workers, sailors, and fishermen.

Harriet tried not to dwell on the fact that they hadn't really said goodbye, because what did it matter? She'd likely never see him again anyway. She didn't even know what he did for a living, but based on his appearance, she guessed logging or shipbuilding. What else could make his shoulders so broad, and his arms so muscular . . . She should probably stop thinking about him, or Vivian would ask why in heaven's name she was blushing.

Besides, she didn't come all the way to Seattle to be caught up in thinking about a man who looked like he could have stepped out of the wild West from fifty years ago. She'd read the accounts of explorers. So she wasn't naïve to what went on in the outer reaches of the territories—horse roundups, cowboy shootings, women of questionable repute.

A young boy bumped into her.

"Oh," Harriet said, backing away as the boy held out a grubby hand. Perhaps he'd mistaken her for his mother in the darkness?

"Do you have any money?" he asked.

Harriet was so stunned, she didn't speak for a moment. Then another child pushed her way in front of Harriet. "My ma is sick, do you have any food?"

"I was here first," the boy said, shoving at the girl.

Harriet was about to intervene, even though the last thing she wanted to do was touch such a filthy child, when a whistle blew. From a policeman somewhere in the crowd. The children scattered. It was then Harriet noticed other small children, moving through the crowd, begging for handouts. They were little things, their faces dirty, their feet bare, their hair tangled. Did these children have homes? If so, where were their parents? She shuddered to think they might be homeless.

"Harriet!" Vivian's voice cut through Harriet's running thoughts.

She turned to find Harriet peering at her with a quizzical look.

"Haven't you heard a word I've said?" Vivian asked.

"I . . ."

"Mr. Mercer wants us all at the hotel right away," Vivian said, an exasperated note in her voice. She leaned closer to whisper. "We're attracting too much attention on the dock to be safe, and he wants to discuss our new job assignments in a more private place."

It was then that Vivian noticed that indeed there *were* many men watching them. Some of them had stopped in their work, congregating in small groups, using their lanterns to get a better look at the women. Speculation, curiosity, and interest in their eyes.

Harriet knew the other women in the company were much more striking than she, with her rather average features of dark brown hair, plain blue eyes, and, like Mr. Munns had pointed out, pale skin. But the men were looking at *her*, too. A new experience, to say the least.

She linked arms with Vivian, and they hurried after the rest of the group, away from the dock. Several crew members from the sloop walked alongside them, holding up lamplight for them to see their way. A cart had been loaded with all of their trunks and luggage, and it rumbled after them along the cobblestone streets. "Mr. Mercer said the hotel's not far, so we're walking."

They turned up one street, then another, Harriet still carrying her unopened parasol. Frankly, the cool evening air felt nice on her face, and the queasiness had already subsided. They soon arrived at the Occidental Hotel, a three-story building. The architecture was simple but appeared clean and well-kept. Stepping inside confirmed her first impression. Rugs scattered about the lobby, giving the place an elegant feel. Groupings of chairs with tables and gas lamps also adorned the space. Mr. Mercer was already at the registration desk, speaking to a clerk.

Some of the women wandered the lobby, peering at the paintings of landscapes on the walls. A couple of the women sank into the high-backed chairs.

Harriet was content to stand and catch her breath for a few moments. The knot of queasiness in her stomach that had been present since San Francisco had abated. For that she was grateful. And she realized she was ravenous. She hadn't felt this hungry for ages, but it seemed that no meals were close at hand this hour of the night. She moved to the windows that looked out onto the dark street, which was illuminated in spots with street lamps.

She stared when she saw a familiar man. His copper hair gleamed in the lamplight, and she didn't miss the wide sweep of his arm as he spoke to another man. The second man had his hat pulled low, and Harriet noted that Mr. Munns was still hatless.

They seemed to be in a bit of a disagreement. Mr. Munns' gestures grew more animated. Next, things happened so fast, that Harriet wasn't exactly sure who shoved first, or who punched first.

She gasped as both men tumbled to the ground, fists flying. Before she could think twice, she ran out of the hotel and headed across the street to the men in the dirt. A few onlookers had stopped, but no one seemed to mind the men beating each other's faces. Was this normal in Seattle?

Someone could be seriously hurt.

"Stop!" she shouted.

Harriet would never call herself the aggressive or bold sort, but her blood boiled, and something hot rose from deep inside her. Indignation. Because the second man had the upper hand over Mr. Munns. In fact, Mr. Munns wasn't fighting back at all. Horror rushed through her, and she pushed past the onlookers.

"Stop hitting him!" she cried, swinging her parasol on top of the second man's head.

The second man turned with a furious growl. His eyes widened with surprise when he saw her. And then he lunged for the parasol. Too late. Harriet had already stepped back, and with a fierce swing she hit him square in the stomach.

The man released an "Oof," then doubled over.

"If you don't stop fighting, I will poke your eye out," she said in a trembling voice, keeping her parasol aimed at him. She wasn't quite sure if the end of her parasol would truly do the trick, but right now the details didn't matter.

The second man slowly lifted his head. Blood stained his cheeks and dribbled from his lip. "Why, you little lassie, you're gonna pay—"

Apparently Mr. Munns wasn't as far gone as Harriet had first thought, and he snaked a hand around the second man's ankle and tugged him off balance. The second man landed with a thud on his backside.

A whistle sounded from somewhere behind her, and a policeman pushed through the crowd. "Break it up. Break it up. What's going on here?"

The onlookers dispersed then, until all that were left were Harriet and the two men.

The police officer looked between the lot of them.

"Fighting over a woman, eh? I s'pose there are worse things to fight over."

"No, sir," Harriet protested. "They were *not* fighting over me."

But the officer wasn't listening. "You're back, Caleb? What's going on? Is ole Bill bothering you?"

Harriet whirled. Sure enough, Caleb Munns had climbed to his feet, no worse for the wear. Unless you counted a black eye and a swollen lip. Not to mention his shirt was torn, revealing a bloody scrape on his firm chest . . .

Harriet blinked and shifted her gaze back to the policeman.

Caleb was out of breath, but he had no problem explaining what was going on. "Bill Sutter here thought he could sell my fishing boat while I was gone."

"You never came back last week," Bill spat out. "Thought you went missing or something. How was I supposed to know you were delayed?"

Caleb turned on Bill. "You very well know that delays happen in travel all of the time. You're a vulture, you know that?"

Bill moved closer, his chest lifted. "You never paid me back for the load from two years ago. I say you owe me."

"We both lost on that one," Caleb said. "We put in the same amount, and we lost equal."

The police officer raised his whistle to his mouth and blew.

The two men stopped arguing, but that didn't stop their glaring.

"You're coming with me, Bill." The police officer grabbed the man's arms and handcuffed him.

Bill groaned, and despite everything, Caleb chuckled.

"You too, Caleb," the police officer said, gripping the man in handcuffs and motioning for Caleb to follow.

Bill smirked, and Caleb scowled.

"Just to get it all sorted out with the captain," the police officer said.

Caleb gave a curt nod. "I'll be there shortly."

The police officer tugged Bill along with him and headed down the road.

Harriet took a step back, because now Caleb was looking at her. She couldn't quite decipher his expression but guessed it to be a cross between consternation and admiration.

When he grasped her parasol and slid it out of her hands, she didn't move.

He closed his fingers around each end, then bent the parasol so that it was straight again. Apparently, it had bowed when she struck Bill. Then he handed it back.

She took the now-straightened parasol and met his gaze. "You need to get cleaned up, sir."

He folded his arms, and she tried not to wince at the scrapes running up his forearms. "You could have been hurt," he said.

Harriet arched a brow. "*You* should look into a mirror."

But Caleb shook his head. "Women don't belong in the middle of a man's fight."

This is how he thanked her? She might have saved his life. Although, right now, he looked as strong and healthy as ever, save for his scrapes and bruises. Perhaps panic had made her think things were much worse than reality.

Harriet could not form a civil reply, and she didn't like that a couple of the women from her group had come out of the hotel, Vivian included. Harriet wasn't interested in an audience.

So she turned from Caleb Munns and crossed the street, then entered the hotel without a single glance behind.

Five

IT TURNED OUT that Harriet had quite the audience. When she walked into the lobby of the hotel, all the Mercer's belles stared at her. "Belles" had been a nickname they'd adopted on the voyage on the way over.

"Are you all right?" Vivian asked, rushing back inside with her.

"Yes." Harriet tucked in the strands of her hair that had fallen from their pins. "I'm fine, thank you." But her breathing was too fast, her skin too hot, her legs a bit shaky.

"You should *not* have interfered with those men, Miss Silverton," Mr. Mercer said next. His dark brows were pulled together as he surveyed her rumpled appearance. "As I explained on the onset of our voyage, the belles need not interfere in a man's business. You're representing all of us with your actions, mind you."

Harriet could only stare. She'd never been reprimanded in public in such a way. She realized she was perhaps an odd duck compared to the average woman. But still.

"We must keep ourselves unsullied," Mr. Mercer continued. "If the belles are to be taken seriously and given every opportunity, all the women must—"

Harriet held up her hand, effectively cutting him off. "I understand," she said. "I don't plan on repeating my actions, and I'm deeply sorry if I've disappointed any of you. Please forgive me."

Some of the belles glanced away, others nodded, and Vivian offered a tremulous smile. "Well then, all's well that ends well, right?"

The other women lifted their chins in approval.

Immense relief swept through Harriet. She was still part of the group. Mr. Mercer's eyes remained hooded, though, and she hoped that he'd still follow through on his promise to secure her a teaching position.

"Well, then," he said, clapping his hands together. "Like I was saying before the interruption . . . we will retire for the night, and tomorrow afternoon we've been invited to a reception at University Hall. The people of Seattle are grateful for our arrival and want to show appreciation. Later that evening, there will be a dance."

"What about our interviews?" Harriet blurted out. She supposed she'd missed an important announcement or two. Were they not here to interview for teaching positions?

Mr. Mercer drew her aside to explain as the other women organized which hotel rooms they'd be staying in. "After the social, Women's Benevolent Society of Seattle will explain which areas in the city need teachers and instruct the belles on writing letters of application. Interviews will take place likely the following day. They've assured me that all the belles will be snapped up for teaching positions almost immediately. We'll also be attending a local dance hall after in order to mingle with Seattle's finest. The belles are expected to wear their best dresses."

"A dance hall?" Harriet didn't know what she thought she'd be doing on her first couple of days in Seattle, but it wasn't socializing.

Once the room assignments were arranged, Harriet followed Vivian to the staircase, but not before casting another glance toward the street through the large windows. No street fighting going on.

"What were you thinking?" Vivian said when they entered their shared room and shut the door behind them.

Harriet moved to the free-standing mirror and began to take out her pins one by one. "I *wasn't* thinking," she said. "I acted before I thought about the consequences." She met Vivian's green-eyed gaze in the mirror. "Are you laughing at me?"

Vivian's cheeks dimpled as she tried not to crack a smile, but she failed miserably.

"You went out on a public street of a city you've only just stepped foot in, to stop a brawl between two strangers?"

Harriet's lips twitched. "One of them wasn't a stranger. He was Mr. Munns."

Vivian's brows arched at this. "The man who pulled you from the bay?"

"The very one," Harriet confirmed, but now her cheeks had flushed pink.

Vivian rested her hands on her hips. "Why, Harriet Silverton, you have a *tendre* for this Mr. Munns, don't you?"

Harriet turned and set her own hands on her hips. "Please don't insult me."

Vivian pressed her lips together, but her eyes were still smiling.

"Now, answer me this," Harriet said. "Why are we going to a dance hall and a social tomorrow night? What are we? To be paraded in front of Seattle like some willy-nilly spinsters who want a man? I mean, we're here for jobs. For independence. To start our lives over."

Surprisingly, Vivian didn't have a comeback for that.

"Viv," Harriet started. "You . . . you're hoping to find a husband."

Vivian dropped her hands and sighed. "I'm twenty-nine, and although I refuse to believe that means I'm a spinster . . . I thought perhaps out here—in the West—men wouldn't be quite so . . . picky."

Harriet blinked. Vivian had been the most vocal on the ship about finding her own path in life without relying on a man. "I thought you said . . ." She exhaled and tried again when she saw the defensive look in Vivian's eyes. "Of course you're not a spinster—that's a term the newspapers throw at us. We haven't married young like other women, but we'll marry as wiser women." *Not I,* Harriet amended to herself. Already in Seattle, she'd proved her unconventional ways. The men who'd been brawling were probably having a good laugh over her right now.

Vivian's gaze became less guarded. "You are hoping to marry as well?"

Harriet knew if she said no right now, Vivian would somehow be offended. "If the right man comes along, certainly." There, that was enough of a concession for now.

Vivian's smile was sudden. "Wonderful. Then we shall have a wonderful time at the dance tomorrow. Mr. Mercer says we'll be outnumbered by the men five to one."

Harriet nodded, trying to pretend that those numbers didn't bother her. Of course, they were in the farthest western territory, and it had been no secret that men—*unmarried* men—were plentiful out here. But *five to one?* Harriet's imagination took off at full train speed as she imagined men lining up to ask her to dance. *Her.* The staunchest spinster of Philadelphia.

She dropped into bed, her body exhausted but her mind a whir. So far, Seattle was full of the unexpected.

The day came too quickly, and Harriet wished she could have had one or two more hours of sleep. The social at University Hall was quite gratifying, since the Seattle residents expressed their gratitude for their arrival over and over. When they returned to the hotel for their meal, Mr. Mercer informed the belles that the Women's Benevolent Society of Seattle would be joining them for dinner.

During their meal, the belles listened to the president of the society, a Mrs. Barton, explain about the education needs in the town and the territories beyond. "Some of these children have never read a word in their lives," she said. "Others have been educated in the East, but due to hard times, they haven't been able to continue their schooling."

Mrs. Barton looked about the room, a soft smile on her face, contrasting to the formality of her navy short jacket and prim white blouse. "Some of these schoolhouses are one or two rooms only. Others are part of the larger farmhouses. You'll be provided room and board. Your salaries will be determined on the number of your students."

Harriet was entranced as she listened, imagining a whitewashed school building, surrounded by green hills dotted with wildflowers. The children would be fresh-faced, wide-eyed youth eager to learn everything "Miss Silverton" taught them. They'd grow up to attend colleges. They'd send her Christmas cards with fondly written letters full of school memories.

"Harriet," Vivian whispered, elbowing her. "Raise your hand."

Harriet blinked away the daydream and lifted her hand. "Why are we raising our hands?"

"To volunteer for meeting the Seattle superintendent tomorrow," she said. "They are looking for teachers for the children of the dock workers."

Harriet frowned and lowered her hand. But it was too late. Mrs. Barton had already pointed at her with a broad smile. "Thank you, ladies, the superintendent will arrive first thing tomorrow morning to meet with the two of you."

Vivian was all smiles, and Harriet didn't have the heart to tell her friend that the last place she wanted to work was near the harbor, where the smell of fish was constant and the children looked like they needed their bodies bathed and their clothing burned. She thought of those begging children. Surely they weren't in school, were they?

Well, Harriet would have to make her intentions more clear in the interview tomorrow. She was paying attention now to what Mrs. Barton said as she set up interviews for others. Rural. That's where she wanted to go. To a place where she could truly start over. Become her own person at last.

But, first, she'd have to get through tonight's dance and the interview tomorrow.

Six

CALEB'S BEST SUIT coat was quite lacking. He'd split a seam more than once, due to the jacket's rather tight fit across his shoulders. Working on a fishing boat day in and day out had built up muscle that he hadn't had living in Montana. So, here he was, using a blunt needle and too-thick thread to repair the shoulder seam before he made an appearance at the Women's Benevolent Society of Seattle dance social.

He'd been roped into this event more than once by his landlady, who was campaigning to join the committee. She told him that if she convinced enough bachelors to attend, then her prestige would raise in the eyes of the board.

It was all hogwash to Caleb. But he didn't mind the food. And dancing with a woman or two with no expectations wasn't too poor of a way to spend an evening. He just had the darnedest time getting rid of the fish smell on his skin. As luck would have it, he hadn't fished today because of all the traveling, so scrubbing up had been a simple-enough task.

Of course, now there was the matter of his black eye. He set down the half-finished seam and glanced in the small, brass mirror he used for shaving. Yes. The bruise had only grown darker, changing from violet to deep blue. Perhaps the ladies would be intrigued and want to know the story. Or perhaps they'd shy away, thinking he'd been in a drunken fight. Which was a quite common occurrence in the taverns after the sun went down.

But Caleb was no drunk.

His marriage to Lucille Baker had lasted thirty minutes. Caleb hadn't been able to say no to the petite blonde, blue-eyed woman who used to visit him at the ranch where he worked as a field hand. Lucille's father was a dairy farmer, and she'd deliver milk to the ranch where Caleb worked. Pretty as a button, she was. But she'd lied about her age.

She'd also lied about her father. Said he was a mean old drunk. Wouldn't let her out of the house except for deliveries. She'd told Caleb her mother had died years ago, and that's why her father was so protective of her. She hadn't ever been kissed. And she'd fallen in love with Caleb.

He'd fallen for every word that dropped from those cherry-red lips of hers.

She'd begged him to take her away from Montana. Wanted to see the ocean, she'd said. And when Caleb proposed marriage to her, she'd jumped into his arms, and he'd fully believed that dreams really could come true.

Up until the moment when a cart came careening toward the train station soon after they left the courthouse. Caleb had picked up Lucille a short distance from her father's ranch, and they'd driven into town to be married by the justice of the peace. Then Caleb planned to take her on to Seattle, where he'd lined up a job, and she could live by the ocean like she'd always dreamed. Far away from her abusive father.

Lucille's father was a burly man, but his words were soft when he spoke to her.

"Sweetheart, it's time to come home," Mr. Baker had said.

Next to her father was a woman who looked like an older version of Lucille.

Apparently her mother. Who was very much alive.

"We're very sorry, Mr. Munns," Mrs. Baker said. "We didn't know Lucille would take it this far again."

"*Again?*"

Mrs. Baker's smile was sad, and Mr. Baker climbed out of the cart, lifted his hat and scrubbed at his receding, thin hair. "Lucille is a fanciful girl. Always creating stories. When a man pays her a bit of attention, she becomes . . . obsessed."

Caleb looked over at Lucille, who was sitting next to him at the train depot.

She had folded her arms.

"I like this one, Pa," she said.

"I know you do," her father said, his tone nonplussed. "He seems like a nice man." Mr. Baker took a tentative step toward his daughter. "What did you tell him?"

Lucille pushed out her lower lip. Caleb was reminded of a small child, who was pouting because her parents wouldn't let her buy a lollipop.

"I told him you were mean," Lucille said, her voice sounding contrite.

Her father sighed. "What else?"

Lucille lowered her head and spoke so softly it was hard to hear. "Ma was dead."

"Oh, Lucy," her mother said. But her voice held no anger, no reprimanding. Just resignation.

Caleb looked between the family members. What was happening here?

Her father held out his hand. "Time to come home, dear. Your mother made pancakes this morning, your favorite."

Lucille jumped up to her feet and smiled. "Really?"

Caleb watched with incredulity as the woman he'd just married hurried to her parents' buggy and climbed in to sit next to her mother. Lucille wasn't even looking at him anymore.

Caleb was speechless.

Mr. Baker crossed to him and placed a hand on his arm. "Sorry you've gotten mixed up in this. Our Lucille had an accident as a child, hit her head and all. The doctors said we should expect episodes now and again. But we never thought they'd turn into *this.*"

"This?" Caleb said. "How many ... men?"

"You're the fourth she's married," Mr. Baker said matter-of-factly.

Caleb blanched.

"Don't worry," Mr. Baker said. "The justice of the peace didn't really marry you. Who do you think sent word to me?"

Caleb opened his mouth, then closed it.

He wasn't really sure what he said to Mr. Baker, or what his reply was. All he knew was that moments later, Lucille Baker rode off with her parents in their buggy, happily chattering with her now-alive mother about pancakes. Completely unaware that she'd left behind a very heartbroken, confused ex-husband.

If they'd been married at all. Which, apparently, they hadn't been.

So Caleb had gotten on that train and headed for Seattle alone.

It wasn't a story he planned to share with anyone, ever. Not just because he'd been so thoroughly duped, but because he couldn't trust his heart. He'd been in love with Lucille. He'd arrived in Seattle with an empty heart and empty soul.

When he'd first arrived in Seattle, he'd been reluctant to attend any sort of social event or dance with other women, who were single and available. He couldn't imagine going through, and surviving, another heartbreak. Thus, he set up his own rules. Dancing with a woman once was his limit. Dancing with a woman twice was something he'd not allow himself.

Caleb tied off the thread of his repaired suit coat, then stood and drew it on. Still snug, but it would have to do. He'd sunk the earnings from his first year of fishing into his own boat, and he didn't have the budget to be buying new clothing, especially something he only wore once every couple of months.

By the time he reached the dance hall, the music was soaring from the open doors, and he caught a glimpse of a good-sized crowd inside. Perhaps his landlady wouldn't miss him at all. He hovered at the edge of the steps leading inside. A few people greeted him as they headed past him. One man asked him about his recent trip.

"Fine, fine," Caleb said, keeping to the shadows to conceal the better part of his bruised face.

There really were quite a few men inside, and the women were being well attended to. He'd be surprised if any of the women sat out a single dance. He was tired, come to think of it. And he ached, mostly from the fight, of course. Going to bed a bit earlier tonight would ensure him a better day tomorrow.

But the scent of food somehow reached him, and his traitorous stomach growled.

Maybe he could eat and leave? Or just dance with one woman and leave? Consider it a duty done?

But as he stepped inside the dance hall and caught sight of a familiar woman, one with blue eyes and dark hair, wearing a dress that was a couple of sizes too small for her, Caleb forgot about the food.

Miss Harriet Silverton wasn't looking at him, but that didn't matter. He was still rooted to the floor. Because Bill Sutter, that snake, was talking to her, his smile oily, his frame leaning too close, his eyes full of things Caleb didn't like.

Then, to Caleb's consternation, he watched as Bill held

out his hand, and Miss Silverton put her hand in his. Was she accepting a dance from him? Or something more?

Before he realized what he was doing, Caleb found himself striding toward Miss Silverton.

Seven

THE MAN'S BRIGHT blue eyes nearly had her fooled. Harriet recognized him, which seemed impossible, because she'd never been to Seattle in her lifetime. But then with an unpleasant jolt, she realized who he was. The man who'd fought Mr. Munns.

"Good evening, miss," he'd started out. "I do apologize if I'm intruding, but I feel that I owe you a deep apology. My name is Bill Sutter, and I'd like to welcome you to Seattle properly."

Harriet couldn't have spoken if she wanted to, because Bill Sutter was a conversationalist, it seemed. He'd cleaned up nicely too. Gone was the sweaty, wild-eyed man, replaced by a slick-haired, twinkling-blue-eyed man. The transformation was quite astonishing, really. And completely unexpected.

"Thank you, uh, Mr. Sutter."

He bowed, rather flamboyantly, and Harriet was aware that several people were looking their way.

"Might you forgive me for behaving so badly last night in the street?" His blue eyes implored as much as did his smooth words.

"Of-of course," Harriet said. "I don't even know you, so there's no reason for me to hold a grudge."

Mr. Sutter lowered his gaze for a brief, contrite moment. Then he focused his blues on her once again. "That is the best news I've heard in all my life."

"Surely not in *all your life*," she repeated.

It turned out that Mr. Sutter had a rather booming laugh. Despite any reserve she might have, Harriet smiled.

"Tell me, might I have the pleasure of learning your name?"

It wasn't like he couldn't learn it anyway. All he'd have to do was ask Mr. Mercer or one of the other belles.

"Harriet Silverton."

"Ah . . . A lovely name for a lovely lady," Mr. Sutter said.

A far-fetched compliment, but Harriet truly didn't mind. She could bask in praise for a few moments. This Mr. Sutter wasn't all that bad. Sure, he'd been in a heated argument with Mr. Munns, and it had come to blows eventually. But Mr. Munns had been in the same fight, done the same yelling, thrown the same punches. And she didn't hold a grudge against *him*. In fact, she'd been wondering how he was faring.

"Would you do me the honor and dance with me?" Mr. Sutter asked, extending his hand.

Harriet really had no reason to say no. "All right." She placed her hand in his, but just then, Mr. Sutter looked past her, and his eyes narrowed.

His hand tightened about hers quite unexpectedly. What was he about?

Then she heard a familiar voice, and a warm shiver whispered along her neck.

"Step aside, Bill," Mr. Munns said.

Her hand still enfolded in Mr. Sutter's, Harriet turned to see the man himself.

He'd cleaned up nicely as well . . . not that he needed to add anymore awareness to his appearance. Mr. Munns was already an imposing man. But in a suit, even one that had seen better days, he was quite possibly the most striking man in the room. His dark copper hair gleamed in the lamplight, and his brown eyes were impossibly black, not to mention she caught the faint scent of pine and fresh air, as if he'd taken a stroll along a wooded path. His hair was no longer windblown, but combed, which only brought more attention to the square set of his jaw and the length of his throat.

"You don't own this woman," Mr. Sutter said, his previously jovial voice now turned decidedly gruff.

"And neither do you," Mr. Munns was quick to say.

The future flashed before Harriet's eyes, of a brawl starting between these two men, once again. How many times could they fight in less than twenty-four hours? By the look in both of their eyes, she guessed more than once. Whatever had transpired between them on the street last night was not finished yet.

"*No one* owns me, gentlemen." Harriet pulled her hand from Mr. Sutter's tight grip. "And I do not have my parasol with me, so I'd appreciate it if you would either leave the dance immediately, or behave as I'm sure your mothers taught you to do."

Mr. Sutter huffed. "I asked her first." He wasn't looking at her, but at Mr. Munns.

When Mr. Sutter had spoken to her alone, without Mr. Munns present, he'd been a decent sort of man. But it seemed his rival, or enemy, or whatever Mr. Munns was, brought out the worst in him.

Mr. Munns' gaze landed on Harriet. "It seems you must choose, Miss Silverton."

"*Choose?*" she echoed. "Choose what?"

"Between us," Mr. Sutter said, his voice a low whine. "You either dance with me, or with him, but you can't dance with us both, because this uneducated fellow is about to blow his top off."

Harriet narrowed her eyes. "I have a better idea." She paused, because she now had their full attention. "How about I don't dance with either of you?"

She stepped away from them. Others in the crowd had diverted their attention now that there were no impending fisticuffs. She gave Mr. Sutter a half-smile, then nodded at Mr. Munns, and before any other words could be spoken, she walked away.

It wasn't hard to escape from their sight, since there were plenty of people to block the way. Another fellow asked her to dance, but she shook her head and continued on her errand. Straight for the refreshment table.

She stopped near the lemonade and poured herself a glass. As she sipped at the cool, tart liquid, she scanned the room for Vivian. Spotting her, Harriet smiled. Her friend was dancing with a rather portly gentleman but seemed to be enjoying every moment of it.

Next, Harriet picked out other belles, also socializing, or dancing. It was gratifying to see the women she'd spent so much time with on the ship enjoying themselves after such a long journey.

"Would you like another refill?" a male voice said next to her.

Harriet didn't turn. She didn't need to. "I thought I told you I wouldn't dance with you, Mr. Munns."

"That you did," he said. "But I'm not asking you to dance, am I?"

"Well, no, but . . ." She turned and looked up at him.

His dark eyes bored into hers, and the too-small dress she'd borrowed from Vivian seemed to shrink another size.

She was suddenly very aware of how close he was

standing, and how he was looking at her like she was the only person in the room. She exhaled, then took another sip of her lemonade She couldn't hide her wince at the tartness.

"Do you want a refill?" he asked. "In case you thought I was joshing earlier."

For some reason, she found his unexpected comment funny. When she laughed one of his brows lifted. "I'm sorry," she said, reigning in control.

His expression remained stoic, yet she didn't miss the amusement in his eyes.

"Here," she said. "Try it."

He took the glass from her fingers, and at the warmth of his brief touch, she felt a longing she hadn't felt for many years . . . the desire to be courted by a man. For a man to look at her as someone he was interested in. But then she blinked, and the longing fled almost as soon as it had appeared.

She watched Mr. Munns raise the glass to his lips and take a deep, and rather brave, swallow.

He went absolutely still.

Then his face twisted into a grimace, and his eyes began to water.

Harriet covered her mouth with a hand, because she knew there was no way she could contain her second round of laughter.

"That was terrible," Mr. Munns gasped.

"Do you want a refill?" Harriet tried to ask the question in a calm voice, but she utterly failed. A giggle burst from her.

Mr. Munns set the glass on the table, half empty. "I think that was the worst lemonade I've ever tasted, and I'm no cook by any means." His eyes flashed to hers, and he wore that amused look again.

"Oh, if you're not a cook, then what are you, Mr. Munns?"

He leaned against the table, his gaze on her. "Guess."

"Guess? How in the world would I guess?"

He shrugged one of those massive shoulders of his, but he seemed content to wait.

Harriet decided Mr. Munns was interesting, if nothing else. She set her hands on her hips and surveyed him. His longish hair, his brutish strength, his twice-patched suit coat. "Are you a railroad worker?"

That brow lifted again, but he shook his head.

"All right." This time she made her perusal of him slower, more obvious. "You're certainly not a tailor."

He chuckled, and the rumble of his laugh sent darts of warmth skittering along her skin. Or maybe it was because the room was so crowded that everything was overwarm.

"I'm most definitely not a tailor," he said. "Guess again, Miss Silverton."

Had he moved closer to her?

Reaching out a few inches would nearly make them dancing partners. "Do you build boats?"

"You're getting closer," he murmured.

They were in a room full of people, with chatter and music surrounding them, yet she could hear his low tones perfectly clearly.

"Are you a sailor?" she asked. "Is that why you swim so well?"

"I swim so well because I spent the summers as a boy swimming the lake that edged my parents' homestead."

She immediately pictured a much younger version of Mr. Munns running full speed across a rickety dock and taking a flying leap. She had no idea why she had thought of him in such a manner, but—

"What are you smiling at?" he asked.

"You," she said. "Thinking of you as a child. I imagine you were quite a handful for your mother."

He shrugged. "She did used to say I'd be the death of her, but that's not what killed her."

Harriet covered her mouth. "I didn't mean—"

"I know you didn't," he said. "Turned out that her tuberculosis was worse than any of us thought. I was nearly thirteen. When my dad turned to the bottle, I left for good. Found myself work and have been on my own ever since."

Harriet's eyes stung with all that he'd revealed. His mother was gone, and his father . . . Mr. Munns was a man who'd understand her broken relationship with her brother. Despite his confession, she didn't want to talk about her family.

And she was desperate to get their conversation back to the first subject. "So, you're a homesteader?"

"Not quite, Miss Silverton," he said.

She tapped her finger against her lip. "Well, that leaves only one thing."

When she didn't finish her sentence, he prompted, "And what would that be?"

"A fisherman."

Eight

CALEB WASN'T SURPRISED that she'd guessed, but he was waiting to see what her reaction would be. "What gave it away? The chapped knuckles? The unkempt hair? The smell of fish about my person?"

She sniffed, actually *sniffed*.

"I don't smell fish, Mr. Munns," she declared, those blue eyes of hers reminding him of the color of the Pacific in the early morning. Deep blue and endless.

"Then why are you opposed to dancing with me?" He knew he was treading on territory he shouldn't be treading on. Flirting with this woman. But he seemed to be having trouble staying away from her. Even when she'd turned both him and Bill down, here Caleb was, talking to her again.

He appreciated the way her lips curved into a smile.

"Do you think I turned you down because you smell like fish, Mr. Munns?"

He leaned closer and was gratified when she didn't shy away. "Yes."

"You are a man with a rather large opinion of yourself, it seems," she said. "Can you think of no other reason a woman would turn down your offer of a dance?"

This gave him pause. "I suppose if she didn't like my looks?"

She raised her brows, as if encouraging him to continue with his list.

"My manners?"

Her brows went a bit higher.

"My poor sewing skills?"

Her lips quirked.

Caleb was quite thirsty, but the lemonade wasn't an option. "Tell me, Miss Silverton, why *did* you turn down a dance from me?"

She didn't answer right away but seemed to be thinking. Then she was the one to lean closer this time. "I suppose it's because I don't want to dance with anyone, now that I really think about it. I didn't come to Seattle for socializing. I'm here to teach school and to start my life anew. Not go backwards."

"Socializing would be going backwards?" Not that Caleb was a master-socializer, but her answer intrigued him.

"*Dancing* would be going backwards," she said. "I've no interest in dancing once, then twice, then becoming friends, then courting, or anything thing like it, with anyone. I'm not here to find a husband, no matter what Mr. Mercer has been insinuating to anyone who will listen. That train passed me by years ago." She straightened but kept her voice low. "In short, Mr. Munns, I don't plan to marry, so all of the preamble at a dance hall is useless."

By Jove, Miss Silverton was perhaps the most intriguing woman he'd ever met. "Then you're in good company, miss. I've no plans to marry either."

She blinked her eyes slowly. "I thought every man wanted a wife."

"Some do, I suppose, but marrying once was enough for me."

She definitely looked curious.

"Don't worry, I'm not some sad widower, and there were no children . . . that would have been quite impossible, since there was no wedding night."

Her cheeks turned a definite shade of pink.

In for a penny, in for a pound. "I don't mean to embarrass you, but I sense that you are a wise woman who is old enough to understand how the world works."

Her blush only deepened.

"Have you been married before, Miss Silverton?" he continued.

"No." Her answer was quick and sharp. "I've never been married, not even for one day, as you seem to be implying."

"Try less than an hour." So, he was confiding in her after all. Interesting.

Instead of looking shocked, she tilted her head, her blue eyes captivated. "Perhaps a dance wouldn't bring any harm then, since we're both not interested in any sort of courting or future relationships."

Caleb could have been knocked over with a tiny gust of wind.

"And it will give you the chance to tell me more about your one-hour marriage," she added.

There was no hesitation on his part, especially since he didn't want to risk that she'd change her mind. So he held out his hand, and when she set her smaller hand against his, he felt like he'd stormed onto a battlefield and successfully defeated his opponent in one fell swoop. And it didn't hurt that as he and Miss Silverton began the steps of the dance, he caught Bill's hard gaze.

Caleb gave his former friend a slight nod, then refocused on Miss Silverton. She might not be the most beautiful and flashy woman in the room, but she was the only woman he wanted to dance with.

The dance was slow, and as the couples moved about them, Miss Silverton didn't shy away from gazing at him. Her gloved hand in his made his palm warm, and his other hand rested on the curve of her hip. Caleb's heart did a little flip at their close contact, but he ignored it. He slowly became aware of her every breath, the length of her eyelashes, the curve of her neck. Not to mention that she smelled like fresh flowers. Was it her essence, or did she wear some sort of expensive perfume? It wasn't something he could very well ask. The question seemed personal, but that didn't stop him from wondering all the same.

"So, Mr. Munns," she said in a voice that tickled his senses. "What could ever possess you to flee your bride of one hour?"

He cleared his throat to cover up his moment of becoming distracted by the physical qualities of Miss Silverton. "It was the other way around, as a matter-of-fact. She fled *my* presence. All it took was the promise of hot pancakes."

Miss Silverton stared at him in disbelief. Well, that's how he'd felt at the time too.

"Those must have been some pancakes."

"Oh, they were," he said. "Possibly the best pancakes known to mankind, although I wasn't able to taste them, so I can't entirely vouch for their deliciousness." He continued to explain in great detail how Lucille's parents had showed up and spirited away their daughter, who apparently wasn't all that in love with him in the end.

He hadn't expected Miss Silverton to laugh, but that's what she did.

"I don't mean to laugh," she said. "But if you look at it from my perspective, can you not see the humor? A big, sturdy man like you, left at the altar—or, er, the train station. While your bride is more excited for pancakes than starting her new life with you."

"It was pathetic, that's what," he said. It was rather funny, now that he saw it from Miss Silverton's perspective. *Hmm.*

"You were fooled, like you said," Miss Silverton said. "But what I don't understand is how the justice of the peace could conduct the ceremony without saying anything to you. A warning would have been nice."

"I suppose he didn't want to be the messenger of bad news."

Miss Silverton bit her bottom lip, which brought his attention firmly to her mouth. "You might be right. What did you do after Lucille hurried off to her scrumptious breakfast?"

"I was already packed. So I left town and continued to Seattle," he said. "And here I am. Now . . . tell me, what brought you on a ship here? What is *your* tale of woe?"

"What makes you think I have a tale of woe?" she asked in a light tone.

He held her gaze. "Don't you?" When her eyes shifted away from his, he knew he'd guessed right. But the music had come to an end, and he couldn't very well dance two numbers with her. He'd be pretty much staking his claim, not that he'd be bothered if all the other men steered clear of her, yet . . .

"Thank you, Mr. Munns," she said, drawing away from him. "It appears that our time is up. We don't want people to gossip about us, especially since neither of us is interested in a relationship."

"No, we wouldn't want that," he said, but he kept a hold of her hand, not leading her off the dance floor. The strains of another dance number began. Still, Caleb didn't move. "When do I get to hear your story?"

She gently, but firmly, tugged her hand from his. "I cannot say. Tomorrow morning I'll have my interview, and I might start my new job as soon as that very afternoon."

"So soon?" He didn't want to reveal his disappointment,

but he was quite sure Miss Silverton could see it in his eyes anyway.

She lifted a shoulder in a shrug.

"I will take my chances, then," he said. "After my work day, I'll stop by the hotel. Perhaps if you happen to be in the lobby, we can sit down for tea—or whatever you easterners do—and you can tell me all about yourself."

Her blue eyes gleamed with amusement, yet there was something else there as well. Hope? *He* certainly had hope. For what, he didn't define. Caleb was curious about this woman, that was all. He could be a good neighbor and answer any of her questions about Seattle. Though she hadn't asked any so far, perhaps she wanted to.

"I hope I don't disappoint you," she said. "Because from the moment we stopped over in San Francisco, I considered myself a westerner."

For some reason, that statement made Caleb seem inordinately pleased. Here was a woman who wouldn't run back to her family. A woman who wouldn't abandon her husband. Wait. Where had that idea come from? He needed to dispel that thought immediately.

And they were still standing in the middle of the dance floor as other couples surrounded them and began to move with the music.

"Oh," Miss Silverton said, as if she'd just realized where they were standing. "I must go now. And tomorrow . . . well, I cannot give any guarantee where I will be."

"I will still take my chances," he said.

Then she was gone. So swiftly that he didn't know exactly which direction she'd disappeared into the crowd. Well, his evening was finished. There was nothing else he wanted to do except continue speaking to Miss Silverton. Since he couldn't ask her to dance again, he moved toward the doors, avoiding the dancing couples and other members of the crowd.

He tugged at his collar. The dance hall really had grown too warm.

And it wasn't until he was outside, striding through the cool breeze of the night toward his rented room, that he realized he hadn't eaten one bite of the dinner. Which had been the main reason he'd attended in the first place.

Nine

"Here? As in *right here*?" Harriet asked, unable to keep the surprise from her tone as she sat across from Mrs. Barton in their morning interview.

"Why yes," Mrs. Barton said, her wide smile revealing her gapped teeth. "Mr. Pinker, the owner of this very hotel, has two children. He doesn't want them mixing in so much with the children from the dock families. He's afraid his children will pick up bad manners, not to mention their poor language. So he's asked for someone to teach his children exclusively three days a week. The other two days, you can help in the schoolhouse by the docks. Miss Little could always use an extra hand."

Harriet blinked. "Vivian, er, Miss Little, has already accepted her position?"

"She has," Mrs. Barton said in a triumphant voice. "And she was eager enough to recommend you. We thought you might be co-teachers, since there are about twenty students of all ages, but then Mr. Pinker made the alternative request only a few moments ago."

Harriet exhaled. She'd been hoping for the rural schoolhouse, but with Vivian nearby maybe it wouldn't be so bad.

But now . . . was she more happy about this new change, or less happy?

She took the plunge. "What else is available?"

Mrs. Barton's brows arched. "Miss Silverton, either you are a teacher or you aren't. Picking and choosing is not a teacher's prerogative. The students' education is what's important here, not convenience."

Duly chastised, Harriet swallowed. She supposed she could give it a shot—although this position sounded more like that of a governess, and not a school teacher. "All right," she said. "I will accept the position."

Twenty minutes later, Harriet was back in her room after being briefed on the duties of her new job, her pay, her living quarters—which she'd share with Vivian—and her days off. Sundays. On Saturdays she was expected to make home visits to struggling students and offer individual tutoring.

But she would be all right. She could do this, and she would enjoy the new challenges. When Vivian returned to their shared room, she was all aflutter with plans, and Harriet didn't want to put a damper on her friend's enthusiasm.

"Our place is not far down the street," Vivian gushed. "We'll need new curtains, but otherwise, it's clean and tidy. We'll make it into a home yet."

Harriet was listening, mostly, but she was also wondering what Mr. Pinker's children were like. She found out soon enough. The very next moment, in fact, when someone knocked on their door.

Harriet opened the door to find a young woman, plainly dressed, and a cap covering her head.

"I'm Jenny." She lifted her brown eyes for a brief moment, then lowered them straightaway. "I've come to fetch you to meet Mrs. Pinker and her children, Rebecca and Wallace. Mrs. Pinker would like you to come right away."

Harriet exchanged a wordless glance with Vivian, who only smiled and nodded.

So Harriet followed Jenny to the top floor of the hotel, through a set of double doors, and into a luxurious living room.

A blonde woman sat in an elegant chair. She lifted her hand and motioned for Harriet to come closer.

"Hello, Mrs. Pinker?" Harriet asked.

Jenny had disappeared somewhere.

"Yes, are you Miss Silverton?" the woman asked, her hand still midair.

Harriet didn't know if she was supposed to take the woman's hand or not.

But then Mrs. Pinker waved her fingers. "Sit down. Jenny will bring the children. I have only two rules to abide by."

"All right." Harriet sat in a chair across from the woman.

Mrs. Pinker was beautiful, but faint violet circles were beneath her eyes, as if she hadn't slept well last night, or for several nights. Harriet felt a twinge of compassion for the woman.

"First," Mrs. Pinker said. "No noise. I don't care where in the hotel you teach them, but I don't want to hear anything, *and* I don't want complaints from the guests."

Harriet didn't know what to make of the request. Surely there'd have to be some noise.

The woman adjusted the doily on the end table next to her as if she was considering her next rule very carefully.

"Second, I don't want them near the water." Mrs. Pinker narrowed her eyes. "I heard what happened to you."

Harriet opened her mouth, then thought better of it and remained silent.

"Ah, here they are now," Mrs. Pinker said. "Wallace, Rebecca, introduce yourselves."

If anything, the two children were spitting images of their blonde mother. Both were impeccably dressed, the girl wearing a pale blue dress with a ruffle hem, and the boy wearing navy short pants and a matching jacket. The boy spoke first.

"My name is Wallace, and I'm eleven." He gave her a small smile that was a bit mischievous, then he elbowed his sister.

She scowled at him, then switched her expression to a contrite smile in the next breath. "I'm Becky, and I'm eight."

Harriet had no doubt that Rebecca, or Becky, would be the one out of the two who'd give her some trouble.

"Very well," Mrs. Pinker said. "Now run along with Miss Silverton. Your lessons will begin right away, then Jenny will fetch you after. I'll keep to my room all evening, so I expect the two of you to behave."

Both nodded mutely, although Wallace stole a peek at Harriet.

"Wait, *right now?*" Harriet said. "I wasn't planning on—" Her words died in her throat as the double doors opened and an older man strode in.

His thinning gray hair was combed severely to one side, and his ferret-like eyes landed on Harriet. "Are you Miss Silverton?" he asked in a commanding tone.

"I am." Harriet had no cause to be nervous, but here she was, nervous.

The man nodded. This man must be Mr. Pinker. "She looks decent, don't you think? Did you tell her the rules?"

Mrs. Pinker was the one who answered. "I told her the rules, and she agreed."

Her husband nodded. "Very well." His gaze landed once again on Harriet.

And that was it. He said nothing else, just studied her with a cocked eyebrow.

"Yes, well, we'll be off then," Harriet said in a slow voice, glancing at Jenny. Perhaps the maid or nanny or whoever she was could help Harriet find where to teach the first lesson that wasn't even prepared. Because the last thing Harriet wanted to do was ask the Pinkers any questions.

Thankfully, Jenny led them out of the living quarters. Once they were in the hallway, Harriet asked her, "Where is our makeshift classroom?"

"In the attic," Wallace promptly said.

"In the lobby," Rebecca said at the same time.

Harriet stopped in the hallway, looking between the children. A faint blush colored both of their cheeks. So she looked to Jenny.

"This way," Jenny said with a briskness she hadn't shown around Mrs. Pinker. "At the end of this corridor is a former hotel room. I've been instructed to get it ready for a classroom, but I haven't had time to accomplish the task yet."

"Understood." Harriet said, not surprised.

They all followed Jenny, and when the young woman opened the door, Rebecca let out a groan. "It will be so boring in here."

Wallace sighed, and his eyes seemed to dull. He crossed to one of the chairs and sat down with a thump.

Jenny ducked out of the room, seeming to be glad to leave the three of them alone.

Harriet eyed the room, then the children. "After our lessons on some days, we could go on a field trip," she suggested.

"A field trip?" Rebecca asked, wrinkling her nose. "What would we do in a field?"

"A field trip is when we go outside, to a museum, or somewhere else to learn about the subject we're studying about."

"Where outside?" Rebecca continued. "Mother says there's crime all over and that it's not safe."

"I'm not scared," Wallace said, puffing out his chest.

Harriet crossed to the hotel window and looked down upon the street below. It happened to be the street where she'd tried to break up a fight between two men. And now... she was thinking about Mr. Munns. Would he really stop by the hotel this evening? She shook that thought away. Turning toward the children, she said, "Well, we could decide about it later then. First, I need to know where you are in your academics so that I can better prepare my lessons."

"I know everything," Rebecca retorted.

Harriet held back a sigh. Maybe if she ignored the girl's impertinence, Rebecca would soften up. "What about you, Wallace?"

As he proudly announced his accomplishments, Harriet was duly impressed. "Who's been your teacher?"

"We went to school until we moved here last year," Wallace said. "Since then, Mother has been our teacher."

"But she stays in her room all the time now," Rebecca said.

Wallace shot her a glare, and Rebecca glared right back.

Harriet didn't want to get too involved with family dynamics, but she had little choice since they were siblings. Trying to change the subject, she said, "What are your hobbies?"

"Painting," Rebecca said immediately.

Wallace folded his arms and scoffed, so before he could say something else negative toward his sister, Harriet asked, "What about *you*, Wallace?"

He looked away, his expression sullen. "Fishing. But Father never takes me."

Stay away from the water, had been one of Mrs. Pinker's rules.

"Well," Harriet began. "I might know someone who could take you fishing." The moment the words left her mouth, she knew it was the wrong thing to say. Wallace's expression lightened up, and Harriet was left wondering why in the world she'd thought she could offer such a thing.

Ten

CALEB SECURED HIS fishing boat to the dock where he'd maneuvered it into its usual slip at the harbor. Three boats down the line, he could see Bill working with old McOwen. They hadn't spoken since the dance. Caleb wasn't sure if it was due to their fist fight or due to their debate over dancing with Miss Silverton.

Perhaps it was both. Caleb was pretty sure their friendship had come to an irreparable end. No matter. He had plenty of work to occupy him, starting with today's catch. After securing his boat, he unloaded the nets with fish into a cart and strolled to the fishing vendor he gave most of his business to.

The fishing had been slower today, and he guessed it was because of the incoming storm. So he was later than he'd planned, and by the time he'd washed up in his rented room, he decided it was too late to stop by the hotel lobby. Dark had fallen, and the decent hour had passed.

Still, he could walk by. Perhaps if he saw her through the lobby window, maybe he could walk in and . . . Caleb knew it was a long shot, but he wouldn't be able to rest tonight without knowing he'd tried. It had been a long time since a woman had so completely dominated his thoughts. Since Lucille, truthfully. And maybe not even with her.

But there was nothing to fear with Miss Silverton, because neither of them was looking to court, and besides, it was perfectly acceptable for men and women to be friends in the nineteenth century. He was curious about her past. He'd certainly told her plenty of his, perhaps too much, and he hoped that hadn't dissuaded her in their mutual accord.

So, it was with these thoughts in mind that Caleb carefully shaved, then wrestled his way into his too-tight jacket again. Perhaps he'd only accomplish a stroll, but the walking would do him good after sitting in the fishing boat for so long.

When Caleb neared the hotel, he was pleased to see that all the first-floor lights were on. He hadn't been sure how active the hotel was at night, but it seemed the restaurant was heavily patronized. People were milling about in the lobby, and Caleb slowed his step outside the windows to peer inside.

Those in the lobby were mostly men, and he guessed there was some sort of meeting or convention going on. A quick scan told him that the women in attendance were likely wives of a few of the men, and Harriet wasn't among them. Neither were any of the other belles whom he might recognize.

Well, he'd tried. Perhaps tomorrow he'd send a note around. Apologize for his change in schedule and arrange another chance meeting. He tried to imagine how Miss Silverton would react to such a note.

"Mr. Munns?" The woman's voice startled him.

Caleb turned around to see a pair of women walking toward him on the sidewalk. One of them was . . . Miss Silverton.

The first words out of his mouth were perhaps not the best. "You shouldn't be out here alone at night."

"I'm not alone, Mr. Munns," she said in a smooth voice. "I'm with Vivian Little."

Caleb glanced at the second woman. They'd arrived in the patches of light spilling from the hotel windows. He didn't care that Miss Silverton was with Miss Little. Neither of them should be out after dark unaccompanied by a man. "Be that the case, it's still unwise to walk the Seattle streets after dark." He nodded to Miss Little, and she nodded back. That introduction was sufficient for the both of them.

The two women grew closer, and Miss Silverton's hair caught the light from the windows, since she wore no hat. She wore a short jacket over her lavender blouse, and her cheeks looked unusually rosy. With a smile, she said, "We only walked a couple of blocks to visit our new accommodations. The sun has barely set. Besides, I had given up on you coming tonight."

He felt the spark of her gaze, or perhaps it was his imagination. Had she implied that she'd waited for him? Perhaps looked forward to his visit?

"The fishing was slow," he said. "Which delays everything else. You have new accommodations?" Did this mean that she'd be teaching locally? He shouldn't let his heart soar, but it did.

"Yes." Her gaze searched his, and he tried not to read into it. "Both Vivian and I are teaching at the schoolhouse near the docks. Although I'll be dividing myself between the schoolhouse and teaching Mr. Pinker's children privately."

This surprised Caleb. "Like a governess? Is that what you want?"

The line between her brows told him what she wasn't saying.

"I'm definitely looking forward to it," she said, her smile not quite genuine. "I already spent the afternoon with the two children. They are very eager to learn."

Caleb glanced at Miss Little to see that she looked bored. He nodded. "Well, then, I wish you all the best." He hesitated, wondering how bold he dared to be. "Might I walk you around the block?"

As expected, her brows raised, but then she nodded. "All right."

Miss Little merely bade farewell and continued into the hotel.

"The night is not too dangerous if I am with you?" she asked, humor in her tone.

Caleb held back a smile. "Avoiding danger completely is impossible, but I'm confident you'll be safe with me." With Miss Little absent, Caleb's guard lowered a bit, and he became more aware of how close they were standing on the sidewalk.

"Well, then, lead the way, Mr. Munns."

"I might not be one of the fancy gentlemen you're used to back east, but I do know how to offer my arm."

She laughed, and he grinned.

"I was testing you, Mr. Munns," she said, slipping her hand around the crook of his elbow so naturally that it was as if this wasn't their first walk.

"Testing me?" he said. "For what?"

"To see if you're more of a gentleman than you think you are," she said, as they took the first steps together.

With her smaller stride, he kept his steps shorter as well. He didn't mind. He was in no hurry for the time to pass. "And what is your conclusion?"

"I haven't formed one yet," she said. "Although I will say that I'm not sad to leave any of the eastern gentlemen behind. They can all have nice lives without me."

Caleb rather enjoyed the press of her fingers against his arm, and the way her clothing brushed against his. The companionship. Of a woman. "Is this revelation part of what you promised to tell me?"

"I don't remember *promising*, exactly."

He looked over at her as they walked past a restaurant. "It was definitely a promise. I don't forget things like that."

Her eyes connected with his, the dark pools of blue in the dimness captivating him. "All right. I suppose this had been your plan all along?"

He chuckled. "Something like that."

She exhaled, then said, "All right. My tale of woe began about five years ago, when both of my parents were killed."

Caleb stopped then and there. He felt awful for making light of her past. "I'm very sorry."

Her smile was sad. "Thank you. Even though it's been five years, sometimes it feels like yesterday." She cleared her throat. "Everything went to my brother, of course, but he made sure I was taken care of. For the most part. Until he started drinking."

They began walking again, Caleb listening intently. This was not the story he had expected to hear.

"It was painful to watch his disillusion grow," she said in a quiet voice. "He blamed everything and everyone else for our situation. He's my twin, you know, so you could say that it cut to the bone."

Again, Caleb stopped walking. He placed a hand over hers on his arm. "You don't have to tell me any more."

"I haven't reached the good part," she said in a voice that betrayed a bit of her emotion.

So they stood there where they'd stopped on the corner, facing each other, touching, while she continued.

"I'm a clumsy person by nature," she said, blinking up at him. "Harry, my brother, used to tease me about it. I never thought I'd miss it. But the clumsiness continued into adulthood, and with it a new awkwardness. I would say the wrong thing, do the wrong thing, even *think* the wrong thing."

"Is that possible?" Caleb asked.

"In Philadelphia society it is," she said. "Women who aren't seeking husbands are ostracized from the social circles. I wanted an education. And I got it, but that also drove the 'gentlemen' away."

Caleb instinctively tightened his hand over hers. She didn't draw back.

"I watched my friends marry one by one, and at the last dance I went to, I was asked by a man twice my age." She shrugged. "After that it wasn't too hard to accept Mr. Mercer's call to relocate teachers. I didn't want to be around my brother anymore, and there was no comfortable place for me in society."

Caleb understood, he really did, but he still had a question. "With Philadelphia behind you, do you regret your decision to leave?"

"No," she said. "The schoolchildren here need me. No one in Philadelphia did. And I think it's important to be needed."

Caleb agreed, although no one needed him. "The students of Seattle are fortunate to have you as their teacher. Forget marriage."

Her smile was much more genuine this time. "Right. I don't need to marry. I already have children, of sorts. I'll be spending plenty of time with my students, day in and day out. Besides, what does it matter that I never get kissed, never married, never have children of my own—"

"Wait," Caleb said, drawing back so he could see her more fully. "You've never kissed a man?"

Her pretty blush returned. "I haven't." She tugged on his arm, and they began to walk again. "There are more important things in life."

"Very true," he said, thinking fast. Why should this

information about Miss Silverton capture his attention so completely? Plenty of women, and likely men, didn't marry, or kiss a love interest, he assumed. But it was hard to believe that Miss Silverton had *never* been kissed. What was wrong with the men back east?

She seemed to be reading his thoughts. "It's all right, you know. I don't mind. Truly. There's never been a man I've expected to marry, so I certainly don't expect to be kissed."

With his free hand, Caleb tugged at his collar. The night was warmer now. "I can see how you'd think that, but it's a shame not to be kissed at least once in your life."

"How so?"

Caleb wasn't prepared for her question. "I... uh, because it's something that can be enjoyable." Now, his face was likely growing red.

"Even when it's not someone you plan to marry?" she asked, her voice genuinely puzzled. "That feels a bit low class to me."

Caleb couldn't let the comment pass. He drew her to a gentle stop. "It wouldn't be low class if the intentions were pure. I mean, if a promise wasn't expected. If..."

She was watching him quite intently.

He swallowed. "I'm not sure exactly what I'm trying to say, but if you ever change your mind, I'm happy to oblige."

Eleven

HARRIET WAS PRETTY sure her eyes were wider than they'd ever been. Mr. Munns had just offered to . . . kiss her. She had no idea how to respond. So she did the only thing that seemed logical at the time. She released his arm and headed back to the hotel.

"Miss Silverton," he called after her, quietly at first. Then again, louder a second time. "Miss Silverton!"

She didn't turn because her face was surely a deep red, and her pounding heart would likely give away what she thought of his offer. His scandalous offer, to say the least. *Kiss?* What could he ever want to kiss *her* for? He'd declared, just as she had, that he had no intention of marrying again.

Harriet picked up her pace, but in truth, her boots were pinching her feet. The walk to her new lodgings with Vivian had been quite enough for the evening. And now she was practically running.

"Harriet," his deep voice was much closer now. "Stop, please."

She was breathing heavily now, and the hotel was within sight. Looking over at him, she saw that he'd caught up with her. He reached out and grasped her arm. Gently, but with a bit of firmness as well.

She couldn't meet his gaze. "I shouldn't have said anything," she said. "I gave you the wrong idea, and now if you would be the gentleman that you claim to be, please step aside and let me pass."

"Harriet," he repeated, his voice softer now, almost a whisper.

She did look at him then, and she wished she hadn't. Because she realized in that moment she *wanted* him to kiss her.

"I didn't mean to scare you off," he said. "The last thing I'd want to do is make you upset. Forgive me. Forget I even brought it up. It was wrong to tease you."

Harriet released a careful exhale and finally met his gaze. "All right. I'll forget about it." She didn't want to forget about it; she didn't want *him* to forget about it. But the blood had rushed to her head, and she didn't trust her mind right now.

He smiled, and her heart did another little flip. She wondered how she could have ever found him intimidating or foreboding.

"Now, let me escort you back to the lobby, as a perfect gentleman would, who is also a *friend*," he said. "A friend who has completely forgotten that he just offered to kiss you."

She swallowed back a laugh as she took his extended arm. She didn't have to look at him to see that he was smiling. The thought sent a dart of warmth to her toes, and her boots didn't pinch quite so much anymore.

They walked the rest of the way in silence, and surprisingly enough, it wasn't awkward. More and more, Harriet felt comfortable with him. "You called me Harriet," she observed, reluctant for the outing to end. "Does that mean I should call you Caleb?"

The smile in his voice was plain. "I think it absolutely does, if that's all right with you."

"It is." She sneaked a glance at his profile. "Tell me, would you be opposed to giving me and the Pinker children a tour of the harbor sometime in the next week?"

His brows lifted. "I don't see why not."

"I hope I can get permission," she said. "Those children puzzle me exceedingly. They've hardly ventured from the hotel due to their parents' rules." They'd reached the edge of the light spilling onto the sidewalk in front of the hotel. Harriet paused, and Caleb paused with her.

"Which rules are these?" he asked.

She released his arm and faced him. Then she told him about the Pinkers' rules.

"If they can't be near the water, how will they see the harbor?"

Harriet puffed out a breath of frustration. "I don't know, and Wallace—the boy—wants to go fishing."

"That sounds like his father's business," he said.

Harriet agreed with him, she did. "But he says his father won't take him."

"Harriet," Caleb said in that maddeningly gentle tone of his. "You're their teacher, not their parent. You can't fulfill all their desires."

She bit her lip and set her hands on her hips. "I know. And I've jumped many steps ahead. We haven't even had real lessons yet. Those will start tomorrow."

His gaze was intent on her. "You're a compassionate woman."

She blinked up at him. He must have shaved again tonight, because his jaw was smooth, so smooth that she was tempted to run her fingers along his skin. "I should go inside. Vivian will be wondering . . ." She didn't finish, because he'd leaned closer, and she thought he might steal that kiss anyway. She took a step back. He didn't move, didn't follow.

But she sensed that something had shifted between them.

"Thank you for the walk," she quickly said. Turning, Harriet took a few steps toward the hotel entrance.

"Harriet," he said, his low voice carrying.

"Yes?" she said, not looking at him, waiting.

"Anytime you want to bring those kids to the harbor, I'll give the tour."

She nodded, then glanced at him a final time. He stood, silhouetted by the yellow light, his shoulders broad, his eyes warm, his presence occupying every spare inch between them. "I'll . . . let you know."

Then she took the last few steps toward the entrance and hurried into the lobby.

The people in their conversation groups didn't pay her mind, and she made her way to the staircase. When she reached her shared bedroom, Vivian had already prepared herself for bed.

Harriet sensed Vivian's expectation about telling her of the evening walk, but Harriet wanted to keep it to herself.

"How was the walk?" Vivian prompted.

"My boots have seemed to shrink." She sat on a chair and unlaced them. "How are your feet?"

"My *feet* are fine," Vivian said, not fooled for a moment. "What did Mr. Munns want to talk about?"

"Oh." Harriet shrugged. "Nothing special. I told him about the Pinker children wanting to tour the harbor. And I told him a little about Philadelphia and my family. He seemed interested in my former life, although I must say, I never thought I'd make such a friend in Seattle."

Vivian didn't say anything as she watched Harriet begin her nightly preparations. "I think he's *very* interested."

"Not in the way you're implying," Harriet said. "There will be nothing between us but friendship. We've both already agreed upon that."

Vivian laughed. "How did you come to that conclusion?"

"He's not interested in marrying, and neither am I. Simple, really." She didn't elaborate further, because she was pretty sure that Caleb's story of his false marriage wasn't something he wanted gossiped about.

Vivian pressed her lips together and picked up a book by the bedside table. After flipping through a few pages, she said, "A man can change his mind."

Harriet felt the slow burn of her cheeks. She moved out of Vivian's line of sight to the closet, where she changed into her night gown. A man *could* change his mind. A woman could too. But *she* wouldn't. She'd made up her mind before getting onto the ship at Philadelphia.

Yet, when she settled into bed and pulled the covers over her shoulders and up to her chin, she was still thinking of Caleb Munns. About his offer to kiss her. An offer he'd taken back, of course, but what did it mean that he'd offered in the first place?

Even in the darkness, and with Vivian's relaxed breathing in the next bed over, Harriet couldn't get her mind to stop mulling over Caleb's words. *Should* she let him kiss her?

No.

She worried that if they kissed, although it would mean nothing to him, it might mean something to her.

Harriet shut her eyes and forced her thoughts to move from Caleb Munns to the tasks tomorrow. Getting settled into her new place, teaching the Pinker children . . . She looked forward to a productive day, one that didn't have room for daydreaming about a particular fisherman.

Twelve

CALEB SUPPOSED HE could inquire at the hotel where Harriet Silverton had moved to, but he wasn't sure that was the best plan. He could stop by the schoolhouse and hope to find her there, but he didn't return to the docks until the late afternoon, well after school would have ended. Or . . . he could aimlessly walk the streets, hoping for a bit of luck, and run into her by happenstance.

Which he was doing right now.

It had been an entire week since he'd seen Harriet, and he realized now that he should have arranged to meet her. The first few times he'd met her had been coincidences. It had almost seemed that providence had kept throwing them together. But now . . . He missed her.

This was a strange thing to admit to himself. Frankly, he didn't know Harriet all that well in the scheme of things, yet he knew her more than he ever did Lucille. Perhaps because everything Lucille had told him had been part-lie.

And he supposed he missed Harriet because when he was around her, he felt lighter somehow. Intrigued. Happier? Yes.

Caleb had arrived full circle, and he was back at the harbor again. The gulls soared about the incoming boats with the evening tide. Caleb had finished earlier today than usual, thanks to an abundant catch of fish.

He stopped and gazed across the activity of the boats, the men, the nets, the fish being dumped into carts to be hauled off and sold to vendors. Gulls screeched overhead, dipping and diving and gobbling up remnants of fish. The day had lost its warmth as clouds moved in, darkening the late-afternoon horizon. The salt on the air was sharp and tangy.

Perhaps he should head to a café, get his supper, and call it a day. Standing here, he felt like a lost soul, which was ironic. The last time he'd felt that way, he'd been caught up in another woman. And now, here he was, again. Caught up.

At first, he wasn't sure the woman speaking to Bill was Harriet Silverton. The distance was too great, and her back was turned toward Caleb. Then he saw the two children on either side of her. A boy and a girl, both towheaded.

Caleb's initial instinct was to stride over to the group and find out if Harriet was looking for *him*. To give that tour. Just as he considered it, another thought entered his mind. Perhaps she'd arranged something with Bill. The idea rankled Caleb, but what if it was true? What if Bill and Harriet were . . . interested in each other? Yes, she'd stated quite clearly that she'd come to Seattle for a job and had no sights on marriage. But Caleb very well knew that a woman's heart and mind could change. Sometimes at the offer of fresh pancakes.

This was why Caleb did not approach the group. And this was why after a few moments of watching Harriet speaking to Bill, and Bill's broad smile as he replied, that Caleb left the harbor. Hands deep in his pockets, eyes trained on the cobblestone road, heart heavy.

She had danced with *him*.
She had walked with *him*.
She had asked *him* to give her the tour.

Once again, it appeared that Caleb had grossly misread a woman's intentions. He'd leapt to conclusions far ahead of reality. And now, the result was . . . nothing. He was alone again, as he'd been for a long time now. Nothing in his life had truly changed. If he cut out the past ten days, scrubbed the thoughts of Harriet from his mind, he was still himself.

No one had been hurt. No one had died. He still had his boat, his rented room, his too-tight suitcoat. He was healthy. A year from now, he'd have enough money in savings to put money down on his own apartment. He'd even considered buying another boat, joining up with a partner. Not Bill, of course. Making a bit of a dynasty for himself. He could add a boat a year, take commissions. Build a home.

Women were . . . well, women were complicated. And it was best he not to get his heart involved with the female race, because his own heart was complicated enough.

"Mr. Munns!" the voice that called out to him was feminine.

He could not believe it was her. No. He stopped in his tracks but didn't turn around.

"Mr. Munns," the woman said again.

There was no doubt it was Harriet. His entire body betrayed, feet pivoting without his permission, and eyes locking on her.

She was walking toward him with the two children. They were dressed to the height of fashion, and now that Caleb thought about it, Harriet was well turned out too. Her navy skirt pinched at her narrow waist, and her pale green blouse curved with her torso. She wore no jacket, and he knew instantly that she was cold, if he were to judge by the pink of her cheeks.

He couldn't explain the immense relief that went through him at the sight of her walking toward him. Perhaps there was nothing between her and Bill, and perhaps Caleb had worried for nothing.

"You're a hard man to find, Mr. Munns," Harriet said.

This only made Caleb's heart soar. Was she talking about today? Or this entire past week? "I returned early today, and I was, in fact . . ." He paused because two blond-headed children were listening to every word he spoke. "I was in fact looking for you."

He didn't miss the upward curve of Harriet's mouth.

"You were?"

"I was." He redirected his gaze to the children so that he didn't stare at Harriet for so long. "Are these your students?"

"Why yes," Harriet said, her tone both formal and amused. "This is Wallace and Rebecca."

"Becky," the girl corrected.

"Becky," Harriet amended. "And they've both earned a field trip, so you can imagine how much we were hoping you'd be able to show us about."

"I'm available now," he said. "Unless it's too late?"

He was answered by Wallace. "Not too late at all, sir. Miss Silverton says that you're a fisherman. Can we go out on your boat?"

"Wallace," Harriet said.

At the same moment, Caleb said, "If it's all right with your parents."

Harriet gave Caleb a sharp look. "No getting onto a boat. We're lucky your mother has allowed us to walk about the harbor in the first place."

Wallace folded his arms. "You just don't like boats."

Caleb frowned. "Do you not like boats, Miss Silverton?"

The children joined him in looking at her in anticipation.

"I, uh, I become quite sick on boats," Harriet said, her cheeks staining a darker pink. "I hope to never step foot on a boat again."

She couldn't be serious, yet her somber gaze and fiery cheeks told him she was absolutely in earnest.

"Well, there won't be any boat riding today at least," Caleb said. "Let's start with the office of the harbor master. We are close to it now."

Harriet cast him a grateful look, and as the group of them headed in the direction of the shipyard office, Caleb couldn't help stealing glances her direction. The wind had picked up, and bits of her hair whipped against her neck. Why wasn't she wearing a jacket or a shawl? The children were warmly dressed, but he was sure Harriet was trying not to shiver.

He shrugged out of his own jacket. He wasn't wearing his heavy fishing coat, so at least this one didn't smell like the ocean and fish. Before Harriet could notice what he was doing, he set the jacket across her shoulders.

Her gaze snapped to his. "I don't need—"

"You do," he murmured. "You're trembling."

She blew out a breath, and for a moment he thought she might be stubborn enough to hand it back. Instead, she gripped the edges of the lapels and drew it closer about her body. "Thank you."

He nodded and said, "Here we are. Now, you must address the man in charge as Captain Kilgon. Respect is due at all times, even though he's a land man now."

"A land man?" Wallace asked. "What's that?"

"Someone who doesn't sail anymore." Caleb tugged open the door and led them into a square, stout building. Inside, the smell of old brine was prevalent, and the walls were decorated with old ship memorabilia.

The harbor master wasn't around, so Caleb showed the children the different items and explained each one.

Harriet listened and walked around with them, but she didn't ask any questions. Each time he caught her gaze on him, she quickly looked away. Caleb wished they could have a private conversation, just the two of them. He wanted to know what she was truly thinking. What she'd talked to Bill about. How her week had been with her new responsibilities.

After they finished with the boat house, they headed outside again, and Caleb was gratified that Harriet kept his jacket on. The clouds were darker now, lower to the earth, and the wind had picked up. "A storm's going to hit soon," he said. "I should escort you back to your home."

"Can we watch it coming in?" Wallace asked.

Caleb ruffled the boy's hair that was already being mussed up by the wind. "I think we should get you back before your mother worries."

Wallace looked disappointed but didn't complain. A glance at Harriet told Caleb he'd done the right thing. As they walked back to the hotel, the children chattered about what they'd seen at the harbor, and Wallace expressed a keen interest in the boats.

Inside the hotel lobby, they were met by a young woman who identified herself as Jenny.

The moment the children were led off, Caleb said to Harriet, "I ought to walk you to your home as well. Unless you'll wait out the storm in the hotel?"

"No," Harriet said. "Vivian will worry about me if I do that." Her gaze slid past him to the hotel windows. "It doesn't look too bad yet."

Caleb followed her gaze. Bits of trash tumbled down the street, and the handful of trees he could see were getting a good shaking. But it hadn't started raining yet. "Let's go, then."

Thirteen

THE STORM WAS faster moving than Harriet could have predicted. After leaving the hotel, Caleb took her arm, and she slipped her hand around the crook of his. She was still wearing his jacket, which helped against the increasing cold wind. But not half a block from the hotel, the rain started.

"Oh," she exclaimed. "I didn't think it would rain so soon."

"The clouds don't look friendly. I'm afraid it's going to get much worse." Caleb pulled her closer, and she leaned into him as they quickened their pace.

They hadn't spoken much since leaving the hotel. She might have been too open with him when they'd met at the harbor—telling him she'd been searching for him.

She'd genuinely been worried they wouldn't find him before night approached. It had been hard enough to get Mrs. Pinker to agree to taking the children on a short visit to the harbor. Of course, now, Harriet was grateful the children were safely inside the hotel in Jenny's care.

The small raindrops soon increased in intensity, and the rain pinged her hat, her face, her neck. Everything covered by the jacket stayed protected, but she was sure her skirt would take some drying.

The wind tugged at her hair, and there was no use trying to fix anything. A strong gust stole her breath, and she found herself practically clinging to Caleb. He didn't seem to mind. No one else was about the streets, so it appeared they'd had the sense to take cover. More trash tumbled along the streets, and the taller trees swayed dangerously.

"How far are you?" Caleb asked above the howling wind.

She named the street, and he said, "I'm much closer. We'll go to my place."

Any protest she might have made was stolen on the wind, and just then, her hat made its final tug and flew off her head.

Caleb turned to grab it, but it had already tumbled out of reach. He let go of her and sprinted after the thing.

"Let it go," Harriet called. The wind felt like it was about to knock her over, and the last thing she cared about was her old hat.

But Caleb either didn't hear her, or he was too focused on his rescue. A moment later, he returned, the crumpled hat gripped in his hand.

Without his protection for a few moments, Harriet was soaked and windblown. She smoothed the hair from her face, but it was useless. The wind was relentless.

If possible, the rain drove harder, and Caleb grabbed her hand and tugged her along. She ran with him while holding up her skirt with her other hand. Her shoes would be ruined, since she'd opted not to wear her boots to the harbor. Vain of her.

They turned a corner, and he led her through an alley that cut the wind in half. The rain didn't lighten, though, and when Caleb turned another corner, Harriet was relieved when he drew her to a stop.

They were in front of a two-story building, and Caleb opened the door. The interior lobby was cold and deserted. But it was dry. Breathless, Harriet walked with him on the hardwood floor, leaving water in their wake. He stopped in front of a door and pulled out a key from his pocket.

Harriet couldn't help but notice his hands trembling from the cold. Harriet herself was trembling all over. Her teeth chattered, and even her legs were shaking.

"Come in." Caleb unlocked the door and pushed it open.

Under any other circumstance, Harriet wouldn't enter a bachelor's apartment alone with him. Yet, Caleb was right. His place was closer, and the storm had turned dangerous. Although Harriet was shivering from the cold, his set of rooms was decidedly warmer. It appeared he had a small sitting room that doubled as a kitchen, with a bedroom beyond.

"Here," Caleb said. "I'll take the wet jacket and get you something warmer."

She got a good look at him then. He was absolutely soaking. His shirt had plastered to his shoulders and chest. His dark copper hair looked almost black now that it was wet, and his trousers . . . She glanced away as she attempted to slip off the jacket, but the combination of her wet clothing and her trembling fingers made it nearly impossible.

"I'll help," Caleb said.

She nodded, because her teeth were still chattering. Despite the deep chill in her body, she felt the warmth of Caleb's breath as he moved close to her and helped her out of the jacket.

"Thank you," she managed.

Caleb stepped away and set the jacket over one of the kitchen chairs. She stood in the entryway, shivering, too cold to do anything else. The room was tidy, masculine, with only the basics of a small table, two chairs, a sofa with an afghan throw over it. She wondered who'd crocheted it.

Beyond, in the bedroom, she could see the edge of a narrow bed, and a nightstand with an oil lamp and a tattered book upon it. She quickly averted her gaze, feeling she had no business looking into the bedroom of a man.

"I'll be right back." Caleb walked into the bedroom, shutting the door partway behind him.

Moments later, he came out, wearing a different shirt, this one dry. His hair was still damp and had begun to curl at the ends, making him look younger. And he carried a heavy coat. One she'd seen him wear on the vessel that took them from Teekalet to Seattle. "This will get you warm."

"I'll look like a drowned rat in that thing," she said.

"Maybe you should check a mirror." Caleb's mouth lifted in amusement. "You already look like a drowned rat."

Harriet smiled, despite her shivering. He was right. The heavy coat was warm, and standing so near Caleb made her warmer still. When he stepped back, a satisfied look on his face, she had the urge to ask him to stay close to her. Keep her warm. But that was entirely inappropriate. She moved another step toward the door. "I shouldn't stay long."

"No gentleman would let a woman go out into such a fierce storm," he said. "You might blow away."

She wouldn't blow away, but she also didn't want to go back out into that rain either.

"Have a seat," he said. "I don't have any refreshment, since I usually eat at one of the cafés."

"I don't need refreshment." Harriet edged toward the sofa. She sat down, and the fishing coat nearly swallowed her up.

"Sorry if it smells." Caleb pulled the afghan from the back of the sofa.

Until that moment, she hadn't noticed the odor. But now, she realized it did smell of ocean, salt, and fish. Apparently the cold rain had dulled her senses. Although other senses were perfectly fine. She was quite aware of Caleb's concerned gaze as he draped the afghan over her legs, and the scent of rain upon him, not to mention the image of his strong, capable hands treating her like she was a porcelain doll.

"Aren't you cold?" she said. "I can't take everything from you."

"I'm fine," he said, his smile slight.

And for a moment, they gazed at each other in the small apartment, with the wind howling and rain driving outside.

Harriet looked away first.

"Would you like, uh, a cup of water?" he asked.

"No, thank you." She adjusted the afghan. Her fingers had stopped their visible trembling, but she still felt a bit shaky. Or was it nervous? It wasn't that she feared being alone with Caleb. She knew he wouldn't harm her or take advantage. It was that she wasn't entirely sure she trusted herself.

Being in his simple living space, with no one else around them, made it seem like Caleb took up the whole of the space with his presence alone. She was aware of everything about him. How his shirt cut across his shoulders, his rolled-up sleeves that displayed the definition of his tanned forearms, the taper of his waist, and the length of his legs. Goodness, she was warming up.

"You can have your coat back," she said, rising to take it off.

"Are you sure?" he asked. "Will you be warm enough?"

Oh, yes. "I'm much warmer, and you're right, the fish smell is quite strong."

He chuckled. "That's an understatement." Taking the coat from her, he returned to the back bedroom.

With the small reprieve, Harriet touched her palm to her forehead. Her skin was rather cool. She could have sworn she was coming down with a fever. Her hair was a mess, that she knew, and her attempts to smooth it out were quite pointless.

When Caleb returned, Harriet had retaken her seat.

He carried a book and handed it to her.

Curious, she took the book and looked at the cover. "You read poetry?"

"Not exactly." He settled on one of the kitchen chairs. "That's about the only thing I have left from my mother. She loved to read."

Harriet opened the cover. The well-worn pages felt fragile. She flipped them slowly, then stopped at one that was earmarked. Without any prompting, she began to read the poem.

When she finished, she looked up and saw Caleb wiping his eyes.

"Are you all right?" she asked.

He gave her a half smile, but it was sad too. "I haven't heard that poem in a long time, since my mother read it to me."

"She read to you as a child?" She looked down at the creased page. It looked like the poem had been read hundreds of times. She gazed at him again. Something in his tone had made her curious. "Can you not read, Caleb?" she asked in a quiet voice.

He didn't answer for a moment. "I learned letters, but I could never figure out how combinations of letters created words."

Harriet tried not to look stunned, and she schooled her features. "Did you learn the sounds of the letters?"

"The sounds?"

She understood now why he couldn't read. "Each letter has a sound, some of them more than one. Once you learn to sound out the letters, it's only a matter of putting the sounds together."

Caleb shifted forward on his chair and rested his elbows on his knees. The action made his shoulders bunch up, made him appear more vulnerable.

"I can teach you," she said into the silence of the room.

His brown eyes snapped to hers. "I've gone this long without reading." He shrugged those large shoulders of his. "Haven't needed to."

Harriet disagreed, but she sensed he'd told her something extremely personal, and she didn't want to embarrass him. "Do you want me to read you another poem?"

The edges of his mouth softened. "Please."

So she read another poem, then a third, which was about the sea and the waves. "Is this what being a fisherman is like?" she asked. "Being at one with Mother Nature, and the patterns of the waves echo the patterns of your heart?"

"Maybe on a very good day," Caleb said. "And that would be dependent on whether the fishing is productive."

"Of course it would." Harriet smiled. She turned another page, read another poem.

He didn't stop her, so she continued to read poem after poem. They were enchanting, and Harriet could see why Caleb kept this tattered book with him, even though he couldn't read a word. They connected him not only to his mother, but they filled the heart and mind with beauty.

"Thank you," he whispered when she finally closed the book. "You don't know how much it means to hear those words again."

Harriet nodded. Somewhere along the way, her heart had

crept into her throat. The man sitting on the sturdy kitchen chair across from her had been nothing but a gentleman. Offering her warmth and protection. And for this short time in his apartment, he'd even shown a bit of his heart.

"If you change your mind about learning the sounds to the letters, I can help you," she said.

Caleb shook his head, but his eyes were shining. "You don't want to take on a stubborn man such as me. Besides, you have plenty of students."

"I think I can handle one more."

He smiled, but his eyes still turned down her offer.

That was all right. Harriet could wait. She'd convince him yet. "The rain must have stopped by now. Vivian might be scouring the streets."

Caleb rose to his feet and extended his hand. It was only to give her a boost to her feet, but his hand remained clasped around hers for a few extra moments. Harriet didn't mind, though she knew she needed to release him. Head back to her living quarters. Breathe in a space that wasn't filled with everything Caleb Munns.

So Harriet slipped her hand from his and turned toward the door.

They headed out of the apartment, and the rain had indeed lessened to a light drizzle. Caleb had brought along an umbrella, and Harriet was reminded of the day she'd tried to stop the fight with her parasol. The thought made her smile, and Caleb noticed. Of course he had.

"Glad to be out of my place?" he asked as they walked along the sidewalk. A few people were out, but the streets were mostly empty.

"No, I was thinking about how handy an umbrella could be, or a parasol."

Caleb chuckled. "Do you want to hold the umbrella? You know, in case I stop being a gentleman?"

She smiled. "I think you've proved yourself well enough by now."

His brows lifted. "Have you reached your conclusion about me yet?"

"Nearly," she teased.

The smile on his face made her heart melt. Thankfully the wind had died down as well, so by the time they reached her lodgings, she wasn't a trembling mess. But she would be happy to find her way into her nightgown and her warm bed, even if nightfall was still a good hour away.

Although she was reluctant to say goodbye to Caleb, it was definitely time.

"Now I know where to find you, Miss Silverton," he said in a low voice as they stopped at her doorstep.

"You do." She rested her hand on his arm, briefly. "Thank you for the tour, and for letting me take shelter."

"Anytime."

Fourteen

CALEB STOOD OUTSIDE the schoolhouse. It had been about ten minutes since he'd watched all of the students leave. Harriet and Miss Little still hadn't come out, though. Did they typically remain for a while? Perhaps to clean up? He wasn't entirely sure what the two women might be doing, because he had scant memories of going to school himself. When he realized he was expected to stand and read aloud, Caleb had started to ditch school.

His teacher never reported him.

The schoolhouse door opened, and out stepped Miss Little. She paused when she saw him, which meant that Harriet nearly ran into her.

"Oh, hello, Mr. Munns," Miss Little said.

"Hello," Harriet said as well, her brow wrinkled with her unasked question.

He nodded to Miss Little, then trained his gaze on Harriet. "Might I speak to you for a moment?"

"I'll meet you later," Miss Little said.

Caleb wasn't going to protest, because he didn't exactly want an audience for what he was about to ask Harriet.

She turned her expectant blue eyes upon him the moment Miss Little left.

His heart did a funny flip. "I wondered if I might inquire after some tutoring services."

Harriet lifted her brows, then she spoke in a coy tone. "Oh, is this for one of your neighbors? A friend, perhaps?"

He held back a smile, pleased that *she* seemed to be pleased. "Not a friend, exactly. He's about my height and goes by the surname of Munns. What would be the price?"

"Well..." She pretended to ponder. "How about we have a trial tutoring session, then discuss the price afterward if both parties are in agreement?"

Caleb nodded gravely. "I think he would agree to that. When can you schedule it?"

Harriet looked up at the sky, then toward the schoolhouse. "Right now will work. There's a convenient schoolhouse behind me that's currently empty. Plenty of chalk and slates to write upon."

"Oh, I don't think he wants to learn to write," Caleb said. "Reading will be enough work."

Harriet smirked and grabbed his hand. Then she tugged him toward the schoolhouse door. Her bold move stunned him, but he wasn't about to protest Harriet's actions. Holding her hand was nice.

She pushed open the door, still grasping his hand, then led him inside.

The interior smelled of warmth, and fresh wood, and Caleb was taken back to what little time he'd spent in the schoolhouse as a boy. The desks were lined up in perfect order, chairs tucked in, and upon each desk sat a cleaned slate.

She released his hand to point out the row of letters written across the top of the chalkboard at the front of the room. "Do you remember these letters?"

"Most of them," he said. "Maybe."

She smiled at him, then turned to pick up a long stick. She pointed to one of the letters in the middle.

"H."

"Yes." She pointed to another toward the end.

"P?"

"Very good." She pointed to a few more. He got them all right except for two. But once she reminded him of the names, he remembered.

"Very good," she said in a voice that she must use on her students. She set the stick down. "Let's practice writing them."

He watched her move to a desk and pick up a slate, something he supposed all children in school used across the territories. "Bring a chair over, and you can sit at my desk. I think you're a little tall for the children's."

He did so, and soon he was seated across from Harriet. "I thought I told you I didn't want to learn to write."

"Oh, this is so you can teach your friend," she said. "This is the letter C, as you know. Try it."

"Aren't we going to start with the letter A?" he asked, taking the piece of chalk from her. Their fingers brushed, and he wanted to forget the chalk, forget the letters, and hold her hand again.

"Every student needs to learn to write his name first," she said primly.

"All right." He formed the C. It looked much more boxy than her curved example.

She next wrote the lowercase a.

Caleb copied. When his name was effectively spelled out, she made him write it several times until he could write it without looking at her example.

"You are doing very well," she said, still using that teacher voice.

Caleb set down the chalk and brushed off his fingers. "It's because I have a good teacher."

Her blue eyes smiled back at him. The room had taken on an orange-gold glow with the late-afternoon sun nearly setting. Such a different day than the one they'd spent dodging the storm. When a faint blush stole over her cheeks, he realized he'd been staring at her for more than a few moments.

"I must say, the first lesson was a success." She set the slate back in its place and gathered the chalk they'd used. She rose to her feet, brushed off her own hands, then clasped them together.

It seemed the lesson was over, and she was ready for him to leave.

Caleb stood as well. He didn't want this time with her to end just yet. He'd come here for more than a lesson. Yes, he wanted to see her, but he also wanted to talk to her. He wanted to tell her that his mind had changed. "Harriet," he said in a quiet voice.

She lifted her chin and met his gaze.

"Do you ever regret our conversation on that night we walked along the hotel street?" he asked.

A small crease formed between her brows. "You mean when you . . ." She cut off her words, and the color in her cheeks darkened.

"Yes, that night. I said some things that might have been true at the time, but they aren't true anymore." Caleb had said he'd never marry again. He'd also said that he was willing to kiss her, if only for experience. But now, he wanted to kiss her for a different reason. "Can a fellow change his mind?"

The edges of her mouth lifted, yet she took a step away from the desk, putting a new distance between them. Was she rejecting him?

"I suppose he might," she said. "I mean, it's a woman's prerogative, but perhaps there can be exceptions."

"I'd like the exception."

She folded her arms and turned from him, then walked slowly toward the door. She didn't open it, though, merely stood near it, her gaze focused on the adjacent window.

Neither of them said anything for a few moments as the orange-gold light faded to a softer peach. He continued walking toward her, and still she didn't turn around. When he placed his hands on her shoulders, his thumbs touched the warm skin of her neck.

Her exhale was like a sigh through his own body.

"Caleb," she whispered.

"Hmm?"

"I've changed my mind too."

He didn't need any more words between them, and when she rotated to face him, he knew exactly what they'd agreed to. He shifted his hands and cradled her face. The blue of her eyes had captivated him from the moment he'd jumped into the ocean to save her. And now, those same blue eyes reached an even deeper part of his soul.

Her eyes fluttered shut, and he closed the distance. The first touch of their lips was tentative, soft. And then she twined her arms about his neck, and he drew her flush against him. Deepening the kiss, he became lost in her warmth, her softness, her touch. He moved his hands up her back, feeling the heat of her skin through her blouse, and she raised up on her toes to pull him even closer.

Her flowery scent surrounded him, pulled him in, and he knew that whatever reservations he'd had after Lucille, every single one of them had fallen away with Harriet.

"Caleb," she whispered against his mouth, "this is much more than one kiss."

He smiled and kissed her again, lingering. "I never meant it to be one kiss."

"Oh?"

He pressed his mouth against her lower jaw, then trailed kisses along her neck. "Did you want it to be one kiss?" he whispered.

"At first I thought I did," she murmured. "But now . . ."

She drew away and locked him into place with her blue gaze.

His heart thudded. "Now . . . ?" he prompted.

"Now I don't want you to stop."

He chuckled and pulled her into a tight embrace. She squeezed him back. He could get used to this; he could reopen his heart and let Harriet in.

Fifteen

HARRIET WAS IN love. She wasn't quite sure how it had happened. Well, she knew *how* it had happened, but she'd never expected it to happen to her. Not with the man who'd pulled her from the harbor waters, and who spent his days on a fishing boat. But the thought of Caleb now, while she was in a room full of students, wouldn't leave her.

Her thoughts were full of his warm brown eyes, the dark copper of his hair, his broad shoulders, and the way his blunt fingertips brushed against her wrist when he held her hand across her desk in the late afternoons during their twice-a-week tutoring sessions.

"Miss Silverton," a young voice said, standing in front of her desk as if he'd been waiting a while for her to answer.

Harriet blinked and smiled. "Yes, Jeb?"

"My ma needs me home early today," Jeb said. "Says her baby is coming soon." The boy's green eyes were bright with anticipation.

"Then you can leave for the day," Harriet said.

He grinned and was out the door in a flash. A few of the other children complained that they wanted to go home early too. But for the most part, the children were content at the little schoolhouse. They adored Vivian, and Harriet could see why as she watched her friend move among the desks, checking on their arithmetic.

Harriet tried to refocus on the short stories she was grading, but her thoughts continually returned to Caleb. He said he'd had a surprise for her today, and after school she was to meet him at the docks. She hadn't slept much last night as she lay in bed wondering what on earth his surprise might be. She wouldn't mind if he stole another kiss.

Over the past few weeks, she'd looked forward to their tutoring sessions for more reasons than just spending time with him. He made her laugh, he made her swoon, he made her feel like all the hardships before coming to Seattle had been worth it. Because he'd been here at the end of it all.

"You're sighing again." Vivian stopped near the desk. "Great story?"

Harriet's face warmed, and she glanced at the paper in her hands that she hadn't been reading at all. "Oh, I'm sure it's lovely."

Vivian smirked. "Do you need to be excused early, too, like Jeb?"

"No," Harriet said quickly. "I'm perfectly capable of focusing on the task at hand."

"Um-hm." Vivian winked, then moved to the board. "Class," she said in an authoritative voice. "Many of you are missing a crucial step in your sums. We need to carry the one this way."

Harriet glanced at the clock on the wall. Less than an hour to go. She could do this.

And perhaps she shouldn't have nearly run to the harbor after the school children left, because her pinched feet would be sore later, but her heart wouldn't stop its fierce pounding.

She spied Caleb where he said he'd be—on his fishing

boat where it was tied to the dock. He was cleaning the boat, and she surmised he'd already brought in his catch for the day. The sun overhead was warm, and only a few wispy clouds scattered across the sky. Otherwise, the barely-there breeze made today pretty much perfect.

The moment Caleb lifted his head and their eyes connected, her heart melted at the smile that spread across his face. He straightened as she approached, his gaze making no secret of his slow perusal of her person.

Already, she was blushing, and he hadn't said one word to her.

He remedied that in the next moment. "Harriet, you're early."

"Oh, am I?" she said, arching her brow. "School got out the same time as every other day."

The edges of his mouth quirked.

"All right, so I left Vivian to do the cleanup," she said. "I'll make it up to her."

He moved to edge of the boat and held out his hand.

"Oh, no," she said, folding her arms. "I can wait on the dock for you to finish."

His smile broadened, and he kept his hand extended.

Harriet considered his hand, then she looked at the boat. As long as they were tied to the dock, perhaps she'd be all right. So she placed her hand in his, and he hoisted her onto the boat.

"Here, have a seat," he said, still holding her hand as he led her to a small bench.

She sat down and gripped the edge of the seat.

"Not so bad, right?" he said.

She shrugged, trying not to grimace. "It's a beautiful day."

He only flashed a smile and continued cleaning.

Would it be impertinent to ask him what his surprise was? She looked about the boat but didn't see anything out of the ordinary, as far as her scant knowledge of boats went.

When Caleb finished the cleaning, he turned to her, holding a thick vest of some sort. "Stand up," he said.

She frowned. "What is that?"

"It's a life preserver." He grasped her hand and drew her to her feet. "Ordered it from a catalog, and it arrived the other day. See, if someone is wearing this and they fall off a boat, or a gangplank, they won't sink below the water. This keeps them buoyant."

Harriet gazed at the thing. It looked bulky and uncomfortable. "What am I supposed to do with it?"

He chuckled. "Wear it."

"No, thank you." Then she paused. "Is *this* your surprise?"

Another chuckle. "Not quite." He lifted her arm and slipped her hand through the opening of the vest.

"I really don't need this," she said. "The harbor is fine. I don't plan on falling off the boat."

Caleb wasn't listening. He continued to slide the vest onto her, then he tied the straps in front. The breeze ruffled his hair as he worked, and she was close enough to kiss him if she raised up on her toes a little.

When he finished, he lifted his gaze. "Ready?"

Her breath stalled at his nearness. "For what?"

"I'm going to teach you how to fish."

She wasn't sure she'd heard him right. Then her mind caught up. "No, Caleb. I don't want to learn to fish."

He closed the distance then and kissed her.

At first, Harriet was stunned. Anyone about the harbor would be able to see them, and by kissing her in public Caleb was making quite a statement. Then, second, she became suspicious. Was he trying to coerce her? Make her forget her protests? Finally, she decided she didn't care anymore. His hands cradled her face, his skin rough and warm against her. If it weren't for the life preserver, Harriet would have pressed against him, but the thing was bulky and prevented such a thing.

As it was, the kiss was all too brief.

"Sit down, Harriet," Caleb said, his brown eyes twinkling.

She didn't even care that he was being extremely bossy. Sitting down, she reveled in the warmth that still coursed through her body from his kissing. Without a word of protest or complaint, she watched him untie the boat from the dock, and soon they were sailing past the other boats.

"We won't go far," he said.

She said nothing, then he came over to her and took her hand. "Are you all right?" he asked in a low voice.

"I think so."

He smiled and ran a thumb along her jawline. "Look around you. It's a beautiful day."

She swallowed. She could do this. Turning her head, she saw that they weren't all that far from the harbor and there were plenty of other boats in sight.

"Ready to learn to fish?"

She blinked. "Here?"

"Yes," he said, his eyes trained on her. "Come on. I think you'll love it."

His words weren't exactly prophetic, because Harriet couldn't say she loved fishing, but she got better at casting the nets. And at the end of the next hour, she could confidently admit she'd enjoyed herself, especially when Caleb hauled up a net that she'd cast, and there were two dozen fish in it.

She watched in fascination as he dumped them into a

holding container. She even helped catch one that got away and slipped across the deck. For that, she earned another kiss.

Of course, enjoying this fishing excursion might have to do with Caleb's presence and the feeling that they were isolated from everything and everyone else. Cocooned by the warm sun, the light wind, the soft creaking of the boat, the deep tones of Caleb's voice, and vast blue surrounding them.

Harriet was starting to understand the pull of the ocean, and she enjoyed watching Caleb in his element. She knew she'd never tire of watching him work the sails, examine the fishing nets, and the look of triumph on his face when fish were a direct result.

She didn't mind this life she was living, not at all.

So, when Caleb joined her on the bench and asked, "Are you ready for your surprise?" she was confused.

"Isn't being whisked away to fish my surprise?"

"No." His mouth lifted at the edges. "It's part of it, because I wanted to make sure that you didn't detest my living."

Harriet was about to argue but stopped herself when she saw the earnest expression on his face. She supposed her comments about never wanting to step on a boat again had really affected him. But now . . . She inhaled the warm, salty air. Somehow, she could breathe freer around Caleb, no matter what they were doing.

"Remember how you agreed that a man could change his mind?"

She nodded. "I do."

His smile widened, and he took her hand in his. "Good. I was hoping you did, because I'm in love with you, Harriet Silverton."

The words drove into her heart, making her head spin. Caleb . . . loved her?

He slid his fingers between hers, and her heart hitched. "I'm still months away from affording a wife, but I hope that you'll take pity on me and agree to a long engagement."

She knew then that it was a matter of pride to Caleb that his wife wasn't forced to remain in the workforce. The school board would release her as a teacher anyway once she married, but in these modern times, some women would take in work at home although they were married.

"You want a wife, Caleb?" she whispered.

"I want *you*, Harriet," he whispered back, his eyes crinkling at the corners.

She looped her arms about his neck. "That's nice to hear, since I'm in love with you too."

He grinned. "Is that a yes?"

She edged closer. "Are you proposing?"

"I am."

"Then, yes, I'll marry you, Caleb Munns."

This time, *she* kissed *him*. Perhaps it was good that she wore the life preserver, because much more of Caleb in her arms would have made her never want to return to shore. With the wide, blue ocean around them, Harriet let herself become lost in his kiss.

It turned out that Harriet hadn't come to Seattle to find a husband, but somehow, she did anyway

Heather B. Moore is a *USA Today* bestselling author. She writes historical thrillers under the pen name H.B. Moore; her latest are *The Killing Curse* and *Breaking Jess*. Under the name Heather B. Moore, she writes romance and women's fiction; her latest include the Pine Valley Novels. Under pen name Jane Redd, she writes the young adult speculative Solstice series, including her latest release *Mistress Grim*. Heather is represented by Dystel, Goderich & Bourret.

Join Heather's email list: hbmoore.com/contact
Website: HBMoore.com
Facebook: Fans of H. B. Moore
Blog: MyWritersLair.blogspot.com
Twitter: @HeatherBMoore
Instagram: @AuthorHBMoore

A Journey to Love

TERI HARMAN

One

January 3, 1866
Boston, Massachusetts

CORA MARTIN WALKED to the edge of the dock and set her small case at her feet. A stiff breeze rolled over Boston Harbor. She smiled, the wind stirring her excitement.

Father Bracewell stopped beside her, folded his arms. "I must ask you once more, Cora. Are you *certain* this is the right thing to do?"

"Yes, I'm certain."

"I don't trust this Mercer character. The papers say he's only interested in the money."

"As are most business men. He's a means to an end, Father. There's a great need for skilled nurses and midwives in the West. I want to work, to help."

"But it's such a long way. Down to the bottom of the map and back. So many things could go wrong."

Cora shook her head. For more than five months they'd circled through this argument. "I survived an orphan childhood, the battlefield surgeries of the war, my husband's death, and Mrs. Bracewell's Irish cooking. A sea voyage will be nothing."

A half smile lifted the reverend's bearded cheek. "You've certainly got a stomach of iron. That'll serve you well on the waves." He sighed. "I hope there truly are good Christian men to marry in Seattle, as Mercer claims. You'll need a husband in order to survive out there. Your age shouldn't be a problem; a smart man will see the advantages of taking a widow as a wife. Women in their thirties are wise and sober."

"I'm only twenty-eight, Father," Cora corrected, unable to stop herself. She didn't feel wise and sober. She felt a childlike giddiness for all the possibilities of the West.

Bracewell waved his hand in dismissal. "Right, right. I know you haven't been eager to remarry, but Thomas has been gone for over a year now. It's time."

Cora's stomach tightened as Thomas's bloodied face flashed in her mind. Even as he'd lain dying, legs mutilated and torso crushed, he looked at her with that cool indifference she'd grown accustomed to over their seven years together. Part of her had longed for a last-breath spark of emotion, some flicker of passion. She'd waited for her own feelings to swell and deepen. But Thomas's death couldn't change how they felt and who they were. Theirs had been a marriage of convenience, nothing more. So she'd sat beside his cot, more nurse than wife, while gunfire echoed over the frigid night and the last of his blood soaked his navy uniform.

When Thomas's body had finally succumbed to his gruesome injuries, Cora marveled at her sweeping sense of relief. Her husband lay dead, but she only wanted to smile at the buoyancy of her heart—a twist of emotion she'd been trying to unravel since that September night in 1864. She was certain there must be something wrong with her, something vital that lay broken in jagged pieces at the bottom of her soul.

What woman smiles sitting next to her husband's deathbed? What woman feels so little for a man she's lived with for seven years?

I'm incapable of love. Real, deep, true love—it's beyond me. My loveless life has ruined me.

The question that confused her most: *if Thomas had loved me would I have been able to love him back?*

She shook her head to clear the dark memories and confounding thoughts. "One thing at a time," she said to soothe Father Bracewell's sweet concern, though she'd silently vowed never to marry again. Her nursing skills would be more than enough to support and provide for her life. She didn't need a husband to survive, and she refused to be smothered under someone else's control again.

Those around her had dictated her circumstances until now. The orphan home, the cotton-mill boss, her husband, Dr. Rand during the war, and, recently, the kind assistance of the Bracewells, who housed and fed her as midwife to the parish. Yet since that night at Chaffin Farm, spurred perhaps by the guilt that followed her relief after Thomas's death, she'd wanted nothing more than to move on. Move forward. Alone and free.

But a family . . .

Cora's lonely childhood had been filled with gossamer visions of a real family. The steel-strong bonds of commitment and blood. A quiet touch, a shared laugh. Connection. She'd hoped for those things with Thomas, naively assuming it'd all come as part of the package of marriage. But she'd found nothing to soothe her soul in Thomas's house.

Mercer's journey west offered her a way to break free, to finally stand on her own two feet. She'd already broken through walls and defied tradition to be a surgeon's assistant on the battlefield. She could do this thing as well, on her terms, in her way.

Or, at least, I hope I can.

"Your face is rather flushed, Cora. Are you feeling well?" Father Bracewell asked, his wrinkled eyes pinched in concern, but also hopeful she'd finally admit to her mistake.

Cora smiled. "I feel quite well, Father. It's this fine sea air. Invigorating, don't you think?"

Bracewell sighed, shook his head. "Women shipped off to the West like loads of dry goods. What is the world coming to?"

Cora held back a laugh and turned away from him to take in the shape of the steamer ship that would convey her to New York. From there, she'd load Mercer's big ship bound for the seas around South America and up to San Francisco. Then Seattle. The possibilities sizzled on the air.

I'm ready. Time to go.

January 16, 1866
New York City, New York

Albert Cunningham checked the scrap of paper one more time to be certain he was headed in the right direction.

Mr. Asa S. Mercer
91 West Street

He was, of course, on track. But Albert was always thorough and careful. It was the very thing that made him an excellent surgeon.

The sun had only been awake in the sky for an hour or so, but the New York streets bustled with activity. Albert savored the buzz of energy and industry, his face alight with the prospect of what was to come.

An adventurous journey.
My own practice in the West.

Albert arrived at Mr. Mercer's small office. He'd yet to meet the famous organizer, but Dr. Charles Barnard, the man who'd hired Albert, assured him Mercer could be trusted. A whirlpool of rumor and controversy swirled around Mercer's name and his plans. Albert would judge for himself, as careful in his relations as he was with his patients. But he was not concerned with Mercer's goals of marrying off women to men in the West. He was only concerned with the experience of assisting Dr. Barnard on the voyage and the chance to break out on his own at the end of it.

The voyage had already been delayed several times, an irritating inconvenience, but the energy in the office as Albert ducked inside told him today was the day. A huddle of men surrounded a large mahogany desk, their voices loud with the morning's activity. Albert was instantly aware of his tall stature in the low-ceilinged room and in comparison to the other men. As a young man he'd often hunched to match others' heights, but his mentor, Dr. Vista, had quickly weaned him off the habit. *Terrible for the spine, Albert. Why be ashamed of all that God-given height? Be proud, stand tall.*

So Albert squared his shoulders and stepped closer.

Dr. Barnard noticed him first.

"Ah, there you are. Come in, come in." The doctor, a solid man with small, active eyes, a bald head, and a fine black suit, waved Albert into the circle. "Gentlemen, this is my assistant for our adventure, Dr. Albert Cunningham. Top of his class at King's College and trained by Dr. Ernest Vista, one of the best surgeons in the country. Albert, this is Mr. Asa Mercer, the architect of our journey."

Albert turned his attention to the man on the opposite side of the desk. Mercer's vibrant red hair, formed into odd pompadours above his ears and on top of his head, was certainly striking. His beard was thick and stiff off his jaw, his suit fine, and his tie neatly arranged. But Albert focused on Mercer's eyes, looking directly at the man. "Nice to meet you, Mr. Mercer." Albert held out his hand.

Mercer gripped it firmly. "Tall one, aren't you?"

"Yes, sir," Albert indulged. People had a compulsive need to point out his height.

"Glad to have you, young man. I expect the highest of standards from the men on this journey. There's to be no flirting with the young women, nothing untoward, if you understand me." Mercer increased the pressure of his hand on Albert's.

"Of course, sir. My new practice comes first; I'm not looking for a wife. I assure you that you have nothing to worry about from me. I'm here to give medical aid, see a bit of the world, and nothing more."

"Good man." Mercer released his hand and turned his attention to another man in the circle. Albert watched Mr. Mercer, forming his opinion. The man was ambitious, with a powerful presence, but there was a glint in his eyes Albert didn't trust. He frowned, wondering if he should be concerned.

"Now, I heard, Mr. Mercer, that you're out of money. Care to comment on that?"

Albert and the group turned to discover the source of the brazen comment. A tall, slender man, face young and fresh, stood in the doorway. His gray suit was expertly tailored, his dusty brown hair and beard neatly trimmed. A small notebook was tucked under one arm. He gave the group a crooked, mischievous grin.

Mercer frowned. "This is Mr. Roger Conant, reporter for *The New York Times*. He'll be joining us for the voyage. To . . . report on our success."

"That's correct," Conant confirmed, his smile growing,

"though success is yet to be determined. I'm here to record everything *as it happens*, which makes Mr. Mercer just a bit uneasy. Now about the situation with your funds—care to comment?"

Albert folded his arms, eager to hear Mercer's response.

Mercer's frown deepened, a blush of anger coloring his cheeks. "Everything is in order, I can assure you. I've recently secured an investor, and we are more than taken care of."

"Ah, yes, the illustrious Mr."—Conant referred to his notebook—"Sniktaw. Such an odd name. Odd man as well, from what I hear."

"Sniktaw is a well-respected mountain man who forged his own fortune. He admires our undertaking and thus offered his generous support. Now, that's enough, Conant. We must get over to the hotel and make arrangements to load the ship."

Conant nodded, an arrogance flickering in his eyes that Albert wasn't sure he should admire or suspect. Either way, he was glad the inquisitive man would be there to keep an eye on Mercer.

Conant, sensing Albert's gaze, turned his direction. "And who's the giant? Sure you'll fit on the ship, my good fellow?"

Albert inwardly sighed. "Dr. Cunningham. Nice to meet you, Mr. Conant."

Conant held out his hand. "Pleasure's all mine. What sport?"

"Excuse me?"

Conant chuckled. "Come now! With that height and those ham-hock arms—you must have been wickedly good at some sport."

Albert half smiled. "Boxing."

Conant gave an excited whoop and clapped his hands together. "Of course! And I bet no one ever knocked you out?"

Unable to help himself, Albert's smile grew. "Not once."

"Magnificent. Well, you and I will have to talk more, and perhaps a little sparring? I'm no match for you, of course, but always up for a workout."

"I'd like that."

Mercer cleared his throat, drawing attention back to him. "We have work to do, gentlemen. You'll have to save your socializing for later."

The men broke apart, off to their individual assignments.

Dr. Barnard chuckled to himself, clapped Albert on the shoulder. "Ready for this, Cunningham?"

"More than ready, sir."

"Well, then ... off to the fortuitously named Lovejoy Hotel, currently bursting with Mercer's hoard of women."

Two

Lovejoy Hotel

CORA MANEUVERED HER way down the wide staircase, weaving around the clumps of chatting women. Pushing through all the wide skirts was like wading through mud. She'd purposefully worn only one petticoat and her most flexible and smallest bustle in anticipation of moving more easily around the ship. Her dress was modest, but Cora had taken great care in making it—and two others—specifically for this voyage. Her launch-day dress was a simple white shirtwaist, lace trim at the sleeves and collar, and an emerald-green skirt with black-velvet ribbon accents along the hem. Her thick coat matched the skirt beautifully. When she'd put on the outfit at home, she'd felt stylish and confident. But now, seeing some of the finer dresses, she only felt out of place. Add that to the fact that she hated crowds, and the first inklings of anxiety tightened her stomach.

What am I doing? I don't belong here.

There's still time to go back to the Bracewells'. Midwife is a perfectly respectable livelihood. What right do I have to go gallivanting off on some grand adventure? The war is over. No one will accept me as a nurse and surgeon's assistant anymore.

Cora took a deep breath and felt for the corner of her black drawstring purse. The shape of her suture kit helped steady her resolve. She carried it with her always, a reminder of all she was capable of and all she'd done during the war.

Everything is fine. It's time to move forward.

I deserve this.

Cora navigated around three women whispering intently, turned the corner, and collided with a solid chest. She stumbled, an apology bursting from her lips almost instantly. "Excuse me. I'm so—"

The shock of his size clamped off her words. She tilted her head way back to find the man's face, and for a moment she didn't remember what she'd been trying to say or why. A steady hand came to her upper arm.

"My apologies, miss. Bit of a madhouse in here," he said with a flash of a smile. His teeth were lovely and straight, his jaw square and made prominent by a neatly trimmed black beard. There was a charming crook to the line of his nose and a thin scar above his right eyebrow. Her nurse's mind instantly wondered what injuries had caused the defects. *Boxer, maybe? With his size ... Or the war?* His vivid eyes, an intriguing shade of gray, searched her face. "Are you all right?"

Cora blinked, remembered herself. "Oh, yes. Perfectly fine. I apologize." She wondered how a man this tall and this broad ever walked through a crowded hall without taking out half the passersby. Thomas had been the same height as her and sapling thin. He'd been uninterested in physical activities, preferring to sit in his study and obsessively attend to the books of his father's cotton mill. A skill that made him brilliant at business but woefully lacking on the battlefield, though bullets felled even the strongest of the soldiers.

But this man was a Goliath. Cora blinked again, suddenly aware of her hands pressed to his boulder chest and his body flush against hers as the crowd compressed around them.

Another man approached and clapped the giant on the shoulder, which brought his body even closer to Cora's. "Whoa there, Cunningham. Didn't you just promise old Mercer you weren't interested in any of our fine ladies?" This man was tall as well, but much more lithe. His suit a bit ostentatious, his smile a bit wicked. He grinned at Cora, raised an eyebrow.

"We had a little run-in," Cunningham answered. "These halls are impossible to navigate."

"Especially when you are . . ." The dashing man looked the large man up and down, face eager with humor. "Well, huge."

"Yes, thank you, Conant. Very helpful."

"My pleasure, Doc. He is impressive, isn't he, miss?"

Cora frowned at the brash man and quickly dropped her hands. This only fueled the man's humor.

"Don't worry, my dear. You'll have plenty of time to get to know our brave doctor." He winked at Cora and passed a conspiratorial glance to Cunningham. "I'll leave you to it. I've other enthusiastic young women to attend to." He strode off and was instantly surrounded by several buzzing females, asking several questions at once.

Cora forgot him instantly and kept her head tilted up to the man in front of her, her pulse quickening even more. "He called you doctor—you're a surgeon? I thought Dr. Barnard had joined the expedition?"

"Yes, you're right. I'm his assistant for the Mercer journey, Dr. Albert Cunningham." Albert took a small step back, gave her a formal nod.

Cora's mouth went dry. *Say something. Tell him you're*

a nurse. "Nice to meet you, Dr. Cunningham." She smiled, trying to feel poised and self-assured. He returned the smile, and Cora felt a warm pulse move through her stomach. "I'm Cora Martin. I'm ... a nurse. I was hoping to assist Dr. Barnard as well. I wrote to him, but he never answered my letters."

"You're a nurse?"

"Yes, sir. I started as a midwife and then assisted a surgeon during the war, performing all types of complicated procedures as well as caring for the men. And I'd like to help—"

"You assisted a surgeon, and he allowed you to perform procedures?"

"Yes, sir."

Albert blinked quickly, his eyes making a quick search of her face. "Well, that's ..."

Cora waited for him to say the things male surgeons always said in response to her experience. *Please don't lie, young lady. That's just not done. But you're a woman!* Albert's lips pressed closed, no more words coming. He had an odd look on his face. Cora asked, "Are you all right, Doctor?"

His smile faded a bit, his eyes lifting to look over her head. "I'm sure two surgeons will be more than enough. I'm sorry, but I must go. If you'll excuse me ..."

With that Albert brushed past her and moved down the hall. Cora turned to watch him hurry out the front door of the hotel. She frowned, confused and a bit discouraged.

I think I would have preferred the words of disbelief.

That was just ... rude.

Cora thought of all the surgeons who had turned her down over the years. All the men who'd dismissed her plea to learn more and do more. *The beds need changing. The bandages restocking. That's what you should do.* It was only

Dr. Rand who'd put a scalpel in her hand, taught her to sew skin and stop a bone from bleeding, and trusted her with the morphine. She'd cut bullets out of flesh and helped amputate more limbs than she could count. But this Dr. Cunningham wouldn't even have a real conversation with her so she might tell him those things.

She wrapped her hand around the corner of her purse. *Keep going. Someone will say yes. Just like Rand. Ask until the answer is yes.*

After all, Cunningham was only the assistant surgeon. It was Barnard she had to find.

Albert pressed his teeth together as he plowed into the open space outside the hotel. His heart raced, and his palms had gone annoyingly damp. *Just a pretty girl. Nothing to be concerned about. The hotel is full of them.*

Yet none had caught his attention like Cora Martin.

She was taller than most women, an instant advantage, and her skin creamy, hair deep walnut brown splashed with highlights. But it was her expression when she'd told him she was a nurse that took his breath. The eagerness, the intelligence. The gleam of desire in her hazel eyes. He knew instantly she wasn't like any of the nurses he'd worked with before.

Her hot palms against his chest had certainly pulled on his attention as well.

And the hope in the tension of her shoulders, which I dismissed by running away. How must she feel right now?

He rubbed at his forehead, the guilt itching the back of his neck. Turning, he looked up at the double glass doors, considering.

Go back in. Find her. Help her.

He wanted to ask her a dozen questions about her experience. He wanted to find the source of her zeal, which had been so evident in just a few words. He wanted to stand too close to her again.

No. No, I can't. I must stay focused.

Albert's family had shuttled many an accomplished young woman his direction over the past few years. But he'd always been too busy studying his profession or disenchanted with the options to consider marrying any of them. He'd yet to meet a woman who could sustain a stimulating conversation. And the day he finished his work with Dr. Vista he'd promised himself not to even think about women or marriage until his practice was heartily established, much to his father's chagrin. But Dr. Vista had supported this course of action. *Good man, Albert. Don't get distracted. There's plenty of time for all that. Get your feet solidly on the ground of your work first, and then grow your family tree.*

An image of the smooth, round curve of Cora's face and her plump pink lips came unbidden and powerful to his mind. His stomach tightened. Had he imagined the spark of interest in her eyes, the flush on her cheeks?

Good grief, what's she done to me?

Shoving his clammy hands in his pockets, Albert called on the rigid, unfailing discipline that had taken him so far in his life already. Through a bleak childhood with his stoic, harsh parents and their cold money. Through years of rigorous boxing training and long, brutal matches. Through hours and hours of bleary-eyed study to rise to the top of his class.

One beautiful woman will not be a problem.

There were a hundred women about to board the *Continental*. It'd be easy to avoid Cora Martin during the voyage.

Very easy. This is not a problem.

It took her another twenty minutes, but Cora finally managed to track down Dr. Barnard. He and his wife were in the hotel lounge, having coffee. Cora stood in the lounge's arched entrance, wringing the straps of her purse as she stared at the back of the doctor's bald head. The room buzzed with animated conversations. Waiters darted among the crowded tables, lifting silver coffee carafes and white plates above the diners' heads. Morning sunlight poured in the tall windows framed by lovely crimson drapes. The light caused the gold-damask wallpaper to shimmer, giving the room a dewy glow.

Despite the gorgeous room and spirited atmosphere, Cora felt only dread. All the determination and courage she'd harbored back home in Boston suddenly seemed a strange dream. She felt as awkward and unsure of herself as the day she'd married Thomas. A nineteen-year-old misfit with no parents, no family, and no idea just how empty adulthood could be. At least at the orphanage there had been other children for companions. Brief friendships. A little laughter and fun between the icy classroom and drudgery of chores. She'd foolishly thought marrying Thomas meant gaining a friend, but she'd been much more lonely in his house than at the orphanage.

At eighteen, she'd been forced from the familiarity of Charity House for Children. The matron, Mrs. Boomer, had looked at her with tired, pale-blue eyes. *You're an adult now, Cora. We need your bed for new children. Children who will hopefully do what you couldn't—attract parents and a new life.* A deep frown had creased the woman's round face, her chin pulling back against her ample jowls. She'd looked at Cora as if Cora were an anomaly, or worse, something broken that there was no chance of repairing. Mrs. Boomer held out a card. *But take this to the man at the cotton mill. He'll give you a job. And good luck, my dear.*

That man had been her future husband, though she'd never have guessed it those first months. Quiet, unobtrusive Thomas Martin, son of Reginald Martin, who owned a moderately successful cotton mill on the Charles River. Thomas, who'd said only a few words to her before the day he stopped at her loom and asked if she might like to have dinner. Over pot roast he'd explained that his father insisted he get married, though Thomas had little interest in family life. The business was his one and only love. But he also wanted to please his father to protect his inheritance. Thomas had said that he admired Cora's work ethic, enjoyed how she looked, knew she had no family, and thought she'd make a suitable wife. Three months later they were married in a simple ceremony, Thomas's austere father nodding his approval.

Even lying in bed beside Thomas, Cora had felt more employee than spouse. His touch had been so clinical, so . . . functional. She'd heard the girls at the mill whispering about their men and the shadowy things that happened between them. But her time with Thomas had been nothing to inspire breathless laughs and flushed cheeks. She'd immediately known she was lacking in some way. That it must be her. She'd never caught the eye of prospective parents. And now, she couldn't even stir her husband's desires. Or her own.

And yet . . .

The man in the hall, Dr. Cunningham. His hand on my arm. My hands on his chest. I'm still a bit breathless.

Cora frowned deeply, yanked her hands from her knotted purse strings. "Stop that at once," she murmured to herself. She pinned her attention back onto Dr. Barnard, sipping coffee with his matronly wife.

I can't do this.

Yes, I can. Just go talk to him.

Cora forced her feet to move forward. She stopped directly behind the doctor, took a breath, and then tapped his shoulder. He turned friendly eyes on her, and a spark of hope kindled inside her.

"Hello, Dr. Barnard. My name is Cora Martin. I'm an experienced nurse and midwife. I wrote to you several times ..." The doctor's brow furrowed with not even the slightest recognition. Her spark of hope puttered out. Cora swallowed. "Perhaps those letters never reached you. I ... uh ... was hoping to assist you during the voyage. I seek no pay, just the experience, and perhaps a recommendation once we arrive in Seattle. I worked on the battlefields, sir, and hope to find a surgeon to assist in the West."

Barnard's expression remained neutral, but Cora saw the rejection forming in his eyes. "That's very commendable, Miss—I'm sorry, your name again, please."

"Mrs. Cora Martin, sir. Widowed. I assisted Dr. Stephen Rand in Virginia. We were at the Battle of Chaffin's Farm. I amputated seventeen legs, twelve arms, and excavated dozens of bullets *on my own* during that battle." Cora glanced at Barnard's wife, whose harsh pass of her eyes made Cora shrivel inside. The older woman's hat was an unsettling explosion of black and brown feathers that made her head seem too big and her shaded eyes threatening.

"That's hardly a proper thing to speak of over breakfast, young lady," Mrs. Barnard snipped. "And nurses do *not* perform amputations." Her tone screamed, *you are a liar.* She looked Cora up and down once more and then turned away to primly sip her coffee.

Just leave. Right now. Go!

"Right," Dr. Barnard said with a sigh. "You performed these procedures yourself? Without Dr. Rand's assistance?"

"That's correct, sir. He trained me, of course, but by the end of the war I was just as capable as he at all the surgical skills required in the field. I want to continue using those skills, learn more."

Mrs. Barnard snorted. She leaned to her husband and in a not-so-quiet whisper said, "This woman is delusional, Charles. No woman wants to do these things."

Dr. Barnard squinted, considering Cora. "Mrs. Martin, I'm sorry, but I do not require a nurse for this voyage. I have a very capable assistant surgeon. We'll mostly be dealing with sickness the first few days as the women adjust to the waves, and then I'm sure it'll be very quiet."

"I see. Are you staying in Seattle, perhaps setting up practice? I could be very useful—"

"My wife, Mrs. Barnard, assists in my office. So, I'm afraid not."

Cora felt the slap of Mrs. Barnard's glare once more but refused to look at the woman. Cora couldn't imagine that woman at a sick person's bedside. She shuddered and covered it up by adjusting the grip on her purse. It was time to withdraw. Any more attempts to elicit a position would only make her sound desperate *and* pathetic. "Thank you for your time, Doctor. Mrs. Barnard. Enjoy your breakfast." It was all she could do not to run from the lounge.

Once out in the lobby, she picked up her skirts and hurried to the stairs, plowing through the clumps of women without the care she had earlier. Thomas's dusty voice filled her head. *I've elevated you from the lower tiers of society. But you must remember your place, always.*

She needed to get to her room, pack, and make the next train or boat back to Boston. Cora bumped shoulders with a man in a gray suit but didn't stop to apologize. He called after her. She ignored him and picked up her pace.

"Wait, Miss! Wait just one moment."

Her eyes burned with suppressed tears. "Please excuse me," she threw back over her shoulder without looking at the man. But he kept up his pursuit.

"Wait! Please." A jovial laugh. "Good grief, you're fast. Are you woman or gazelle?"

Cora rounded on him. "What do you—" She stopped when she realized it was the man who had spoken to Dr. Cunningham earlier in the hall. She couldn't recall his name, though she was certain Cunningham had said it.

He stopped in front of her, grinning his wicked grin. "I thought that was you. Did Cunningham treat you poorly? Is that why you're fleeing looking simply devastated? I couldn't let you go without offering my services." He bowed dramatically. "Roger Conant. And if Cunningham did dismiss you he is an addled fool." His eyes took her in with appreciation.

Cora held back a grimace. "I don't even know Dr. Cunningham. We collided in the hall. Nothing more. Now, please excuse me, I have to go." Cora turned, but Conant leaped in front of her.

"Have to go? Where? Aren't you one of Mercer's girls? The boat isn't quite ready yet. We are all stuck here for a few more hours, I'm afraid."

"No, I'm not going on the boat. I'm going back to Boston."

His brow furrowed, eyes sharp with curiosity. "Changed your mind? Why?"

Cora huffed out a sigh of frustration. "Please, Mr. Conant, leave me be."

"I'm sorry. It's the reporter in me. I like to dig into things. Ask questions. You see, you don't strike me as the cowardly type. I see a bit of adventure longing in those pretty eyes."

An unbidden flush heated her cheeks. She was not accustomed to men flirting with her. But her pride was riled. "I'm not a coward, Mr. Conant. Just a realist. And this was a huge mistake."

"Why?" He flattened his palm to the wall, barring her way past him. "Oh, come on. Indulge me, please. Tell me your story. Perhaps I can help."

Cora studied his face. He seemed genuinely interested, which only confused her. Part of her wanted to shove him and run, but nothing about that was proper, so she took a breath to call on her patience. "I'm a nurse, and Dr. Barnard doesn't need a nurse as I had hoped. So there is no point going on the journey."

"You're not here to snag a husband?"

"No, sir. I'm a widow and have no intention of marrying again. I want to use my nursing skills, help others."

"I see." He nodded thoughtfully. "Are you a good nurse?" There was a challenge in his tone, daring her to tell him the truth.

"The best, if you must know. As good as most surgeons." She bit her lower lip. *Know your place. That was arrogance.*

"I believe it." His face lit up, followed by a throaty chuckle. "Your name, almighty nurse?"

"Mrs. Cora Martin." She felt a tug of pride from the look of admiration in his eyes. She wanted to enjoy it, but a tiny voice of warning told her Roger Conant was nothing but trouble.

"Tell me, Mrs. Martin, is Dr. Barnard the *only* doctor in the country?"

Cora scoffed, folded her arms.

Roger went on. "I've heard there is great need for medical people in the West. So why run home when you can come with us? Who cares if you can't work for Barnard; he seems a bit of a stiff anyhow. And that wife of his . . ." He rolled his eyes and then grinned. "Opportunity awaits, madam. How can you turn away from *that*?"

Pressing her teeth together, Cora hated that he was right. And that she'd been acting impulsively, childish even, by thinking of running home. *I decide who I am, Thomas. I'm free of you.*

"Ah. I see it." He leaned toward her. "A change of mind." Conant dropped his arm, smirking with satisfaction. "I know I would very much enjoy your company on the long voyage."

He took a step closer, and Cora's throat constricted. Her awkwardness returned in a sudden fell. She stumbled back a couple steps, uncertain how to react to his interest. She'd rather he went back to challenging her skills. She'd rather stitch up a deep wound than flirt with a handsome gentleman. She pulled her hands to her chest, gripping her purse. "I . . . uh . . . I had better check my room." She stepped to the other side of the hall. "Make sure I haven't forgotten anything. Excuse me, Mr. Conant."

He let her pass. "See you soon, Mrs. Martin." His tone was arrogant, self-satisfied.

Cora glanced back to see him strolling down the hall at a leisurely pace, hands in his pockets. She let out a shaking breath as she ducked into the safety of her room.

Three

The *S.S. Continental*

ALBERT STOOD ON the main deck of the impressive ship that would carry Mercer's ambitious party. He'd hurried around to the opposite side of the pier to avoid the crowd and looked fervently toward the open sea. He had a fondness for boats, a fascination that had started as a young boy when his father took the family abroad for the summer. During the long voyage across the Atlantic his father had walked him around the ship, pointing out each part and explaining how the steam engine functioned, and he had even found a way into the engine room. With all its levers and knobs, gray steel, and oil residue, Albert had felt like he'd stepped into another world. One he didn't want to leave until he understood every piece. He felt the same kind of zealous fascination for the human body.

So he was quite pleased to be standing on a fine screw steamer, with three wide decks, ample lighting and ventilation, and the chug of the stroke pistons warming up in her belly. He looked forward to getting to know the ship better and increasing his skills as a surgeon.

The *Continental* had been expected to set sail at eleven this morning, but it was now almost three in the afternoon. Albert's legs ached. He'd spent the last several hours walking the New York streets to avoid the Lovejoy Hotel and Cora Martin. Waiting impatiently to be underway.

With a huff of breath, Albert crossed his arms and let his eyes roam the harbor. It wasn't the delayed departure that had him so irritated; he still couldn't get Cora Martin out of his head. She kept drifting into his thoughts, riding on the current of his mind, always coming to the surface. With those intelligent, radiant eyes and warm hands.

Albert harshly tugged at his tie and collar, suddenly too warm despite the crisp January air. He pulled off his coat and draped it over the railing, bracing his hands on either side. Other people had found their way to this side of the deck. A tingle at the back of his neck made him turn. Cora stood several yards down the railing, her face upturned to the breeze, eyes closed. He froze, unable to take his eyes off her. Her deep-green coat and dress were a marvelous complement to her pale skin. Most of her rich-brown hair was tied back into a black netted snood, but she didn't wear a hat. He watched the sun play with the highlights along the crown of her head. And once again, it was the expression on her face, the position of her body that transfixed him. She reminded him of the heroines in his grandmother's stories. Seated by the fire, the children at her feet, Grandma Dolly had recounted daring adventures, favoring gritty tales of the Vikings and their conquests. One of her favorites had told the sorrowful tale of a shield-maiden, a woman who'd lost everything dear to her and was forced to fight for her home. A warrior as powerful as any man. An image of Cora, shield braced on her forearm, hair wild around her shoulders, and blood on her hands burned sudden and powerful in his brain.

Albert blinked in shock. He wasn't much for fantasy and imagination. At least, not since those days at his grandmother's hearth. He was a man of science, disciplined and practical. He pressed his eyes closed, forcing the brazen image away.

What is wrong with me?

When he opened his eyes, his gaze slammed into Cora's. She'd finally noticed him, and the displeasure in her expression brought a sharp ache to his chest. She narrowed her eyes slightly, thoughtfully, and then spun on her heel and disappeared around the corner. Albert took a few steps after her before he reined in his senses. With a grunt, he snatched his jacket off the railing and went in the opposite direction to find the doctor's quarters.

Focus on your work. Just focus.

Cora's heartbeat tripped over itself. Her foot caught an uneven spot on the deck, and she stumbled, cursing under her breath—a bad habit she'd picked up listening to the men on the battlefield. A gentleman and his wife scowled at her, but she hurried past, ignoring their silent reproach. Finding Dr. Cunningham—Albert, as she thought of him despite hardly knowing him—standing in the winter sun, no jacket on, hair askew from the breeze, and eyes closed, had a strange cocktail of adrenaline pulsing in her veins. She'd caught him with his body turned toward her and his eyes closed as if bracing himself against some twisted pain. She'd instantly wondered if he'd been a soldier on a ship during the war and memories had come back to haunt him. She'd felt compelled to go to him, to smooth the contours of his face with her comfort. But then he'd opened his eyes. The intensity directed at her had been more than she could stand.

Did I imagine it? I must have. I'm being ridiculous.

"Ah, the courageous Nurse Martin decided to join us after all."

Cora jerked to a halt to find Roger Conant standing in front of her, looking smug and dashing with his black derby hat angled over his eyes. She shot back an expression of annoyance. "Yes, I did. Thank you for the advice. Now, if you'll excuse me—"

"Why are you always about to run off?" He stepped closer, leaned forward slightly. "This is a boat. Not many places to be alone." His tone, though intended to be playful, soured her stomach. He went on, "Besides, this is an historic occasion. Why would you want to miss it by hiding belowdecks? Stand with me and wave to the dulcet crowd."

Not waiting for her to agree, he took her arm, looped it through his, and towed her along to the rails. He found a small opening in the crowd and wedged them into the tight space, pressing her forward into the rail. People pressed in on both sides of her, Roger behind. *Trapped.* Cora gripped the rail so tightly her knuckles ached. Her stomach turned, and her pulse raced uncomfortably again. The crowd below blurred into a wash of colors.

I'm not trapped. I'm fine. I'm fine.

"How sad to be one of *them*?" Roger said close to her ear, nodding toward the people on the pier. "The ones left behind. *Tsk, tsk, tsk.* Much better to be the ones leaving, don't you agree?"

Cora tucked her chin, pulling away from his hot breath. The smell of salt and brine was replaced with the overwhelming scent of dust and raw coal. *This is not that place. I'm safe. I'm fine.*

"Mrs. Martin? Are you all right?"

Cora closed her eyes, shook her head. "I don't like

crowds," she managed to choke out. Roger immediately extracted her from the press of people. She tried to catch her breath as he swung her back and maneuvered below one of the hanging lifeboats. The cool shade and space were an instant relief. She leaned into the wall, Roger's hand on her arm.

"Shall I fetch the doctor?" he asked urgently.

She thought of Dr. Cunningham, and her breath caught. "No!" Much too loud. She swallowed, throat dry. And then, softer, "No, thank you, Mr. Conant. I'll be fine now. Really."

Conant's eyebrows pressed together at the bridge of his nose. "I'm not sure I believe you, Mrs. Martin. You can't catch your breath, and your face is dreadfully pale."

A flush of embarrassment broke through her panic. Her eyes flitted up to check Mr. Conant's expression. "I'm sorry. I—"

"No need to apologize. My mother hated crowds. I've seen her face look just like yours many a time. But I feel I should fetch a doctor to be safe."

She shook her head, gripping his arm as he moved to turn away. "Mr. Conant, may I remind you that *I'm* a nurse and more than capable of taking care of myself? I do *not* require the doctors. I just need a moment to recover."

The edge of Roger's mouth quirked up. "How dare I forget?" He settled beside her. "Any better?"

She straightened, dropped her hand from his arm. "Yes, better."

The ship's horn blew, and a chug of movement made them both shift their footing. Cora felt Roger's penetrating gaze. "It will not be easy to find open space on this crowded ship," he said with concern. "I'm afraid it will always be a bit tight quarters."

She knew that fact all too well, and she had been preparing herself to face the crowded, small rooms. "I know. I promise I'll be fine." Cora waved toward the railing. "Please don't miss the fun on my account. I'll be content right here."

Mr. Conant pressed his lips together, looked back over his shoulder at all the laughing, waving women. Cora knew he couldn't resist it, and she was relieved it would pull him away.

"You're certain?" he asked.

She smiled. "Yes, Mr. Conant. Off you go."

"I'll check on you later."

"Thank you, but no need."

He gave her a dashing smile and then bounded off into the waiting attention of several young women. Cora watched the bustled skirts and feathered hats huddle around him like hens to a pile of corn, and she smiled.

She didn't want to miss this moment bogged down by old panic. *Those days are long past. I'm not a frightened child locked in a basement room for hiding books under my pillow.* With a long breath, she squared her shoulders, moved a few steps from the wall, and watched the pier slide away.

No turning back now.

She gripped the shape of her suture kit through her purse. *Time to move on. From so many things.* Her mind tried to stray back to bloody battlefields and dark basements, but she anchored it to the present. A thrill she'd never experienced swelled in her gut as they broke out into the open harbor. She looked around at the crowd, all these women daring for a different future. A sudden grip of kinship brought happy tears to her eyes.

"We are on our way, ladies," she whispered.

A tight group of men went hurrying past her, their faces grim, conversation hushed. Two women trailed behind them, obviously listening, but then veered off when they saw Mr. Conant. Cora stepped forward to listen. "Oh, Mr. Conant, you'll not believe it," a young woman in a baby-blue skirt and white coat began dramatically.

"What is it, my dear lady?" Conant asked, eyes alight with intrigue.

"There's talk on the ship of . . . of people who have *not paid their passage*. Mercer has demanded proof from *everyone*. We may even stop to let off the guilty."

"Stop the ship? But we've just started," Conant exclaimed. "Surely this is a mistake."

"Everyone is to gather in the saloon to have their tickets examined."

"That's preposterous! Everyone's tickets were checked as we boarded." Conant shook his head. "I'll find Mercer and sort it out. Has anyone seen him?"

Several women shook their heads.

One woman began to cry, which drew more attention. "I *must* go west," she sobbed. "There's nothing left for me here. I must go! I know I paid, Mr. Conant. I saved every penny."

"I'm sure you did, my dear. We'll sort it out."

Despite Conant's attempts to calm the women, soon the whole deck buzzed with panic. Cora watched one woman fly past her, vowing to lock herself in her room. "I'll not leave this ship! They'll have to break down my door." A few more followed her. Cora frowned as she felt the crowd's energy shift.

This is not good.

One of the running women tripped and fell at Cora's feet. Cora reached to help her. The woman lifted her face, eyes wide and mouth pouring blood. "I've got you," Cora said confidently, pulling the woman to her feet and examining her face. "You've split open your lip." Cora pulled her hankie from her sleeve. "Press this to your mouth."

The young woman blinked tears onto her cheeks. "I paid," she mumbled. "I swear I did."

Cora sighed. "Don't worry about that right now. We've got to get you to the doctor." She pulled back her hankie to check the cut, and the girl finally saw the blood.

She began crying in earnest. "I'm bleeding! My lip!"

"Yes, I know." Cora grabbed the girl's hand and pushed it to the hankie. "Hold that!" The command in her voice got through, and the girl's eyes focused on Cora. "Now, come with me." Keeping a hand on the girl's arm, Cora started for belowdecks.

"What's all that racket?" Dr. Barnard grumbled, looking up from a stack of papers. He sat behind a simple oak desk, in the small office area of the medical rooms. A matching oak cabinet with a lock stood to his left, filled with medicines and the doctor's personal alcohol stores. To his right, a small sunlit porthole.

Albert stuck his head out of the medical office into the hall. The pounding of feet echoed all around him. "Sounds like everyone is coming belowdecks."

"That's odd. We've just started, and it's a fine day."

Albert nodded, equally confused. He watched and listened for another moment, an instinct telling him something was wrong. "I'll go find out, sir."

"Good man."

Albert had made it halfway down the hall, the noise increasing considerably, when two women burst from the stairs, coming his way. He recognized Cora right away and then registered the bloody cloth at the second woman's mouth. "What happened?" he called out, jogging to close the distance.

"She fell," Cora called back. "Her lip requires two stitches."

The injured woman whimpered, eyes big and glossy with tears. Albert took her weight, lifting her into his arms, and turned to take her to the exam room. "What's going on up there?"

Cora quickly explained the cause of the panic and asked, "Have you seen Mercer? Do you know anything about this?"

"No. I haven't seen him since this morning at his office," Albert grunted. "I hope he's not trying to cheat anyone."

"You don't trust him?"

Albert glanced back at Cora. "I don't know him. So no, not entirely." He easily lifted the young woman into the room and put her on the exam table. Her whimpering had not stopped. He turned to reach for some fresh strips of cloth and found Cora already holding them out to him. He blinked, surprised, but then quickly moved back into action. He eased the woman's hand away. "It's all right; I need to inspect the wound."

"Her name is June," Cora said, appearing on the other side of the table.

Her presence flustered him; Albert tried to focus on his patient. "Miss June. You've opened your bottom lip just a bit. It'll need ... two stiches. Just as Miss Martin said." He met Cora's eyes. She looked back stoically, her left eyebrow quirking up slightly in the smallest of *I told you so* expressions. Albert cleared his throat. "This will only take a moment, Miss June. Nothing to worry about."

Cora pulled off her coat, draped it over a chair, and rolled up the sleeves of her white shirt. She quickly washed her hands in the basin. Albert dabbed at Miss June's lip—the bleeding had slowed a bit—and watched Cora out of the corner of his eye. She pulled something from her drawstring purse and crossed back to the table.

"You're doing very well, June," Cora smiled sweetly.

"We'll have you back to your friends soon." June, still wide-eyed and nervous as a cat, nodded. Cora held out the small bundle to Albert.

He recognized the piece of yellow buckskin leather instantly. "A suture kit?"

Cora's gaze reached out to him, a challenge, a desperate request. "Yes. It's the one I used during the war." She unrolled it to reveal a set of eight pristine needles of various lengths and curvatures, two neat rolls of silk and wire, and a triangle of butter-yellow bone wax.

Albert's heart rate quickened. He'd only ever seen experienced surgeons carry such a kit. His own was not as nice. *Why does she have that?* He smoothed his expression, focused on his patient. "You know how to perform sutures, Miss Martin?"

"Yes, sir. And it's Mrs. Martin. Not Miss."

Albert blinked, a hook of disappointment grabbing his throat. *She's married.* "I'm sorry. Mrs. Martin. Is your husband aboard, then?"

"No. I'm a widow."

He couldn't help the wave of relief, and then he instantly scolded himself. *You're not looking for a wife, remember? Focus on your work.* He lowered his chin and looked at June but was still too curious about Cora. "Which hospital did you serve during the war, Mrs. Martin?"

"I didn't. I worked in the field, sir. With Dr. Stephen Rand."

Albert's hand slipped as he dabbed a wet cloth over Miss June's lip. "Dr. Rand—who cared for the men at Chaffin's Farm?"

"Yes."

Albert stilled, straightened up slowly. *This is impossible.* He had a split second of cold doubt, which was quickly swept away by her penetrating eyes. He leaned slightly toward her.

"You're the surgeon nurse who worked for Rand at Chaffin's Farm?"

"Yes," she repeated, with a conviction that took his breath away.

His heart beat into his ribs. *Extraordinary.* "I heard about you."

Cora's lips twitched as if she wanted to smile but suppressed it. She held his regard for a brief moment and then looked to June. "Are you doing all right, dear? We are ready to suture now."

"Will it hurt?" June whined, her words a bit mushy from her swollen lip.

Cora took the girl's hand. "Yes, but not terribly. It'll be over quickly."

June's face collapsed. "I don't think I can . . . it hurts so much already."

"Of course you can!" Cora gave her a wide, genuine smile, and Albert held his breath. Cora went on, her voice light but commanding. "You are a woman, June. Your body is built like a warrior's. It can give birth, chase little ones, and wear a corset every day. What's a few pinches of the lip?"

Albert immediately thought of the Viking shield-maiden from Grandma Dolly's story. His face heated, and he turned away to hide it under the guise of cleaning up the cloths.

June gave a little laugh. "It'll be over quickly? You *promise*?"

"I promise."

"Might I have a *tiny* drink to help steady my nerves? My father had several of his teeth pulled, and he could laugh through it after a few glasses of whiskey."

Cora laughed and then looked up to Albert. He'd been so intently thinking about the nurse that he barely registered what the patient had said. "Uh . . . yes. Of course, Miss June.

Dr. Barnard has some bourbon in his office. I'll fetch it." Albert bolted out into the narrow hall and hurried into the office next door.

Dr. Barnard looked up from his desk. "Did you discover what's happening?"

"Yes, sir. Mercer claims some passengers have not paid; they're checking tickets. It's caused a bit of a panic. A woman fell, split her lip. I'm treating her in the exam room."

The older doctor frowned. "You look a bit flustered, Cunningham. Do you need any assistance?"

Albert almost laughed. "No, sir." *I have more than enough assistance.*

"Then I guess I'd better go check on the situation. Make sure Mercer is handling this correctly."

"May I take some bourbon for the girl? She's a bit anxious."

Barnard waved to his cabinet as he stood. "Help yourself; it's unlocked. I'll check in later."

Albert grabbed the liquor and a glass, his mind wheeling. *Cora Martin is the surgeon nurse I heard rumors about during the war. The woman who performed battlefield amputations. Cora Martin is no ordinary nurse. No ordinary woman either.*

Stepping back into the exam room, Albert stole a glance at Cora while she chatted with June. A flash of heat moved through him. He swallowed hard. "Here we are, Miss June." He offered her a finger of bourbon; she accepted it with shaky hands. Albert turned to the nurse. "Mrs. Martin... would you care to perform the sutures?"

Her hazel eyes flashed, head snapping up to gauge his sincerity. He relished the surprise and desire she couldn't manage to hide. He watched her consider him, probably a bit suspicious of his motivations. He offered her a little more incentive. "Miss June is quite comfortable with you, and if you are who you say you are, you could do this with your eyes closed."

She narrowed her eyes, but he knew she couldn't resist. "Thank you, Dr. Cunningham. It'd be my pleasure."

Cora pulled her suture kit closer, selected a curved needle and the thin silk. June held out her glass for more bourbon. Albert frowned but gave her another serving. Cora had the needle ready before he was finished. She turned to the patient. "June, lie down for me, all right?"

June grinned, the bourbon taking effect. "Of course, Cora. *You* are going to do my stitches? I didn't know nurses did that. How fun!"

"I am. I'm very good and very fast." Her eyes cut a glance at Albert, and he crossed his arms over his chest, hiding his anticipation and challenging her to prove it. She smiled down at their patient. "I have a clean needle all ready. I'll make the two tiny sutures, quick as you like, and then you'll be done. You'll need to wash your lip with some warm water twice a day, keep it clean so it heals nicely. And you may not want to smile at the handsome crewmen for a few days." June giggled. She started to bring a hand to cover her mouth, but Cora gently pulled it away from the clean wound. "I want you to look at Dr. Cunningham—"

"He's handsome too." Another giggle. "And he carried me like I was nothing! Look at those arms!"

"Yes," Cora said, half smiling but not looking at Albert. "He's much better to look at than this little needle, so keep right on looking and hold still. All right?"

Albert held back a grin. He stepped closer to help hold June's attention while Cora set to work. "You're doing very well, Miss June," he said, though his focus was on Cora. Her hands moved with astounding agility. One stitch done, already on the second. "Mrs. Martin is almost done, Miss

June." And then she was done. Two even, expert sutures. No puckering of the skin, and clean, tight knots. Better than his own, which both thrilled and annoyed him.

Cora patted June's shoulder. "All done. You did marvelously. Do you remember my instructions?"

June nodded slowly, her eyes drooping. "Clean it, and no smiling at men."

"Good girl. Now, I want you to rest here. Take a little nap, if you please. Does that sound good?"

June's eyelids slid down. "Yes, Cora." With that the patient fell asleep.

Cora's pulse still hadn't slowed. Hers palm were sweaty, her chest constricted in her corset. Holding the suture needle made the whole world fall away. Performing the simple procedure filled her soul with joy. She looked over at Dr. Cunningham.

And he allowed me to do it. Trusted me. Why?

"Doesn't hold her liquor too well, does she?" Albert whispered, nodding to June.

Cora laughed and then caught the edge of her bottom lip between her teeth to silence the sound. "It made my job very easy," she said quietly.

"You really could do that with your eyes closed." Albert leaned down to inspect her work closely. "Excellent work. Truly."

Cora blushed, busying herself with washing the needle. "Thank you, Dr. Cunningham. Dr. Rand was a gifted teacher." She rolled up her kit and went to return it to her purse.

"And you're an excellent student, it seems. You're obviously a natural talent," he offered. "You'd do marvelously at medical school."

Cold bitterness filled her chest, her happy face suddenly rigid. "Yes, I would, but none would take me."

Albert blinked, as if for a moment he'd forgotten she was a woman and not allowed to attend. His voice turned achingly soft. "I'm sorry for that. It isn't right."

Cora gasped quietly, the words—so unexpected but so longed for—hit her dead center of the chest. She studied him intently for a short moment. "Do you mean that?"

He took a step forward, rounding the exam table to close the distance between them. He took up so much space in the small room, his head barely missing the ceiling. "Yes, of course," he answered sincerely. "Those stitches are better than mine, and I actually went to medical school." He smiled again.

An unexpected laugh bubbled up her throat. "You're kind to say it. I've yet to meet a doctor who would admit such a thing. Even Dr. Rand would not say when I became better than him."

Albert shook his head. "You should assist Dr. Barnard and me during the journey." He took another step toward her, his expression earnest. "And you must tell me all about your work during the war."

Cora swallowed hard, trying to calm the response of her body with his so near. "That was my intention, but ... Dr. Barnard said no."

The shock on Albert's face endeared him to her even more. "Why? That doesn't make sense. Was it the money?"

"I offered to work for free. It's because ... ." She paused, took a breath, but then found she didn't have the energy to finish the sentence. She met Albert's gaze and gestured to her skirts.

His brushed-metal eyes narrowed, turned gloomy. "I see."

Miss June gave a soft snore, and they both turned. The

room suddenly felt too small, too crowded. Cora reached for her coat. "I'd better go."

Albert lifted a hand toward her and then dropped it to his side. "I'll talk to him. Once he sees those sutures—"

She shook her head. "Please don't compromise your own position, Dr. Cunningham."

"It wouldn't. I'll simply—"

Hurried footsteps sounded in the hall. Dr. Barnard stepped into the office, another young woman behind him. "Cunningham, I have another patient for you. What a mess! Everyone is crammed in the saloon—" His eyes surveyed Miss June, passed out on the table, and then snagged on Cora. "What's going on? Are you injured, Mrs. Martin?"

A lightning flash of guilt went down her spine. Cora gripped her coat and her purse. "No, sir. I ... I was just leaving."

Albert stepped slightly in front of her. "No, wait." He turned to Barnard.

Cora's panic fluttered. "Don't," she whispered, but Albert didn't listen.

"Mrs. Martin brought this patient to me and performed those smartly done sutures. She's a brilliant nurse. We really ought to—"

Barnard lifted a halting hand, his face red. "You allowed this woman to *suture a patient*? My patient, in my exam room?"

Albert blinked slowly and then folded his arms, using his solid size and thick arms to emphasize his stance. "Dr. Barnard. Miss June is *my* patient, and we share this exam room. I am *not* your employee; Mr. Mercer pays my salary."

"That may be, but *I* am head surgeon. You work under me, and I have final say in *all* medical matters. Mercer gave me that privilege, and I have his ear; he only met you this morning. The man is a simpering fool, yes—he's hiding from the current drama as we speak—but he is still the leader of this voyage and will do whatever I ask of him. Including letting go of my assistant if he does not meet my standards."

Albert's jaw clenched. "Mrs. Martin is no ordinary nurse. Did you even look at those stitches?"

Cora was certain she was about to faint. The room had shrunk three sizes, her corset five sizes, and she couldn't calm her heart. *I'm trapped.* Albert and the exam table blocked her way to the door. She couldn't escape without crawling over June or plowing past Albert's considerable size. *I climbed up the coal shoot the second time Mrs. Boomer put me in the basement. Climbing over June would be easy. Awkward and improper, but easy.*

June shifted in her sleep, a sigh escaping her swollen lip.

Barnard scoffed. "Nurses do *not* perform suturing of any kind. It's just not allowed, Cunningham. You know that."

"With all due respect, Barnard, that's old thinking," Albert said harshly.

It was a step too far. The room stilled. The woman behind Dr. Barnard inhaled sharply, reminding everyone of her forgotten presence. The dark-haired woman cradled her arm. Cora knew instantly she had a sprained wrist and knew exactly what to do to help her, but that didn't matter. She wasn't the nurse here.

Cora watched Barnard's whole body stiffen and his eyes burn. "We are pulling up along Staten Island to let off the scoundrels who didn't pay their tickets. You *both* will join them."

Cora lunged forward. "No, wait!" She leaned over June, no longer worried about waking her. "Please, Dr. Barnard. No, please don't. I'm so sorry. I asked Dr. Cunningham if I could do the sutures. It's *my* fault—" Albert grunted in protest, but

Cora whipped him a hard look of warning, and he pressed his teeth together. She went on, "I had no idea you'd be so angry. I promise to stay away from your offices and your patients for the rest of the journey. I promise. Please don't punish Dr. Cunningham; he was simply being kind."

Barnard put his hands on his hips and let out a huff of breath. "At the hotel this morning, I informed you I didn't need a nurse. You had no right."

"Yes, sir. I only wanted to help during a chaotic moment. It won't happen again." Cora lowered her eyes sheepishly, wishing with all her soul that she could rage at this arrogant surgeon. But years of experience had taught her to pander when she'd pushed too far. She could not allow Dr. Cunningham to be punished. She felt the tension coming off Albert in hot waves and hoped he'd control his temper.

Barnard sighed. "This is your *only* warning and your *only* chance. If I catch you in this room again for any reason other than your own medical needs, I will have Mercer drop you at the nearest port. Do you understand?"

"Yes, of course. Thank you."

"And you, Cunningham—you wouldn't want to be responsible for the lady being left in a foreign place all alone, would you? Or risk your own future as a surgeon?"

Albert was silent for a long moment. Then, voice low and vibrating with resentment, "No, sir. I understand perfectly."

Cora breathed a sigh of relief. She scooted to the edge of the table, her shoulder nearly touching Albert. He leaned ever so slightly toward her. She wanted badly to look up at him but didn't dare. *Just move, Albert. Get out of my way.* He finally stepped aside.

Cora ducked out of the room and ran all the way up the stairs and to the railing, where the sounds of the engine drowned out the sound of her crying.

Four

January 18, 1866
At sea

ALBERT LAY IN bed in his stateroom, hands behind his head, staring at the ceiling. His body was exhausted but his mind intent on turning those moments in the exam room over and over. Two days later, Albert was still furious with Dr. Barnard—and himself. He hadn't seen Cora since she'd fled the crowded exam room.

I should have fought harder. But I would have lost my position. What good would it have done to get tossed off the ship and destroy my plans? But she's an incredible nurse. She deserves to work.

With all the seasick women, he didn't have time to go searching for her. Part of him hoped she'd be among the sick and come to him. But so far she hadn't.

Outside, a chopping wind and heavy cross sea churned up, snatching at the ship, tossing it side to side like toddlers fighting over a toy. Any chance of sleep for him and the whole ship vanished with that wind. Albert heard the women stirring. He climbed out of bed, bracing his arms against the wall to keep from falling. After dressing, he made his way to the medical offices. He heard women pounding on Mr. Mercer's stateroom door, calling out in frantic voices. "Mr. Mercer! Get up, get up. We will all be drowned. You must save us!"

Albert scoffed. Mercer probably wouldn't even come out. In the last two days Mercer had hidden from problems, forced people off the ship, yelled at crewmen for laughing with the ladies, and taken to lecturing like a father-preacher. Albert hoped the man did stay in his room.

An hour later, the whole ship smelled of vomit. The moans of women drifted on the air like the complaints of ghosts in an old house. Dishes clattered on the shelves, and furniture banged into the hull. Even Albert's seaworthy stomach felt uneasy. Dr. Barnard had never shown up to help with the patients, probably too sick himself.

Roger Conant staggered into the exam room with a half hysterical woman in his arms. "Cunningham, my good doctor, you'd best give this woman something to make her sleep, or she's going to jump off the ship." The woman wore a white nightdress, her black hair falling out of its braid. Her face was astonishingly pale and her arms flailing about at random so that she looked like some horrid specter.

"Please!" the woman begged, reaching clawed hands out at Albert. "I can't take another moment. Put me in a row boat, and I'll make my own way back to New York."

The men exchanged an incredulous glance over her head. Albert shook his head at the absurdity of it. He said, "I have some laudanum. Hold her while I fetch it."

Roger nodded. To the girl, he said, "My dear, we're *one hundred miles* from New York. Rowing is quite out of the question."

Albert wished Cora were here to assist him, to help divide

the turmoil. He wondered how she was faring in the rough seas. He wanted badly to go find her. What if she needed help?

Laudanum in hand, Albert went back to his hysterical patient.

"I'll swim. Let me swim!" she yelled, voice raw from screaming and vomiting.

"No, my lovely, you'll drown." Even on such a horrible night there was humor in Conant's eyes.

"I *must* get off this awful boat before it sinks to the depths."

"The waves will calm soon, I assure you," Albert soothed.

She put her hands over her face and wailed loudly.

"I see you're not bothered," Albert said to Roger as he measured out the medicine.

"I've spent many hours on ships. Though these conditions will rattle even the strongest sailor."

"Indeed. I wonder if Captain Winser will have to change course."

"I think he already did."

Albert nodded, turned to the patient. "Miss, this will help. Can you open your mouth?"

She dragged her palms from her face. "If I open my mouth, I'll drown." Her icy-blue eyes pulled unnaturally wide, and Albert suppressed a shiver. He put a hand on her arm. "The medicine will put you to sleep, and you won't feel the boat anymore. It will make everything better."

She blinked quickly; Albert doubted he'd reached her sanity. But then she opened her mouth wide. He quickly slipped in the medicine, and she swallowed.

"Fantastic work, my friend," Roger said with a chuckle. "I'll get her back to her room."

"Thanks, Conant." Albert turned away but then stopped. "Roger?"

"Yes?"

"Have you seen Mrs. Martin in all this mess?"

Roger flashed him a knowing smile, which only made Albert frown with discomfort. "Oh, yes. Our valiant nurse is flittering from victim to victim, making them all drink water. She's got the cook staff churning out endless plates of dry toast, as well, so that no one starves to death. She tasked me with bringing this poor creature to you."

Albert wanted to smile, to sigh with relief, but he kept his face blank and said only, "She's not sick?"

Roger grinned. "I think she's the strongest of us all."

Albert nodded, in full agreement. "Thank you." A crack of jealousy marred his relief. He wished he could follow Roger up to find Cora. *Stop acting like a lovesick fool. Your place is here. Forget her.*

Roger gave him a sly wink and then swept the already calmed woman out of the room.

Cora dragged her sleeve over her forehead to clear the sweat. She longed for some fresh air and silently prayed the waves would soon give up tossing the ship. She wasn't sure how much more she could take. She bent down over yet another pale, sick woman, and helped her to take a few sips of water.

"Good girl. Try to rest."

"Thank you," the victim murmured. Cora gave her a weak smile, though it always warmed her to hear thanks. She hurried to the next stateroom. Two women were huddled together in the small bed. One lifted her head at the sound of Cora's footsteps, her blond hair in disarray and eyes rimmed red.

"Why doesn't Mr. Mercer *do something*?" she complained.

"Not even Mr. Mercer can command the waves." Cora smiled calmly. "It will pass soon. Have some water?" The room pitched suddenly to the left, and Cora scrambled to keep her feet. The two women screamed and latched onto one another. Cora banged her elbow on a chair back, spilled a little water, but otherwise managed to survive the ship's efforts to knock her down. As she helped the women drink, her mind strayed to Albert. *How's he faring in all this?* She'd heard someone say Dr. Barnard was too sick to leave his room.

Poor Albert, all alone down there.

But there was nothing she could do. She'd kept to the other side of the ship for the last two days. She'd taken her meals in her room and kept a watchful eye whenever she walked the decks, not daring to even be seen by the doctors. She felt much like her younger self, hiding from Matron Boomer when her mood turned stormy, but Cora refused to bring harm to a doctor's career. And she did not want her own chances of reaching Seattle taken away.

Yet Albert's handsome face refused to leave her mind, despite her best efforts.

I must forget him. He was kind and curious, nothing more. He means nothing to me, and I nothing to him.

Cora took a quick look at the two women and then made to turn, but an instinct stopped her. She stepped closer to the bed. "Is everything all right?" she asked, trying to see the second woman better.

The blond woman adjusted to block Cora's view, which answered her question: something was not right. "Just the sea sickness. She's fine," the blond hurried to say.

Cora leaned closer over the second woman, small, thin,

and hair the color of late-autumn pumpkins. "Miss, I'm a nurse. Is there something I can help you with?"

The girl shook her head, curled into a ball. Cora eyed the way she seemed to clutch at her stomach. *Oh dear. Not that.* She sighed, put down her bucket, and crossed her arms. "When is the baby due?"

The red-haired girl jerked her head around, eyes instantly filled with terrified tears. "Oh, please, nurse. *Please don't tell.* No one can know. Mr. Mercer will throw me off the side of the ship."

Cora scoffed. "He'll do no such thing." She took a step closer. "When was the last time you kept down any food? You and the baby must have enough to eat and drink, especially while the waves bother you."

The girl's lip quivered. The blond spoke up. "It's my fault. This was my idea. Please don't tell."

"What do you mean? Are you stowaways?"

"No ma'am! I paid fair and square. But ..." Her eyes shifted to the floor. "The money I used for the tickets wasn't exactly mine."

Cora looked between them. "I see."

The young woman took a loud breath and then launched into her story, a floodgate opened. "Our daddy brought us over from Ireland to New York when we were small. But ... things were hard. We lost Ma years ago and Daddy this last fall. It was just Pearl and me—I'm Sally—and then ..." Sally looked at her sister's swollen belly.

Cora blinked, a little overwhelmed by the purge of information coming from the poor waif.

Sally went on. "Then Pearl ... well, it was the landlord of the place where we had a small room. I had a job in a factory, but then the factory caught fire. We didn't have money for rent, so he ... always had an eye for Pearl. So he—"

"I understand," Cora said gently, relieving Sally from explaining further.

"We hid it for months, but when he found out about the baby he beat poor Pearl. I managed to stop him before it was too bad." She winced, swallowed hard. "So I packed our bags and stole money from his office. I'd heard about Mercer's ship. I knew it was a risk bringing Pearl on like she is, but we . . ." A shaky breath—so much worry in one small sound. "Mercer promises there are men to marry in Seattle. We are good workers." Sally blinked quickly, as if shocked by all her own words. She winced. "Please don't tell Mr. Mercer. He thinks we are all . . . pure. This is our only chance."

Cora sighed, her empathy aching for the sisters. "Well, Mr. Mercer thinks a lot of things that aren't true."

"Do you think we will find husbands in Seattle?" Pearl asked, her voice weak. "Even with the baby?"

Cora's heart broke a little. "I don't know, but lots of women and children lost their men during the war. So I think . . . perhaps." She gave a little smile. "But right now, we have to get you through this voyage. How far along are you, Pearl?"

She winced. "About eight months."

Cora's eyes went wide, a stab of panic cutting her gut. The girl looked much too small for eight months, and that meant she'd deliver before the journey's end. Cora rubbed at her forehead. "You realize that you will give birth on this ship?"

Both girls nodded, eyes wide. Sally said, "I helped a few neighbors with births. I thought . . . I thought I could help her."

Cora held back a reprimand; the girl didn't know any better and was only trying to make a better life for her and her sister. "Sally, many things can go wrong during a birth. This is not something you want to do on your own. I will help, if you'll let me. I'm also an experienced midwife."

Sally and Pearl nodded again. Pearl whispered, "Yes, please. I'm so scared."

"I know, but you're not alone anymore. My name is Cora Martin. It's a pleasure to meet you both." The girls smiled shyly. Cora asked, "I assume you didn't tell Dr. Barnard?"

"No, ma'am," Sally answered, her face still tight with guilt.

"Good. And don't. He'll go straight to Mercer. Dr. Cunningham would likely help, but that's still risky. I will keep your secret, as long as we can, anyway. And once the baby comes ... leave Mercer and the doctors to me." She knelt beside the bed. "May I listen for the baby's heart, Pearl?"

Pearl scooted closer, lifted her nightshirt away from her small, round belly. Cora put her ear to the skin and listened intently. It was hard with all the noise from the ship and the storm. She held her breath. *Come on, little one.* She laughed when the strong rhythm finally found her ear. Pearl and Sally smiled big. Cora then felt Pearl's belly, checking the size and position of the baby. Small for eight months, but the mother was a tiny thing, so Cora reserved her worry for now.

"Very good, Pearl. The baby is moving well and has a strong heartbeat. How old are you, dear?"

"Seventeen, ma'am."

Not as young as she looked, which was a relief. Younger girls had harder births. Cora nodded. "And you, Sally?"

"I'm twenty, just a few weeks ago."

"Pearl, you need three meals a day and plenty of water. You also need good rest at night, perhaps a nap in the afternoon. Exercise and fresh air are important, but we can't risk anyone seeing you above decks. So pace the room several times a day, open the porthole regularly."

Sally nodded. "Anything you say, Nurse Martin. I'll make sure she does it all."

"Take care of yourself too, Sally." Cora smiled. "You can't help Pearl if you're not healthy."

Both girls smiled in return, some of the terror gone from their gazes. They had the exact same eyes, big, round, and a beguiling shade of jade green. Pearl had more freckles than Sally on their matching white skin. Pretty, both of them. *Maybe they will find those husbands in Seattle without a problem. They'll certainly need someone to provide for them.* Cora said a silent prayer of thanks that she had not been with child when Thomas died, that he'd not left her with the burden of another life. Seven years and not a single pregnancy. Cora saw it as yet another failure on her part, another way she was found wanting. She was deeply familiar with other women giving birth, but would she ever know it for herself?

Cora had started training as a midwife shortly after her marriage. Thomas would not allow her to work in the mill anymore, but she longed for something to fill the hours. When she heard that the local midwife was looking for an apprentice, she'd carefully broached the subject with her husband. In the end, he liked the idea of extra income and had given permission. It had soured Cora's stomach to need his permission. But at least she had found something that ignited fire in her soul like nothing ever had. A fire that grew tenfold when she stepped into the battlefield surgery tent.

Cora pressed up to standing. "First thing—you both need food. I'll go to the kitchens myself and be back soon."

Cora picked up her water bucket, stumbled to the door as the room rocked side to side.

"Nurse Martin?" Sally called out.

Cora turned. "Yes?"

"Thank you. We feel so much better now."

"Good. I'm glad. Rest while I go fetch the food."

Cora stepped into the hall, leaned against the vibrating wall, and took a long breath. *A pregnant woman on Mercer's ship of virgins. Poor girls. What will we do when the baby comes?* She looked up and down the empty hall. *I guess there's nothing for it. Good thing I brought my midwife bag.*

She wanted to run and tell Albert, to have a second set of capable hands caring for the girl, but she started toward the kitchens instead. Pearl needed her; Cora certainly couldn't risk her place on the ship now.

Roger Conant came around the corner. "No one will be leaping off the railing tonight, fair nurse. Our tragic girl is all settled into bed, snoring like a pirate thanks to Cunningham's laudanum."

Cora shook her head at his tireless humor. "Thank you." Another slam of water rocked the ship. Roger helped steady her, his hands gripping her shoulders. When the world leveled, she noticed he looked at her with his token curiosity. "What is it, Mr. Conant?"

"He asked after you."

A roll of heat moved through her core. "Who?"

He clicked his tongue. "You know exactly who. Our gladiator doctor."

She kept her face neutral. "Well, I'm sure he's overrun."

Roger shook his head. "He wasn't asking for a nurse, silly woman. He asked after *you.*"

Cora quickly looked down at her bucket. "I must fetch some more water."

Roger didn't release her shoulders. "I might be persuaded to convey a message back. What would you say?"

Caught off guard, Cora's jaw dropped open. "I . . . uh . . . I don't think—"

Roger lifted a hand. "He is my friend. You are my friend.

I feel it my duty to help while you are parted by circumstances." He smiled at her increased shock. "Oh, yes. He told me what happened."

"Mr. Conant, I appreciate your concern. But there's no . . ." A swell of desire filled her chest. She pressed her teeth together, considering. She looked up at Roger; he leaned forward expectantly. She steadied her resolve. "Please tell Dr. Cunningham that I appreciate his concern and hope he is faring well."

Roger's eyes warmed. "I'll let him know."

Cora nodded, nervous energy bubbling in her blood. "Now I must go, Conant." She stepped back. "Go write in that ever-present notebook of yours."

He half grinned. "I think I shall. I'll write all about our savior nurse, her battered water bucket, and her hidden emotions. And then about our giant of a doctor and his yearnings for a tall nurse at his side."

Cora rolled her eyes. "You're obnoxious."

Conant threw back his head and laughed. Then he bowed dramatically. "Thank you, Nurse Martin."

Cora shook her head and maneuvered around him, leaving him laughing as he walked in the opposite direction. She forced her mind off Albert and back to the poor pregnant woman and her sister.

What will Roger write when a baby's cry echoes down this hall?

January 29, 1866
The Upper Saloon

CORA SAT IN the saloon, the favorite gathering place of the passengers, and focused on the book in her hands. The saloon was long and narrow, dotted with square tables at one end, with an open space in the middle and a sleek grand piano on the other end. The walls were paneled in yellow oak, the floor dark walnut. Simple, wide chandeliers hung from the ceiling, swaying slightly from the movement of the ship and casting a lovely glow throughout the room.

The ship had a small library, and Cora had managed to find a book on herbal remedies for common ailments. Content to listen to the background sounds of Miss Ida Barlow at the piano and the comforting hum of conversation, Cora enjoyed her quiet corner table. Several of the women had pulled chairs into a large circle in the middle of the room and were busy knitting with the great skeins of yarn Mr. Mercer had produced for them. Everyone was in high spirits, the sickness of the past weeks forgotten.

"Do you not wish to knit, Mrs. Martin?"

Cora looked up from a page on the pain-relieving qualities of St. John's wort to find Mr. Mercer standing over her table. His fiery, strange hair always caught her off guard, but his greasy smile made the effect far worse. She stiffened so as not to flinch away. "No, thank you, Mr. Mercer. I prefer to read. Alone."

Alone, Mercer. Go away.

"That's too bad. You really should socialize with the other women; you're on your own far too often. And it's important to work on your domestic skills. Don't you want your new husband to have some nice warm socks?"

Cora gripped the edges of the book. Mercer walked the halls of the ship with a thick air of superiority, dispensing unsolicited advice to all the ladies like some impressive father figure, pulling apart couples, breaking up card games, insisting on early bedtimes, and gathering groups to spout sermons about purity and honesty—only to be found sneaking off with his own choice of young lady soon after. He'd become quite a joke among the crew and passengers. Roger Conant had taken to calling him Old Red and often sent groups of girls into fits of giggles with melodramatic impressions of the odd leader.

Bite your tongue. Be polite. Even if he's a detestable twit.

Cora forced a ladylike smile. "You forget, Mr. Mercer, that I'm a nurse and a widow. I have many skills and no need for another husband. Enjoy your evening." Cora lowered her head and focused her eyes on her book, hoping he would honor her dismissal and go pester one of the younger girls. He stood there for a brief moment and then spun away in retreat. Cora half smiled and sighed with relief. She flipped the page and read only a few sentences before another masculine shadow fell over her book.

"Good evening, fair nurse." Roger Conant grinned down at her, looking dashing in a black suit and tan waistcoat.

"Hello, Mr. Conant."

"Please save me from the infernal clicking of these knitting needles and take a turn with me up on deck. It's a pleasant evening."

Cora smiled, suddenly noticing how loud the needles had become. Some fresh air sounded nice; she shut her book. "I'd love a walk." She took his offered elbow and let him guide her to her room, where she dropped off her book and retrieved her coat. Tonight she wore a cream shirtwaist and indigo-blue skirt. Simple, with no embellishments except the enchanting depth of the color. Her green coat was a fine compliment to the skirt. She'd braided her long hair and coiled it at the base of her neck.

"You look lovely, Mrs. Martin."

"You've a silver tongue, Mr. Conant. I look quite normal."

He laughed heartily, the noise echoing in the stairwell as they ascended. "I promise my tongue is true and my words sincere. You are a beautiful woman, unmarred by all the fancy frippery most women insist on donning."

Cora blushed, unable to ignore his generous compliments. "Thank you, Mr. Conant."

"Roger, please. We've become friends these last weeks, and I'm not much for stiff formality."

"Neither am I. I'll call you Roger if you'll call me Cora."

"With pleasure, Cora. The name suits you."

They strolled toward the front of the ship, walking slowly, the crisp winter air a pleasant relief from the hot saloon. Several other couples and groups had come up to enjoy the night air. Cora tilted her head back to admire the vast fabric of stars, brilliant and thick. The ship cut a steady line through the waves, a stiff wind from the south gaining strength. She'd come to relish the solitude of being at sea, the vastness of the ocean all around and sky above. Freedom scented every breath.

"Mercer plans to sell all those knitted goods," Roger said, "in order to help make up some of his costs."

Cora's brow furrowed. "He told me they were gifts for the future husbands." She shook her head. "The man is a confusion of schemes."

Roger grinned. "Well said. I might have to borrow that for my writings."

"Be my guest." She gave him a shy, pleased smile. "Will you go back to New York, Roger? Or stay on in the West?"

"I'm not sure yet. San Francisco may prove too irresistible. I've heard so many great things. Last night, Albert told me all about the mile-wide Golden Gate Strait connecting San Francisco to the Pacific and the beguiling fog and crush of new buildings."

At the mention of Albert's name, a spark of heat sizzled on the back of Cora's neck. She'd yet to see him face to face, but the time away from him had done nothing to cool her attraction. Albert and Roger had become close friends, and she wondered if Roger made it a point to talk to her about him.

"Sounds incredible," she said calmly.

"For certain. Albert went there for—"

"MAN OVERBOARD!"

Cora and Roger froze, the burst of words knifing through the air. They looked at each other in shock and then took off toward the call for help. Cora picked up her skirts and ran, keeping pace with Roger. They flew past several other people, who'd been paralyzed by the unsettling declaration. Cora saw the shape of a life preserver hanging in the shadows and cut over to rip it off the wall. She met up with a small group leaning over the railing near the front bow. "Take this!" she yelled, shoving the preserver out. The man who turned to her was Albert, his face wide with fear, dark hair windblown across his forehead. His eyes flashed at the sight of her.

"Cora," he breathed.

She blinked back at him, reveling at the pleasure on his face before she remembered what they were doing. "Take it. Throw it out to him." She pushed the rescue device into Albert's hands. If anyone had the strength and coordination to get it to the man in the waves, he did.

Albert startled, looked at the white ring, and then snatched it from her hands. Cora moved to the side, giving him plenty of space. She squinted down at the black water, trying to find the man. "There!" Roger yelled from the other side of Albert. He pointed to the left. Cora marveled at how small the man looked, bobbing in the waves, arms thrashing.

"We must get him before he's pulled back to the screw," a young crewman yelled as he ran toward the railing. "Captain is slowing the ship, but it takes time."

Albert wound the ring's rope in his hand, leaned over the railing, gauged the distance, and then hurled with all his might. The target looked dead on; the man reached out. But a heavy wave rolled up behind him, surging out of the darkness to push him violently sideways. The ship took the brunt of the wave's strength, rocking sharply. Everyone on deck lurched backward, scrambling for footing. Cora spread her feet wide and barely stopped herself from falling. She rushed back to the railing, Albert beside her.

He swore under his breath. "Where did he go?" Albert yelled out, reeling the icy preserver back in, his face hard with disappointment. "Can anyone see him?"

Cora worried the poor man had been slammed into the side of the ship by the wave. Or worse, pulled under to the mercy of the slicing screw. Everyone along the rail searched, heads and eyes snapping back and forth. The wind had chopped up the sea, and Cora strained her eyes, panic building in her gut. She looked at Albert. "The water is freezing."

He knew instantly what she meant. The man's body had little chance of surviving the cold waves while he waited for rescue. "I know," he whispered back. "Keep looking, Cora. It's all we can do." He nodded toward the unforgiving sea.

"Can't you lower the boats?" Roger begged the young sailor.

He shook his head, face grim. "Not until the ship stops."

"It'll be too late by then," Roger countered, shoulders sagging.

The sailor just stared back, blinking helplessly.

Cora knew exactly how he felt. She leaned farther over the railing, trying to find the man in the chop, her mind telling her he was already gone, her heart holding out hope. *What a horrible way to die. I'd rather face the battlefield than the waves. Going under the black water would feel like that basement room...* She shuddered, her hand slipping from the rail. Albert caught her around the waist, pulled her back. The momentum made her turn, so she faced him, fully enclosed in his arms.

"It'll do no good to go swimming after him," Albert said, his voice low and deep. He made no move to release her.

Flustered and not sure she was breathing correctly, all she could say was "I'm sorry." She lifted her chin to look up at him; he looked down, his gray eyes made dark in the shadow of night.

"Are you all right?" he asked, voice gruffer than before.

Cora nodded. "We had... uh... better..."

Albert nodded back. "Yes."

At the same moment, they parted, moving away from

each other. Cora tried to find her breath and ignore the heat left behind by Albert's arms. Albert moved back to the rail, picked up the preserver again. She stood for a moment, unsure what to do.

Stop it! A man is dying or already dead.

The *Continental* had slowed significantly. Sailors readied the boats.

Cora stepped next to Albert. "Dr. Cunningham, should I ready hot water and blankets?"

Albert scanned the rough waves, cringed. "No, Mrs. Martin. I'm afraid it's too late for our man."

She nodded, allowing a rush of emotion to sting the back of her eyes before she pushed it back down—a well-practiced professional skill that brought back painful memories of the battlefield and Thomas. She remained at Albert's side as the rescue boats hit the sea, lanterns held out from the bows.

The crew searched valiantly for two hours. Albert stayed by Cora's side most of that time. He replayed the moment the man fell into the water over and over in his head. Albert had been walking alone, hands deep in his pockets, thinking seriously of finding the woman now standing beside him, when a noise had lifted his head. He'd looked up just in time to see the man pitch over the railing, legs tumbling through the air. No one had seen exactly what made him fall. It was soon discovered that his name was Kinny Foster; he was a new cook, his first time aboard, and likely not more than eighteen. That was all anyone knew at the moment.

Cora shivered beside Albert. He took off his coat and wrapped it around her shoulders. "Go to bed. There's no more to be done."

She lifted weary eyes to him. "I can't sleep. It's so . . . awful."

"It certainly is." He let his hands linger on her shoulders for a brief moment and then folded his arms to keep from touching her more. "If only I'd thrown the ring a few moments earlier."

She shook her head. "It wouldn't have made a difference. Even if he'd had a hold on it—that wave . . ." A frustrated grunt. "I hate that we couldn't do anything to help him."

"Me too. So like the battlefield."

Albert nodded, sighed as the image of the young man's frightened eyes filled his head. He'd seen that look many times on the men in his tent surgeries during the war. He'd seen it on dozens of patients. The fear of pain, the paralyzing terror of death. The hope it would all be avoided, while knowing it could not. He would never grow accustomed to that look, no matter how many times he confronted it. It was a great comfort that Cora shared that feeling, understood it.

Turning slightly, he studied Cora's profile, realizing that she understood the complicated depths of that look and the moments that caused it more than anyone else he'd met. She knew hardship as intimately as he. Few people understood the complicated emotions of being a surgeon, of being the person who faced that haunted look over and over, often with no solution or relief for it. But Cora Martin did.

He stepped closer to her, allowing his arm to press into her shoulder. She didn't move away.

"I knew Kinny," she whispered.

Albert's mouth dropped open. "What? How?"

"During the sickness, he made the toast when I asked. He filled my water bucket. He was so sweet and eager to help. His apron was always so clean." She cringed, shook her head. "I can't stop imagining him under the water, pulled down, unable to . . ." She swallowed hard, lifted her eyes to Albert, as if gauging if he was worthy of more. Albert waited. Finally, she took a long breath and said, "I watched my husband die at Chaffin Farm." She shuddered, took a shaky breath. "He was too close to a cannon explosion and riddled with bullets."

Albert shuddered with her. "I'm so sorry," he whispered.

Cora wrapped her arms around herself. "He and I were . . . not close. It was . . ." She shook her head, the dark emotions filling her expression. Albert felt an instant burst of anger toward her husband. How could anyone be cruel to such a woman? She sighed and went on, "Thinking of Kinny in the water, frightened, it makes me wonder if Thomas was frightened. Even as he lay dying I could not tell what he felt." She looked up, her eyes widening in embarrassment. "I'm sorry. I didn't mean to—"

Albert put his arm around her shoulders, pulled her close. He knew he shouldn't, but the night opened a window of possibility that the day would surely slam shut. And her empathy touched him deeply. "I understand," he said quietly. "I watched a close friend die after he lost his legs to a cannon shell." He shuddered at the memory of Gabe Hutton on the bloody cot, shaking uncontrollably and eyes wide with that fear. Albert pulled her a little closer. "Gabe was my closest friend and sparring partner. We grew up together. He's responsible for this crooked nose. He thought I had stolen a girl from him and caught me with a nasty jab. For the record, I had nothing to do with his romance troubles. It was another of our friends." A half smile, followed by a heaviness in his chest. "Yes, I understand, Cora."

Cora let her head rest against his biceps. "I'm so sorry, Albert." After several quiet moments she said, "Kinny was a good sailor. The waves didn't bother him. On that horrible night, when the waves were the worst, he helped me get some extra food for—" She flinched and pressed her mouth shut.

Why had she stopped? "For what? Are you not getting enough food?"

She sighed, pulled away from him. "Not for me. Never mind."

"Is everything all right, Cora?" He realized he'd slipped into using her first name without her permission or the social connection to warrant it. It felt so natural...

She looked up at him, her eyes still luminous in the oily darkness. She seemed to consider something and then said, "Everything is fine. Thank you, Albert. Just a girl who took longer to get over the sickness than others."

He relaxed at her return of his first name but was still curious what she meant. He knew her answer was a lie, and he was certain she knew he'd picked up on the falsehood. But there was a warning in her expression, so he asked nothing further. He circled back to the lost cook. "Good sailors don't fall over the railings. It's so strange."

"The ship was rocking a bit. Perhaps he just lost his footing? An unfortunate accident?" Cora pursed her lips, unsatisfied.

Roger Conant approached, face stern. Albert asked, "What is it, Roger?"

"I've discovered the whole story," he announced solemnly. "The boy had fallen in love with Miss Barlow, our piano-playing songbird. Earlier this evening she jilted him for one of the older sailors. Kinny took it badly and also took a whole bottle of whiskey as medicine for his broken heart."

"But there's no alcohol on board," Cora said, "except for Dr. Barnard's supplies. Did Kinny steal it from the medical office?"

"No, he wasn't a thief," Roger answered. "Mercer *declared* none was allowed served to the *women*, but plenty of the crew have their own collections of libations. The head cook, apparently, harbors the largest. Kinny took the bottle from his cabinet."

"He was drunk," Albert confirmed, heart heavy.

"The only mystery left," Roger said softly, "is whether the alcohol made him clumsy or . . . hopeless."

Cora sucked in a breath. "You don't think . . . Miss Barlow is charming but not worth his life."

Roger gave a weak smile. "Oh, fair nurse, a woman has no idea the sway she can have over a man." He looked between Albert and Cora. Albert pressed his teeth together, worried what the outspoken man might say.

"Thanks for telling us, Roger," Albert said to avoid any comments about him and Cora.

Roger nodded. "And so the *Continental* endures her first tragedy." He glanced at the ocean. "And the evening started out so lovely. Such a shame." He took a loud breath. "I hear there's hot coffee in the saloon. You both look like you could use a cup. I certainly could. Shall we?"

Cora felt the chill of the night down to the center of her bones; a hot coffee sounded amazing. And she knew she wouldn't be able to sleep, so she might as well feel awake after the exhaustive worry of the last two hours. She hated that young Kinny had died; sorrow weighed down her heart. Or at least part of it. The other part had been thrilled to stand next to Albert. His body-heat-warm jacket around her, his shoulder pressing close to hers. The quiet kinship of enduring the bleak tragedy and sharing others.

She walked between Roger and Albert, Roger in the lead. They descended the stairs and stepped into the hall toward the saloon. A chilling scream burst from one of the rooms.

Cora jerked away from the sound and closer to Albert; Albert's hand came to her waist. "What is that?" Cora whispered, her heart rate kicking up.

Roger grimaced. "It's coming from Miss Barlow's room. She must have heard the news."

Cora shivered. "She'll feel responsible. Oh! Listen to that crying." With a shy glance back at Albert she stepped away from him, brushing at her skirts to hide her awkwardness.

Roger nodded. "I'll go to her, help calm her. Save me some coffee, friends." With that, the reporter hurried down the hall and into one of the staterooms.

Cora's awkwardness increased without the buffer of Roger between her and Albert. Standing beside him at the railing, under cover of the dark and chaos, hadn't bothered her—it'd felt normal, natural—but now, belowdecks, reality crept back into her mind.

You're supposed to be avoiding him.

He smiled, his gaze knowing, his eyes tired. "I'd still very much like that coffee. Join me, Mrs. Martin?"

A warm tremor teased her spine. "My pleasure, Dr. Cunningham." She turned away quickly to avoid her attention lingering on his face too long and led them to the saloon. The cook had set out coffee with some bread and honey. A few others congregated at the tables, palms pressed to the warmth of their cups, heads bent low with whispers. Cora poured two cups, handed one off. Albert nodded his thanks and led her to the corner table. Did he know it was her favorite spot?

How could he? We've never been in here at the same time.

He sat with a sigh. "I like this spot. A little more privacy, but you can still see the whole room."

Cora gripped her cup tighter, hesitated a second before lowering to her chair. "I know. I always sit here." She imagined that each time she'd sat with a book or a meal Albert had been there moments before or after. Passing trains, ghosts sharing a haunt but never meeting.

His eyes widened a fraction before his gaze lowered to his coffee. "We seem to have much in common, Cora."

She nodded slowly, sipped, unsure what to say. Instead of responding directly to his intimate observation—which felt somehow dangerous and definitive—she asked, "So Gabe was responsible for your nose, but where did you get that scar above your eye? Looks like a nasty laceration."

Albert's hand wandered absently to the diagonal gash above his right eyebrow. A flicker of a smile moved his lips, but the expression was melancholy. "My father was my first boxing instructor," he started slowly, eyes glassy with reminiscing. "He'd boxed at university and wanted me to do the same. A family legacy, I suppose. Well, he was ... very *serious*." He gave her a significant look, which Cora took to mean his father was not only serious but also cruel. She nodded somberly, and he went on. "When I was ten he said I was ready to fight him, ready to face an opponent. He was"—his fingers stroked the scar—"merciless. He fought me as if I were a man his same size. And at the time I was not. I didn't yet have this height or bulk. I was ... scrawny." A small smile. "Two minutes into the fight he caught me with a left hook. My forehead split open, gushing blood in my eyes. Of course, he saw that as no reason to stop."

Cora gasped. "He made you continue fighting?"

Albert nodded, sighed with disappointment. "It's probably why it scarred so badly. It was left gaping open for nearly an hour before he allowed me to shuffle off to our gardener, who was handy with a needle and thread."

"The *gardener* administered your sutures?" Cora leaned forward to examine the old scar. Albert obliged and leaned in as well. She shook her head. "That explains the uneven margins." Her hand came up before she could stop it, fingertips brushing the textured skin. "It didn't heal straight or flat."

Albert met her eyes, their faces only a few inches apart. "No, it did not," he whispered.

Cora dropped her hand, sat back, and paid extra attention to her coffee, working hard to ignore the tingle in the sensitive pads of her fingers and insistent flutter in her belly. "I'm sorry," she murmured. "My curiosity has no manners."

Albert remained leaning over the table, studying her intently. "It's quite all right," he finally said. "I have that same problem." He said it with significance, pointing out yet another thing they shared. He finally sat back, picked up his cup.

Cora took a shaky breath. She knew she should get up, go to the safety of her room, but she felt rooted in place under the spell of Albert's mist-gray eyes and their shared stories.

After a few moments of silence, he cleared his throat. "I was supposed to be at Chaffin Hill."

Cora's head lifted, her pulse skipping oddly. "What do you mean?"

"I had been assigned to help Dr. Rand, but then my services were diverted to Peeble's Hill. Their surgeon caught a bullet to the head."

Cora's stomach tightened. "I heard that, poor man. To think . . . we might have met before." In her mind, she saw the round enclosure of Fort Harrison, the legions of soldiers stacked deep all around it. *He would have been in that medical tent . . . with me. He would have been there for those long bloody nights, for Thomas.* She shivered again, unsettled. She didn't like that her mind was throwing out the idea that she and Albert were fated to meet.

My life is not that charmed. This is just coincidence.

"So that's how you heard about me," she said slowly.

Albert nodded. "I'm sorry I couldn't be there to see your work firsthand."

Cora took a long pull of her hot drink. She realized she still had Albert's coat draped around her shoulders. It now felt a burden, an obligation, instead of a comfort. Too many things were already trying to weave her life together with his. She slipped the fine black coat off and held it out. "Thank you for that. I almost forgot I had it on."

"My pleasure." He tossed the coat over an empty chair, his expression suddenly urgent. "Cora, I'm sorry about that day and the stitches . . . Dr. Barnard—"

She held up her hand. "No, don't. You must protect your career. Truly good surgeons are hard to come by." She regretted the compliment. *Stop that. Stop encouraging this ill-fated connection.* She licked her lips, adjusted her cup. *Find something neutral to discuss.* "What are your plans after assisting Dr. Barnard?"

"I'm bound for Seattle, to establish my own practice. There's great need, and I have a fondness for forests." He smiled, eyes alight with the anticipation of his future.

Cora couldn't smile back. An unsolicited image of working side by side with Albert, building the practice together, raided her thoughts. Reason was swept aside as she imagined their life . . . *together.* A powerful ache pinched her gut.

"Are you all right, Cora?"

She flattened out her expression. "Fine. Fine. Just . . . tired."

Albert nodded, still suspicious.

"I think I'd better—"

"Nurse Martin! Nurse Martin!"

Cora spun in her chair at the frantic sound of her name. Sally, nightdress flapping around her legs and black shawl half fallen from her shoulders, came running into the saloon. She skidded to a stop as Cora stood to catch her. "Sally? What's wrong?"

"You must come." Her worried eyes flitted to Albert. "You must come *now*," she repeated instead of explaining.

Albert stood too, looking from the wretched girl to Cora. "What's the problem, Mrs. Martin?"

She didn't look at him. "Nothing. Everything is fine." Cora stepped away from the table.

"Obviously it is *not*," Albert asserted, authority in his voice now. He turned to Sally. "I'm Dr. Cunningham. Is someone injured, sick? Do you need assistance?"

Sally gripped Cora's hand, her eyes wide with panic. She opened her mouth and then closed it. Cora answered for her. "Albert, I'll attend to this. Sally's sister requires some assistance. I've helped her several times before. Nothing to worry about."

Albert narrowed his eyes at Sally, who trembled by Cora's side. Cora was just as anxious to get to Pearl as her sister, but she couldn't have Albert suspicious or, worse, following.

He started to shake his head, "Cora, I can—"

"Perhaps you had better check in on Miss Barlow." Cora put a warning in her voice and then met his gaze. Albert stared back, none of his suspicions put at ease.

His expression hardened. "Perhaps you're right." He nodded, snatched his coat from the chair so roughly the chair hopped and landed noisily. "Good evening, ladies." He marched out of the saloon.

Cora winced, feeling totally deflated. Sally tugged on her arm. "We must go!" she hissed. "Something's wrong with Pearl."

Six

ANGER FORCED TINGLES of irritation down Albert's arms. He flexed his fists over and over as he made his way to Miss Barlow's room. *What am I so upset about? Cora was right, I should check in.* But he knew the frenzied girl who'd come for Cora meant something serious.

He stopped walking.

I'm mad Cora turned me away. I'm angry I'm not still with her.

The source of his irritation turned his stomach.

How did I become so attached so quickly?

Albert rolled his shoulders, took a breath. Cora's ties to the blond woman meant nothing to him. Cora was more than capable of dealing with problems. His attention and skills were required for other matters.

Albert tried to make this narrative erase Cora's floral scent and full lips from his memory. But all he could think about was how it would have felt to kiss her standing at the railing above decks, cold winter air swirling down from the stars. The power of the daydream nearly made him turn to seek out Cora. Instead he stood tightening his fists so fiercely his arms trembled.

No more fantasy! You're a doctor, not a silly boy.

Albert turned into the open door of Miss Barlow's room, and chaos smacked him in the face. Barlow was face down on her bed, wailing and rocking while three other women knelt around the narrow bed, trying desperately to calm her. Huddled against the wall, Roger and Mercer were face to face, locked in some heated debate. Albert blinked quickly, surveyed the mess once more, and then folded his arms.

"That's enough!" he boomed.

Roger and Mercer's heads swung his direction, both faces red with fury. The kneeling women startled with tiny yelps, eyes blinking up at him. Miss Barlow's wailing did not change in the least. Roger stepped forward. "Oh, thank God you're here, Cunningham. Will you please use those boulder fists to punch Mercer in his insipid face *at once*?"

Mercer balked. "Now, see here, Conant—"

Albert lifted a warning hand at their red-haired leader. "This woman is suffering, and you stand here arguing with Conant. Explain."

Mercer scrunched up his face. His hair was more wild than normal, and he looked a bit too much like a circus clown. "I was merely helping Miss Barlow understand her actions and the dangers of flirting with men. She caused this—"

Albert was across the room and Mercer's thin lapels were locked in his grip before he could stop himself. He knew only half this anger and energy came from Mercer's gross behavior. The other half was tied to a tall nurse somewhere else on the ship. Albert put his face in Mercer's. "How dare you put that man's death on this young girl. Foster's death is *no one's fault* but his own. He chose to drink. He chose to walk topside."

"Yes, but . . ." Mercer sputtered, his face going cherry red, "if she'd only controlled her base desires—"

Albert yanked the man's lapels, lifting his polished shoes

off the ground. He threw him out into the hall, restraining himself enough to keep Mercer on his feet but stumbling into the wall opposite the door with a somewhat satisfying thump. Albert spun back around, displeased to find Roger grinning from ear to ear with blatant satisfaction. Albert shook his head. "Please leave Miss Barlow to me. Everyone out. Now!"

The women sprang to their feet and scuttled away like crabs on the sand, keeping their eyes averted. Roger clapped him on the shoulder. "Thank you for that, friend. Made my whole week."

Albert grunted. "Get out, Conant. Let me help this poor girl in peace."

"As the doctor orders." Roger walked to the door and then turned back. "Did you leave our fair nurse unattended?"

"Of course not. She . . . went back to her room."

Roger's eyes narrowed slightly, picking up on the lie. "All right then. I'll say good night." He closed the door behind him.

Albert turned to his patient, surprised to find Miss Barlow sitting up, legs straddled out under her skirts, face splotchy, and eyes pulled wide at him. "Doctor, is that true?" she asked, her voice rough from her lamentations.

"Is what true, Miss Barlow?" he asked gently. He grabbed the chair from the small desk and sat at the end of the bed.

"Was Kinny drinking?"

"Yes. More than his share, I'm afraid."

"So he didn't leap from the railing, calling out my name?"

Albert flinched. "Of course not. He was drunk. We think he fell when the ship took a rough wave."

Miss Barlow's whole body collapsed forward. She let out a rush of air.

Albert asked, "Is that what Mercer told you?"

"Yes. He said Kinny jumped because I'd played with his feelings. I didn't mean to—I was just having fun. I didn't think... I never thought..." Her face started to crumble.

Albert leaned forward. "Miss Barlow, this is *not* your fault. Mercer has some strange ideas about directing you women and your behaviors. My professional advice: ignore him."

A hesitant smile lifted the woman's swollen cheeks. But it fell just as quickly as it came. "Kinny was a sweet boy. I still feel awful."

"We all feel awful; it's a tragedy. But it's not made better by dramatic displays. So are you quite finished?"

Miss Barlow straightened her back, folded her hands in her lap. "Yes, sir."

"Good. Now I suggest you get some rest. Tomorrow perhaps you'll play a few songs in honor of Mr. Foster?"

"Yes, I would love to."

Albert nodded, stood up. "If you need anything else, please come to the medical rooms."

"Thank you, Dr. Cunningham."

"You're welcome." He opened the door. "Good night."

In the hall, Albert found Dr. Barnard hurrying toward him and felt his own exhaustion deepen. Dr. Barnard said, "Is the girl all right?"

"Yes, fine."

"Good. Come with me. We've got a few men with a touch of frostbite from searching out on those freezing waters." The older doctor started off toward the medical rooms. Albert allowed himself a single glance toward the saloon, a single moment of wanting to find Cora, before he focused his attention on the tasks ahead.

Pearl lay on her side, gripping her belly and rocking slightly. Her eyes pinched tightly closed. Cora knelt by the bed, tugging off her coat to start rolling up her sleeves. "Pearl, dear, tell me what's wrong." She touched Pearl's forehead, cold and clammy. "Pearl?"

"It hurts," she managed to squeeze out through her teeth.

Please don't be birthing pains. It's too soon.

"What hurts?"

"My belly. And I've got a raging headache."

Cora held back a frown. "All right. Let's figure this out. I'm here to help." She stroked Pearl's pumpkin hair back from her face as she spoke. "When did the pain start?"

"An hour or so," Pearl grimaced. "But my head's been poorly all day."

Cora helped the young mother-to-be roll onto her back. She held Pearl's wrist to check her pulse: a bit too fast.

"Her feet are all swollen, Mrs. Martin," Sally said, hovering over Cora's shoulder.

"When did the swelling start?" Cora felt Pearl's belly, relieved when the child gave a few annoyed kicks in response to her pressure.

"I noticed it this afternoon. Not sure when it started exactly."

"How often are the pains in your belly, Pearl? Regular or come and go?"

"They come and go."

This time Cora did frown. She leaned closer to Pearl. "I need to check under your nightdress, Pearl. Do you understand?"

Pearl had relaxed a bit but was still pale with worry. "Yes, ma'am."

Cora quickly checked for bleeding and any signs of active labor. She didn't see anything that alarmed her, though there was a bit of thinning of the barrier to the womb. She lowered the nightdress back into place and sat beside Pearl. She wiped her hands on a towel Sally handed her. "In the final months, the body practices for labor. So it's natural to have birthing pains that come and go. They aren't dangerous. It's just your body getting ready."

"The baby's not coming right now?" Pearl asked, voice wavering.

Cora didn't have an answer. So she asked, "Have you vomited?"

"No, ma'am, but my stomach is a bit uneasy. I thought it was from the pains."

"Perhaps, yes. But I'm a little concerned about your headache and ankles." Cora pressed her finger into Pearl's ankle, a shallow dimple remaining for a few seconds. *Not good. Not good.* "Do the pains cause your stomach to tighten and then release?"

"Yes! It's so strange. But that's just . . . practice?"

"If they aren't regular and strong, then usually. But it may also be early labor. We need to watch you very closely."

Pearl caught her bottom lip in her teeth, eyes going watery. "I'm sorry. I've been careful. Doing everything you said—"

"Oh! No, no. You haven't done anything wrong, Pearl. You've done a wonderful job. The last month is always a bit precarious, and I'm only being cautious. All right?"

"Yes, all right." Pearl nodded, eyes still tight with anxiety. She looked past Cora to her sister, who hurried over to the bed to take Pearl's outstretched hand.

Cora stood. "Let's start with your poor ankles." She gathered a blanket and pillow and propped them under Pearl's feet. Then Cora adjusted another pillow under her patient's head. "I'm going to make you a special tea. Some ginger powder to help your circulation and some willow bark to help ease your pains. I have everything I need in my kit." Cora moved to the door. "I'll fetch it and be right back. After you've drunk the tea, I want you both to rest. I'll sit with you."

"Thank you, Mrs. Martin," the sisters said in unison, and then they laughed quietly. Tension evident in the edges of the sound.

"Of course. I'll return as quickly as I can."

Cora rushed down the hall, concern coursing through her. She'd seen these symptoms before, and it would likely make Pearl's delivery come early and hard.

Please let her and the baby survive. Please help me do everything right for them.

Hastily, Cora retrieved her small brown leather valise from her room and went to the kitchen. The galley was empty, much to her relief. She started the kettle to boil and found a mug. A few minutes later, as she was steeping the tea, footsteps sounded in the hall. She looked up, unsure what would happen if anyone caught her making a simple cup of tea. She set her eyes on the door.

Please don't come in here.

The door pushed open, and she straightened. "Albert?"

He startled and stopped just inside the door. "Cora? What are you doing?" He was down to just his white shirt, sleeves rolled up to expose thick forearms. The top two buttons of his shirt were undone, and Cora's eyes went to the smooth skin of his chest. Heat flooded her body as she imagined unbuttoning the rest and pushing the shirt away.

Shame on you, Cora Martin.

Not once had she had such a brazen thought about Thomas—or any man, for that matter.

Thomas was the wrong man. Albert is the right man.

The thought shook the walls she'd placed around her heart and challenged the belief that she was incapable of love. Standing in the night-quiet galley, Cora felt something significant shift inside her. Without realizing it, she'd allowed herself to fall in love with Albert Cunningham. She cleared her throat, begged her face to cool. "Just making a cup of tea," she answered. Not a lie. "Something to help me sleep." Definitely a lie. Albert moved forward, coming into the light of the flickering lanterns hung along the wall. Stress had etched deep lines between his eyebrows. Cora's gut twisted. "Are you all right?"

He nodded slowly, sniffed the air. "A few of the rescue crew have mild frostbite. Dr. Barnard has disappeared—again. So I came to get some hot water myself."

"Can I help?" The words came automatically, before Cora remembered that, no, she could not assist with official ship medical problems. "At least, help boil the water, that is."

Albert looked from her to the cup again. "Are you in pain, Cora?"

Cora pressed her teeth together. "No, of course not."

"Ginger and willow are for pain. Chamomile and lavender are for sleep. You're brewing the wrong tea."

Cora winced, holding back a sigh. Part of her admired his knowledge, and part of her hated that he was so perceptive. She considered her next words carefully. Albert took another step forward, waiting. Cora said, "That woman, from before, her sister is having . . . womanly pains. Her monthlies cause her a great deal of trouble. The tea will help."

He kept his gaze on her face. "And that is all?"

"Yes, of course."

His gaze shifted to her open valise. After a tense pause, he said, "Because if there is a serious medical problem, I hope you'd tell me. It would only be right, after all. Ship's doctor should know these things. And this ship's doctor would help, no matter what."

Cora kept any reaction from her face, and nodded. "Of

course." She wanted so badly to tell him the truth. The slime of lying to Albert coated her throat. But the risk to all involved was too great. *Not yet, Albert. Soon you'll know I'm lying. But not until that baby cries for the first time. Then if I'm kicked off the ship, left in Brazil, so be it. At least I'll know Pearl's baby was brought safely into the world.*

Albert kept looking at her, and Cora felt he could read her thoughts. She busied herself with the tea and with closing her suspect midwife bag. "Do you need any assistance with the hot water?" she asked, voice smooth.

"No, thank you. I'll manage." His voice matched hers, chill for chill. "I hope your patient recovers soon."

Cora nodded once, swallowed down her thick throat. "Thank you. Yours too. Good night, Dr. Cunningham." She hated how formal, how cold it sounded.

"Good night, Mrs. Martin."

The sound of her full name cut a chasm in her heart. Did his voice sound dejected, or was she simply reflecting her feelings onto him? Cora forced herself not to look up as she walked toward him to get to the door. His hand lifted to circle her wrist—the wrist of the hand holding her bag. She nearly gasped at the shock of pleasure his touch sent rocketing up her arm. He looked at the bag and then held her eyes. She forced herself to stare back.

After a moment, he said quietly, "If things go badly, Cora, come get me. Please. We'll figure it out."

The soft, genuine kindness in the words made her knees go weak. A flash of inexplicable tears misted her eyes. Had anyone ever looked at her that way? Offered help without an underlying demand? Allowed her to decide what was best without forcing their rules on her?

"Thank you, Albert," she whispered, her shock preventing any more words.

His head lowered a fraction, leaning so near hers. His gaze moved to her lips and back. She mirrored his action and looked at his tender lips, desire building in her so swiftly a gasp escaped her throat. The teacup faltered in her other hand, nearly forgotten. A splash of hot liquid on her skin pulled her back to reality.

Cora moved away from Albert, her arm slipping from his grip. Part of her wished he'd refused to let her go until he'd satisfied this furious craving heating her blood. The quickness of his breath, the fervor in his gray eyes suggested he was considering it.

Cora faltered, almost dropped the cup and valise to rush into Albert's arms.

But then he stepped to the door, opened it. Eyes on the floor, he waited for her to leave.

Cora fled into the safety of the hall, allowing a few tears free at the sound of the door closing behind her.

Albert stood behind the galley door, palms pressed to either side of it and head dropped between his shoulders. He dragged in slow, measured breaths, willing his body to forget the flame he'd seen in Cora's eyes. He'd almost lost control, almost anchored his arms around her slim waist and let loose his craving to kiss her with wild abandon. But he knew if he kissed Cora Martin, the ground beneath all his well-made plans would crumble away to dust, leaving him free-falling. But he badly wanted to explore the passion brewing between them.

She has addled my brain. Think clearly. Think rationally.

But all Albert could think about was the cool silk of her wrist against his palm.

With a loud groan, he pushed away from the wall. He had

to get that hot water to the waiting patients. He refilled the kettle, working to calm his thoughts. Some logic finally broke through his lust.

There's a pregnant woman on board.

He felt certain that was Cora's secret. He'd recognized the midwife tools in her bag. Of course, he might be wrong. She'd needed the herbs from the bag, perhaps nothing more than that. But his well-trained instincts, that slight hesitation in Cora's tone, and the look on that younger woman's face when she came rushing into the saloon told him it was not a simple case of painful monthlies.

But how could there be a pregnant woman on board?

"What would Mercer say to *that*?" Albert whispered to the empty kitchen. He sighed heavily. The kettle whistled, and the shrill tone of it helped urge him into quick action. There were men in pain waiting for him. No more time for his carousel of thoughts.

Seven

PEARL SLEPT FITFULLY for a couple hours before she woke with a loud groan. Alert, Cora saw the young woman's stomach tighten. "It's all right, Pearl," she soothed. "Take slow breaths." Cora dove a hand into her bag and pulled out an old pocket watch. Fourteen minutes past midnight.

Pearl gasped. "It's passing. That one was different." She looked across the murky darkness at Cora, the whites of her eyes visible with her shock.

Cora took a steadying breath. *This is it. It's starting.* She smiled at the mother-to-be. "It's starting, Pearl."

Sally groaned from the floor, where she'd curled onto a blanket to try to sleep. "What's wrong?" she murmured.

"The baby's coming," Pearl said, the tone of her voice part awe, part terror.

Sally sat bolt up, her gaze going from her sister to Cora. "Will she be all right?"

"I'll do everything I can." She turned back to her patient. "I want you to relax as much as you can between pains. You'll need all the strength you can find. Here . . . take some water and then lie back." Cora helped Pearl drink.

Pearl swallowed loudly. "Will it hurt terribly?"

Cora didn't believe in lying to her patients. "Yes, dear, *but* your body was made for this. It's strong and amazing, and it knows what to do."

Pearl nodded, considering. "Do you have children, Cora?"

"No, I don't. My husband and I never became pregnant, and then he died in the war."

"I'm so sorry," Pearl whispered.

Sally added, a mischievous glint in her tone, "You should marry that handsome doctor you were with earlier tonight and have lots of beautiful, tall children."

Cora rounded on her, surprised. "Sally!"

She laughed, relieving some of the tension in the room. "Come now, Cora, I saw the way he looked at you and the way he *looked*." She lifted her eyebrows, challenging Cora to refute it.

Of course, she couldn't. A flutter in her stomach pushed a smile to her lips. The sisters laughed again. "See that, there!" Sally pointed at her. "You know exactly what I mean."

"Who are you talking about?" Pearl asked. "Tell me! I've been stuck in here the whole journey."

Sally grinned. "Dr. Cunningham, one of the doctors on board. The young, handsome one, not the old, stuffy one. He looks like those Greek heroes Mama used to tell stories about—so tall and so strong. I think every girl on board is secretly in love with him."

Cora felt a twist of jealousy. "Good grief, Sally. Don't be so silly. Dr. Cunningham is a nice man and an excellent surgeon."

Sally snorted. "A nice man! That's all you can say?"

Pearl hissed in a breath, the next pain saving Cora from the awkward conversation. She looked at her watch. "Five minutes apart. A good start. Take deep breaths, Pearl. I'm here. Sally is here. We'll do this together." Cora turned to Sally. "Do you have the clean sheets and water basins we talked about?"

"Yes, ma'am. Everything is there under the desk. And we already knitted a few blankets and booties for the baby." Sally's blue eyes went wide. "I can't believe it's happening." She crawled across the floor to sit at her sister's side. They exchanged a loving expression, no words necessary. Cora marveled at their closeness. She'd never known that depth of connection. Her heart ached to experience it, that same ache that had lived inside her as long as she could remember.

Is Albert the cure for this ache? Could he be . . . the one?

Cora frowned. Did she even believe such things? Wasn't marriage more about survival and mutual support rather than passion and fulfillment?

"Cora!"

Cora jerked her wandering mind back to attention. "What, Pearl?"

Pearl's cheeks had flushed red. "I . . . uh . . . I think I wet myself." She caught her bottom lip in her teeth.

"No, dear. That's probably your waters." Cora stood to do a quick check. "Yes. Your waters, for sure. Another sign that the baby is on the way."

Pearl groaned with another pain. "It's worse," she said through gritted teeth.

"They grow more powerful as you progress." She turned to Sally. "Run to the kitchen for some hot water. We need to clean up and ready everything."

Sally nodded and bolted out of the door.

Cora leaned down and put a hand on Pearl's sweaty forehead. "You're going to do wonderfully. And soon you'll meet your little one."

"What's wrong? I know something's wrong!" Pearl cried. She rolled onto her side, her hand coming to her lower back. "It hurts so much."

Cora rubbed at her forehead, thinking. Pearl's labor had been strong for the first four hours, her body progressing quickly. But during the last three hours things had suddenly come to a halt, the pain in her back worsening significantly. "Pearl, I need to check the baby's position." Pearl rolled back onto her back and opened her legs, all modesty forgotten. Cora reached into the birth canal. *Oh no. Just as I thought.* "The baby is positioned face up."

"Is that bad?" Sally asked.

"It is preferred that babies are born face down. They move better down the birth canal, and there's less pressure in the mother's back."

"Can you fix it?"

"I can try to turn the baby, but . . ."

"But what?" Sally breathed, her face growing pale.

"It's better with two experienced midwives. One helping from the inside and one on the outside."

"Can I do it?" Sally asked, quickly looking at her sister's belly.

"Perhaps, but . . ." *Get Albert. He offered help. Use it!* "Sally, I need you to go get Dr. Cunningham."

Sally and Pearl both went rigid. After a tense moment, Sally whispered, "We can't. He'll tell Mercer."

"He won't tell. But Mercer is going to find out soon enough anyway. I need Albert's help." Cora gave Sally a significant look, silently communicating how dire the moment had become.

Sally blinked a few times. "Are you sure?"

"It's what's best for Pearl. She's nearly spent. We must get the baby out soon."

Sally swallowed hard, got to her feet. "I'll be right back."

Albert stood at the exam table, checking the bandage on the worst of the frostbite victims. The surface of the fingers was mottled and dotted with several swollen blisters. But the skin would recover. He was about to announce this good news to the sailor when a woman burst in the room.

"Dr. Cunningham!"

Albert spun around. It was the same woman who'd come for Cora in the saloon. His pulse quickened. "What's wrong?"

"Cora—Nurse Martin. She . . . needs your help. *Right away.*"

Albert left the sailor blinking in surprise, grabbed his doctor's bag, and gestured to the woman to lead the way. They ran through the halls, heads and whispers turning their way. The woman stopped at a stateroom door, looked around, and then swept him inside. He took in the sight of Cora standing next to a young woman, a child, really, who was lying on her side, sweating and moaning. Cora rubbed at the girl's low back and murmured comfort. At the sound of the door, Cora looked back over her shoulder.

Albert crossed the room in two strides. "What can I do?"

"Have you ever turned a baby?" Cora asked.

Albert winced. "No. But I can if you'll guide me."

"The baby is lying face up and needs to be face down. We have to roll her over. I'll manipulate the head from inside. I need you to help the body follow by pushing on Pearl's belly."

Albert put down his bag. "All right. Is there—" He saw the wash basin and quickly washed his hands.

Cora turned to her patient. "All right, Pearl, this will be

uncomfortable, but once it's done things will go much better. Okay?"

Pearl, eyes mashed shut, only nodded. Albert wondered how long they'd been at it. From the disheveled, exhausted look of all three women it must have started soon after he saw Cora in the kitchen last night.

Cora positioned herself at Pearl's legs. Albert stepped up to the side of the small bed. "Hello, Pearl. I'm Dr. Cunningham."

Pearl, eyes opening a slit, gave a weak smile. "You're as handsome and tall as she said."

Albert smiled back, a warm flush of heat moving through his chest. He looked briefly at Cora, who avoided his eyes. He said, "Let's help this baby come out, shall we?"

Pearl nodded.

Albert turned his full attention to Cora, unable to stop the rush of admiration when he saw the look of focused determination on her face. He put his hands on Pearl's tiny belly; it hardly seemed big enough. "Is she early?" he asked.

"Yes," Cora answered quickly, her quick look telling him just how much she was concerned for the young woman. "She had swelling of her feet, a bad headache, nausea, irregular pulse."

Albert blinked, understanding blooming as tension in his neck. "I feel the child. I'm ready when you are."

Cora nodded. "Pearl, grip the sheets tightly and try not to move. Breathe through it. Sally—" The other woman positioned herself next to Albert, kneeling down to put her face near Pearl's.

"All right, sister," Sally said. "Look at me and just keep breathing. You can do this."

"But Mama . . . she . . ."

Sally's face fell. "No, Pearl, no. You're not Mama. Don't even think that. *You're* going to be just fine."

Albert's heart went out to the sisters. How terrifying it must be to be a woman giving birth.

How strong they are. How amazing.

"Albert, are you ready?" Cora called back his attention.

He met her eyes. "Yes."

"Carefully, toward you. You must be gentle but firm. Only working between her pains. And now . . . slowly . . ."

Albert felt the shift Cora initiated and followed it, applying firm pressure to the infant's shoulders through the thick barrier of Pearl's belly. Pearl gritted her teeth, a scream trapped behind them. Sally whispered comfort.

"Good," Cora breathed. "Keep going. A little more."

It was both harder and easier than Albert expected to turn the child. Would they injure the baby, the mother? He was certain his hands would leave bruises. He watched Cora closely, matching her effort and movements. The little flutters of tension around her eyes seemed to tell him everything she was thinking.

"A little more . . ." Cora whispered.

Pearl let out a guttural scream. "No more!" She huffed. "Please!"

"All done!" Cora announced. Albert instantly retracted his hands, took a step back. A birthing pain immediately followed. Cora added, "Pearl, it's time to push. Come on. Work to do."

Pearl gritted her teeth, face red with effort.

"Good girl!" Cora cheered. "Baby is moving down much better now. On the next pain, big push. All your might!"

Albert watched in a haze of wonder as Cora soothed and commanded and as Pearl struggled and triumphed. He'd only assisted on one other birth in his first years of medical school. The mother had been under the influence of ether, a newer practice, and the attending doctor had used forceps to pull the baby free. But this . . . this primal, glorious battle . . .

No wonder so many women die. Please, God, help Cora and young Pearl.

Pearl pushed again and again, for what seemed like an age but may have been only an hour. Albert had to remind himself not to hold his breath in anticipation. Cora was tireless, never wavering. And suddenly, there was a tiny baby in her arms, slick with blood and birthing fluids. Cora rubbed the little chest, and a strong cry burst forth from the infant.

First breath.

They all laughed in relief. "It's a girl!" Cora announced. "Healthy and strong, even if she is a bit small." She quickly wrapped the child in a white knitted blanket and laid her on her mother's chest. Pearl and Sally were both crying and cooing at the infant, who'd settled the moment she felt her mother's skin. Her big deep-blue eyes were wide open, taking in her new world. A smear of reddish hair adorned her head.

Cora went to the basin to wash her hands. Albert looked at her back, at the tension in her shoulders, the damp curls of hair at her neck. When she finished washing she didn't turn around but instead opened the porthole and leaned toward it to suck in long breaths. Albert went to her, pulling her into his arms. She let him take her weight and tucked her head against his chest. Her arms came around his waist, and quiet sobs escaped her throat.

He held her tighter.

Eight

A HESITANT KNOCK came at the door. Cora jolted away from Albert, immediately missing his solid warmth. She looked to Sally and Pearl, who stared at the door; Pearl gripped her baby closer. They all exchanged a worried look.

Albert, seeing their anxiety, said, "I'll talk to whomever it is," and went to the door. "Conant?"

"Doc? What are you doing here? I have three women telling me stories of the sound of baby cries coming from this room. What's going on?"

Albert angled his body, blocking the reporter's view of the room with himself and the door. Cora went to the bed and sat at Pearl's feet. "It'll be all right," she whispered. *Please let it be all right.* She swiped at her wet cheeks, adjusted her rumpled dress.

Albert said, "Roger, I need you to be very discreet about what I'm going to tell you."

"Of course," he answered, voice low and sincere.

"A young woman has given birth. The baby and mother are fine and under my care."

"Goodness, Cunningham. A baby? I assume Mercer doesn't know. He'll—"

"Doesn't know what? What's this about a baby?" Mercer's voice cut into the conversation. Cora jerked in surprise, her hand reaching for Sally's. Albert's hand on the edge of the door tensed.

"Mr. Mercer," Albert began. "All is well."

"So a woman gave birth on my ship? One of my virgins? How can this be?" The man's voice pitched louder with each question. "This will tarnish my reputation. This will—"

"This has *nothing* to do with you, sir," Albert cut in, his rock-solid authority coming into his voice. "A young widow gave birth to a child. She and her sister are traveling to Seattle to find husbands, just like the rest of your group."

Cora nodded. *The right lies. Good, Albert.*

Mercer huffed. "But I should have known! Even if she is a widow."

"Why? How is this your concern? The young woman's condition was her and her doctor's business alone. I knew, as the doctor, and that's all that matters."

Cora tightened her grip on Sally's hand. They exchanged a shocked look. "He can't take responsibility for this," Cora whispered. "Mercer might kick him off the ship." Sally only shook her head in response.

Mercer huffed out an exasperated breath. "I didn't promise those men in the West women *and* children. This is appalling. Does Dr. Barnard know about this?"

"No. I chose not to tell him."

"So you didn't tell your supervisor or me? How dare you, Cunningham!"

"I did what I thought was best for the young lady."

Cora couldn't stand it a moment longer. She jumped up and rushed to the door, ignoring Sally's whimper of warning. She ducked under Albert's arm. "It's my fault, Mr. Mercer. I attended the mother. Dr. Cunningham didn't know until an hour ago when I needed his assistance to save her and her baby's life." Mercer blinked at her, confused. Albert put his hand around her upper arm, a warning. She ignored him.

Dr. Barnard came rushing down the hall, pushing through the crowd that had gathered. "What's the problem here?" he demanded.

Mercer turned to him, face red. "This troublesome nurse and your assistant just delivered a *baby on my ship*. One of my young ladies now has a baby!"

"These women do not belong to you, Mercer," Cora spat back. "She and her sister are seeking a better life. Fleeing a dangerous situation. You have no right to interfere."

Dr. Barnard glared at her. "I told you that you were not allowed to participate in the medical situations on this ship."

"Tell me, Doctor, how many babies have you delivered?" Cora's heart punched her ribs so hard it hurt, but she would not back down.

Barnard flinched. "I do not have to justify myself—"

"Well, I've delivered over seven hundred," Cora cut in.

All the men balked in surprise. Albert was the first to speak, his thumb stroking the back of her arm. "Mrs. Martin was the only person aboard this ship qualified to deal with this matter."

Cora felt a surge of gratitude. "I will continue to monitor the child and the mother. They need not bother any of you."

Mercer's scowl deepened. "I want them *all* off the ship. When we dock in Brazil, I want all of you gone."

"You cannot do that!" Cora argued. "They won't survive there. They need knowledgeable care for at least three months, to ensure everything is all right."

"Then the baby and mother stay, under the care of the *doctors*. But you, Mrs. Martin, you may leave my ship." Mercer pointed a trembling finger at her face.

Cora's stomach dropped to the floor. Even though she'd suspected this might happen, her throat went dust-dry in an instant.

Will I survive there, in a foreign land?
Without Albert.

Albert's hand dropped from her arm, and he stepped in front of her, closing the distance between him and Mercer. Mercer's jaw clenched as he looked up. "Don't try to intimidate me, Cunningham. I'm in charge of this voyage."

"Then be a leader, not a fool, Mercer. Mrs. Martin has done nothing but offend your and Barnard's egos."

"How dare you!" Barnard cut in.

"She performed those excellent stitches the first day. She and I treated all the sick during that first week, while the two of you hid in your rooms. Cora and I were there at the railing when Foster went over. Where were you? And now Cora has saved this young lady's life and brought a new baby into the world. Why would you deprive your ship and passengers of such a valuable asset? Of *two* valuable assets—because if she goes I go."

Mercer scoffed. There was a tense pause. "Fine. We don't need you. Dr. Barnard can handle everything."

"Really?" Albert turned his head in Barnard's direction. "Did you know, Mr. Mercer, that your valiant doctor hasn't seen *one* patient?"

"What do you mean?" Mercer asked, looking over his shoulder at his doctor.

"I mean that I'm certain Barnard is either *not* a doctor or incredibly lazy."

A gasp sounded from the gathered crowd. Mercer swung around to face Barnard. "What is he talking about?"

Barnard's face turned apple red; he backed up a step. "I *am* a doctor . . . of sorts. I'm a . . . dentist."

"A dentist! So you lied to me?" Mercer spat. "All those qualifications you spouted?"

"All in dentistry, not medical. I wanted to go west; there's so much opportunity. I didn't think it would matter, especially with a capable assistant. I—"

Mercer's hand flew up to stop further explanation. "That's enough. I've had enough for one night. Barnard, you and your wife will disembark in Brazil. Cunningham, you're now the head and only doctor on this ship."

"Only if Mrs. Martin is my nurse."

Mercer cut a glance at her, frowned. He threw up his hands. "Fine. If you think it's best. But I don't want to be bothered about this baby. I don't want it making chaos of this ship. Women lose all reason around babies."

"You won't be bothered, Mr. Mercer," Cora assured him. She felt weak in the knees.

Mercer spun on his heel. "I'm going to my room, and I'm not to be disturbed," Mercer boomed. Barnard trailed after him, begging. Mercer yelled back at him, "I'm sure the good people of Brazil can use a fine dentist who thinks so highly of himself. You'll be fine."

"But my wife, Mercer. She'll be furious."

"Not my problem!"

The two men disappeared around the corner, along with most of the onlookers, who wanted to follow the drama. Albert, Cora, and Roger were left alone outside Sally and Pearl's room. Cora put a hand to her stomach, a flood of emotions making her dizzy.

Roger was the first to speak. "Well, that was loads of fun. I never liked that Barnard fellow. And his wife . . ." He rolled his eyes. "Brazil will certainly humble them both." He laughed lightly. "At least Mercer's erraticism worked in our favor this time. Nicely done, Cunningham. Oh, I can't wait to write about this."

Cora was only vaguely aware of what Roger had said or his attention now. She was staring at Albert in utter surprise. He stared back. "You . . . why did you do that?" she asked.

Albert held her gaze. "Because it was the right thing to do."

"No one has ever . . ." She couldn't finish the sentence. Tears slipped down her hot cheeks. "You really want me to be your nurse?"

Albert stepped closer. "No, I want you to be my partner."

Chills raced up her spine, lifting goose bumps along her skin. "What?" she breathed.

"You are as good a surgeon as I am. Better in some ways. So I propose this: when we get to Seattle, you and I open a practice *together*, equal partners."

She went cold from head to toe. "Truly? Albert, are you sincere, because . . ." Sudden fear gripped her. *No, this is too good to be true.*

He took another step closer, nearly touching her. "I've never been more sincere in my life. You are a miracle, and I want you working by my side. But there is one thing we must do first."

Cora's stomach tightened. Her breath came in small gasps as she looked up at him. "What is that?" she murmured.

"We must go to the captain right now and be married." His eyes roamed down her body and back to her eyes. "Because there are some things that can't wait until we get to Seattle."

In one swift movement, Albert pulled her into his arms and crushed his lips to hers. Insistent passion poured out of him, which Cora answered with equal enthusiasm. Her hands came to his neck, pulling him closer.

"Whoa, my friends!" Roger laughed. "Sorry to interrupt, but I feel it my duty to make sure that proposed marriage actually happens before you two drop to the floor right here in the hall." He laughed again.

Cora reluctantly pulled back from Albert, meeting his heated gaze. He smiled, and she started to laugh, all the exhaustion, relief, and joy bubbling out of her. He kissed her forehead. "Roger, you're a valuable friend," Albert teased, his eyes still on Cora.

Roger clapped Albert on the back, much like the first day they'd all met. "And now I'll be your best man. Off we go! Let's get you two married."

Nine

May 29, 1866
Seattle

CORA AND ALBERT stood on the dock, looking back at the *Continental*. Cora had hoped that stepping onto that ship would change her life, but she never imagined just how much. She lifted her gaze to her husband, her partner. He was everything she never believed she'd have and more. She imagined that the little orphan girl inside her finally had a reason to jump for joy and shed her melancholy shell.

Albert smiled, eyes still on the ship. "That was quite the journey, wasn't it?"

"Life-changing," she said, "just as Mercer promised in all his advertisements."

Albert laughed heartily, turning to face her. A stiff breeze came off the sea and loosened a bit of her hair. Albert tucked it behind her ears. "Roger promised to come visit in a few months. After he's explored the depths of San Francisco's delights. His words, not mine."

"I bet that takes him more than a few months."

Albert nodded, smiling. "We have many of our own delights to look forward to. A practice to build, a home to establish, patients to save, perhaps children one day, and more of this..." He leaned in to kiss her slowly, unashamedly, until she was thoroughly breathless. It was only when he pulled back to smile at her that she remembered they were still surrounded by people getting off the ship.

Cora blinked quickly, gave his chest a playful shove. "Mind your manners, Doctor."

The corner of Albert's mouth lifted in a mischievous grin.

"Mrs. Cunningham! Doctor!"

The couple turned toward the call and found Sally and Pearl hurrying toward them. Cora waved. The girls' faces were flushed with excitement. "You'll not believe it!" Sally said. "We've found husbands!"

"Already?" Cora gasped. "We've been docked less than an hour."

"A group of men were waiting, as Mercer promised," Pearl explained, bouncing her babe in her arms. Lottie slept peacefully, cheeks plump and pink.

"And we've been talking with two kind and good-looking brothers, both in need of wives," Sally went on. "They own a large farm a couple hours outside the city. So we both have husbands, Lottie has a father, *and* we get to stay together. It's a miracle!"

Cora laughed. "It really is. I'm so happy for you."

"Thank you for all you did, Cora," Pearl said, eyes suddenly teary.

"My pleasure." Cora hugged the sisters. "I'm so happy for you. I'll check on you soon."

They said their goodbyes, and Albert and Cora watched the girls hurry away. Albert put his arm around her shoulders. "Are you ready to go, my love?"

Cora took a long breath, looking over the *Continental* once more. *Quite a journey, indeed.* She lifted to her toes, gave Albert a leisurely, lingering kiss, and then said, "I'm ready. Let's get to work."

Teri Harman is the author of The Moonlight Trilogy, a witch fantasy series, and the magic realism romance, *A Thousand Sleepless Nights*. For many years, she's written about books for ksl.com, reviewed books for *The Deseret News*, and contributed book segments to Utah's number one lifestyle show, "Studio 5 with Brooke Walker." Her fiction won first place in the "Romance Through the Ages Contest" in 2016 and Kirkus Reviews called her work "unusual and absorbing." She has taught classes and workshops for writers all over Utah.

Teri is also a certified yoga instructor (RYT-500) and has a degree in exercise and sport science from the University of Utah. She lives in Utah with her husband and three children. Visit her at www.teriharman.com

A Faraway Love

LINDA CARROLL-BRADD

Lowell, Massachusetts
December 1865

THE FLICKERING LIGHT from the oil lantern danced shadows across the pages of the *Courier-Citizen*. Sorcha leaned an elbow on the scarred dining room table of her parents' two-story house, where she'd spread the newspaper. She scanned columns containing advertisements for sales of furniture, bolts of fabric, and premium butcher cuts. Wedged amongst the ads were announcements of available job offerings. Since the War of the Rebellion ended, any job she might be qualified for went to a returning soldier. The company name of her former employer, Raybourne's Textiles, headed the next column. Just seeing the words made the scars on her disfigured left hand throb. Never again.

"Saints alive, Sorcha Geraghty. Where be yer spectacles?" Maveen bustled into the room, carrying a basket of mending on her ample hip. "Why must ye scrunch up yer face in that way? Hasten wrinkles, ye'll be doin'." She settled into the upholstered chair with Queen Anne legs and opened the basket.

Straightening before an anticipated reprimand for poor posture, Sorcha grinned at the way her mother's Irish accent broadened when she became irritated. They'd lived twenty-five years in America, and neither parent had lost their accent from County Mayo. "I wouldn't be squinting if someone on the newspaper staff saw the importance of grouping and labeling the ads. I posted a note on that very correction to the publisher last week."

"Pish posh, ye and yer notes. Are ye thinkin' ye know better than the man who makes his business runnin' the paper?" Tsking, Ma lifted a wooden oval from the basket and slipped a holey woolen sock over the smooth end.

"I figured a businessman would welcome a suggestion for making the reader's experience more enjoyable." She flipped to the last page, then smoothed the creases. Under her hand, bold print with the name *Asa S. Mercer* popped into focus. A skitter of interest tingled her spine. Leaning closer, she scanned the article from *The New York Times* with a reprint date from several days earlier. The announcement stated space remained on a ship, the *S.S. Continental,* for a second group of "petticoat brides" leaving the following month for Washington Territory.

Quick footsteps snapped on the hardwood floor before becoming muffled by the carpet. A loud huffing of expelled breath followed. "Are you still reading, Sorcha?"

"That I am. I told you I needed to review the ads for a job." Sorcha planted a finger in the article to glance up at her black-haired cousin. The tapping shoe and fists planted on rounded hips left no doubt about how Blinne felt about her activity.

"You were to be my partner in the parlor for charades. Our sisters and brothers are waiting." She scurried to the table and rested a hand on the table, leaning close. "Why a job?

Aren't you too busy with your studies for your teacher's certificate?"

"In these final weeks of the course, we're concentrating on our individual projects. I'll make time. Look at this news, Blinne." Sorcha tapped a finger on the headline. "Remember when we heard this gentleman speak two years ago?"

"Huh." Blinne dropped into the adjacent chair. "*Asa Mercer, Female Emigrant Agent.* That man who convinced women to travel across the country to marry those frontiersmen?" She turned, her eyes flashing. "I remember sitting with you in the Unitarian Church for his presentation and thinking he, as a bachelor, was an odd choice to convince women to go forth and populate the West." A giggle escaped before she shot a frowning glance toward her aunt across the room. "I mean, travel so far away from the bosom of their families."

Sorcha turned a wide-eyed look at her capricious cousin, then scrunched her face into a frown. That fact was not one she wanted planted in Ma's head. When Sorcha first broached the subject about joining the original group on the *S.S. Illinois*, she'd met only opposition. Her parents had argued that grief over her beau's death in the Battle of Chancellorsville colored her thoughts.

Ma stood and approached the table. "Just the other day I was chattin' with Dorothy Ordway." She pointed the darning needle toward her niece. "Ye must be knowin' her, Blinne. She has her dresses made at Dinah's shop, where ye work."

"Of course I know Missus Ordway. Nice lady." Blinne nodded, then ducked her head and glanced sideways, then mouthed, *Sorry.*

"Well, she'd had a recent letter from her niece, Lizzie, who traveled on Mercer's first trip." Ma rested a hip against the edge of the table. "Saints be praised, Dorothy worried so that Lizzie would never marry. She reported the independent young woman loves teachin' and is quite happy out west."

"I remember Miss Ordway. She taught my Sunday School classes at Reverend Abner's Unitarian Society meetings." A sigh slid between her lips before Sorcha could hold it inside. To be in charge of her own classroom—to gaze upon a sea of young, eager faces and share facts to give the children the means to prosper in the world—was her dream.

Ma sucked in a breath. "Sorcha Donelle, yer not thinkin' on this emigration madness again, are ye?"

"Why not?" The use of her middle name worked as Ma intended—to make her feel about six years old. Wincing, Sorcha angled her head to meet her mother's gaze. "I've not seen a single ad for a teaching job locally. Why did I spend my trousseau money on the teaching academy if I can't get a job? Since the war ended, all the schools are only hiring men."

"But the Pacific Coast . . . 'tis so far away." Ma blinked fast, her eyes watering.

Being seated and looking upward created too much of a disadvantage. Sorcha rose, careful not to step too close and tower over her ma's petite form. Ma was the parent to convince, then Da would go along with whatever she decided. "As was America when you and Da and Uncle Eoin left the family farm in the Doo Lough Valley and climbed aboard an oceangoing ship." Suddenly, traveling west presented the logical solution to her dilemma. The article claimed Mercer again offered teaching jobs to the women who joined his expedition. Plus she knew women moving to the sparsely populated region were much sought after as wives.

"But we had no other choice."

Irritation squared her shoulders, and she narrowed her eyes. "Don't be shaking your head, Ma. I've been raised on the dire potato-famine stories you tell."

Gasping, Maveen reached for the hem of her apron and dabbed her eyes. "The forties were tryin' times ... dyin' times ..." Scowling, she shook a pointed finger. "And well ye know it."

The word *dying* tightened Sorcha's throat. More than two years of grieving were behind her, and she didn't want to upset Ma more by mentioning the hated war that stole her Tully and two of her brothers, Shea and Odran. For the past several months, she'd felt restless. "I do, Ma. And I'm seeking calmer times. What could be more peaceful than living near an ocean and listening to soothing waves at the end of a day?" After hearing Mercer's talk, she'd looked up details in Lowell's library about the faraway territory and learned about the city of Seattle. She'd even found a copy of the pamphlet he'd written, titled *Washington Territory, The Great North-West.*

"Ah, lass, family is everythin'." Ma tilted back her head and reached up a hand.

Like when she was young, Sorcha nestled her cheek against the work-roughened palm for comfort and looked into her mother's pale-blue eyes. "A fact I know well, Ma. But so is wanting to feel like I'm making a difference in the world." The more she argued, the more she was convinced her future lay in that distant territory. If Ma was worried about her being far from family ... *The solution is so obvious.* Sorcha straightened and rested a hand on her cousin's shoulder. "Blinne will come along too."

Blinne jerked her head around, and her eyes popped wide. "I will?"

"Of course. Women with seamstress abilities will be in great demand in a city where men have been making do with their own sewing." Although calling Seattle a city stretched the truth, the lack of seamstresses rang as logical. "They've been limited to buying whatever gets shipped to town and hoping it fits well enough."

"Where is yer father? I'll get him to talk sense into ye two." Maveen spun toward the hallway. "Padraig!" Her skirts swished with a hiss as she dashed from the sitting room.

Sorcha slumped into the chair, suddenly drained of her initial spunk, but her thoughts whirled.

"Are you serious about this trip, then?" Blinne clasped her hands and shifted her gaze from the table to the doorway where her aunt had disappeared.

"I wanted to go the first time. Two years ago, the trip represented escape from constant news of the war and how the blockades choked the textile industry. Then the accident occurred." She held up her maimed hand with the missing ring and pinky fingers, frowning at the puckered scar. Only within her own house did she expose her injury to others.

"Mama and Papa were still alive then." Slumping in her chair, Blinne sniffled. "And we lived in the big house overlooking the Concord River."

"Let's join this group of women." Hoping to dissuade a mood that could turn to melancholy, Sorcha reached for Blinne's hand and squeezed. "Let's be bold and be the individuals who steer our own future. I have some money saved, and you could use part of your inheritance."

"My dowry?" Shaking her head, she wrung her hands in her lap. "Papa left me that money so I could make a good marriage."

The old-country ways. Sorcha fought to keep a disparaging note from her voice. "Blinne, haven't you noticed that life isn't like it was before the war? Marriages for people like us aren't arranged anymore. Besides, you could pay your passage and still have funds remaining to bring to a marriage. *If* that's what you want." She thought of the women's suffrage speeches she'd heard this summer at the city auditorium. The eloquent orators spoke of the importance of women valuing their abilities and sparked a fire in Sorcha's soul to seek her best potential. "Or you could open your own seamstress shop."

"No. I couldn't." Blinne shook her head, then frowned. With shaky fingers, she pleated the fabric of her skirt into rows before turning with a gleam in her eyes. "Could I?"

"Of course. You've learned everything about running a shop from working with Dinah. And I've seen how good you are with the customers."

"I do have a way with bestowing compliments that turn into sales." Blinne flashed a smile. "Dinah's been letting me take the remnants from the end of fabric bolts home. I'd thought to make them into a quilt, but maybe I could sew men's shirts instead."

Blinne is making plans. Hope burst in her chest. Sorcha turned back to the table, running a finger along the lines of text. "The ship leaves from New York City the second week of January for a four-month journey. Passage costs three hundred dollars." She winced, her enthusiasm waning. Her bank account held only two-thirds of that amount. Could she convince Da to supply the remaining funds? Or did Mercer have financial backing from supporters in his native territory to assist the eastern women?

"Sorcha!" Wavy-haired Padraig strode into the room, wispy smoke trailing from the pipe clenched in his teeth. "What's this I hear about ye wantin' a sea adventure? Is me bonny girl ready to spread her wings?"

Biting back a smile, Sorcha jumped to her feet and rushed to her da's side. She rose on tiptoes and kissed his whiskery cheek, then leaned back and looked into flashing green eyes that mirrored her own. In that moment, she was ready to risk anything to earn herself a coveted teaching position—even traveling the high seas. "You heard right, Da. I wish to become one of Mercer's belles."

Two

CHILLY BREEZES TUGGED at Sorcha's skirt as she topped the shaky gangplank and stepped onto the solid deck of the *S.S. Continental*. After several days of nervous waiting, she was glad when Mister Mercer finally appeared at Lovejoy's Hotel this morning a bit before noon. Local newspapers ran articles doubting Mercer's motives for the trip. Rumors abounded among the ladies in the group that he controlled insufficient funding to start the expedition. But his cheerful salutation on the morning of January 16, 1866, absolved all of those fears.

Thankfully, he brought men from the ship's crew to oversee loading trunks, crates, and valises. The same crew also arranged multiple coaches and taxis to transport the passengers from the hotel at Beekman Street and Park Row to Pier 2 NR on the North River.

All told, their group—comprising seven widows with children, three childless widows, and thirty-six unmarried women—presented quite a smaller contingent than the seven hundred women Mercer boasted about in his interviews. Sorcha had come to the conclusion the man loved to exaggerate. The captain, his wife and daughter, crew members, and several others not associated with the Mercer party accounted for the remaining people, to bring the total to exactly one hundred souls on board. Carrying only her reticule and a small valise holding her teaching supplies felt wrong. However, she rationalized the fee she paid for her passage covered being escorted.

"Oh, Sorcha, we're finally here." Blinne stumbled at the ship's rocking motion in its berth, then grabbed onto the railing and looked all around. "I've never been on a ship before."

Overhead, a short sail flapped in the wind in rhythm with the water slapping against the hull. Gulls swooped low among the masts, and their high-pitched shrieks filled the air.

The cries drew her attention, and she looked up, the sight of the tall mast setting her stomach tumbling. A breeze tugged at her bonnet, so Sorcha retied the silk ribbons until she felt the pinch under her jaw. Her gloves, with two padded fingers, made the task a struggle. "As you keep saying." Obviously, Blinne didn't count the Fall River Line steamboat they rode overnight to travel from Newport, Rhode Island, to New York as a ship. Sorcha widened her stance to compensate for the movement, remembering Da's advice from trips long ago on a friend's fishing boat.

"Ladies and gentlemen." Mister Mercer held up his hands and scanned the group. His attire of a suit and tie befitted a former university president. Tall and thin, he wore a full beard and moustache, and his reddish hair was styled with a wavy clump on top, above his broad forehead. "Welcome to your new home for the next three months, until we reach our destination of San Francisco."

Several titters and whispers passed among the women standing nearby.

Sorcha glanced around and spotted the Peebles sisters, who looked to be ignoring Mister Mercer and instead smiled and flirted with members of the crew carrying the luggage onto the deck. She'd noticed them flirting with the hotel staff and wondered if the lack of parental supervision was the reason for their brazen behavior.

"Let me tell you of the ship's features before I release you to choose your rooms. Captain Winser would count me remiss if I didn't inform you that the steamer *S.S. Continental* is two hundred thirty-five feet in length and thirty-six feet wide. Its three decks are well lit and ventilated. On both sides of a middle passageway are situated large and pleasant staterooms with an attached bathing room for each one. One cabin has been set aside for exclusive use by the women with no male admittance allowed. Another cabin holds two sewing machines bolted to the floor for your shared use."

Bouncing on her toes, Blinne leaned close. "How wonderful. I can—"

"Later." Frowning, Sorcha raised a finger to her lips.

"Please be aware an inspector will visit the living spaces each morning and report to the ship's doctor on any signs of illness." Mister Mercer scanned the group, then stretched an arm to point. "Doctor Charles Barnard will tend to any medical issues. A surgeon, Albert Cunningham, will be assisting in the designated sick room."

Heads bobbed, and women shuffled to get a look at the gentlemen.

"The ship is equipped with ten lifeboats and a life preserver for every single passenger. Books have been donated, and a library will be set up once we're underway." He smiled at the gathering.

Sorcha shivered at the mention of lifeboats, but the last announcement excited her. She loved to read and never found enough time in her parents' busy household. Three months on the ocean would provide ample time. Plus she looked forward to finding a quiet place somewhere to play her Celtic lap harp.

"Seek your rooms, and keep in mind those with children should receive the ones with trundles or cots." Mercer waved toward an open doorway. "Once you've selected one, let the crew know so your belongings can be delivered."

Hours later, Sorcha and Blinne had their trunks and valises arranged to their liking. A second mate who delivered their belongings warned them not to leave items loose on surfaces where they would be tossed around in rough seas. Putting away items after each use might take an extra moment or two, but Sorcha wished to keep her belongings in one piece.

A shrill whistle around three in the afternoon drew them to the top deck, and Sorcha watched as the *Continental* sailed free of the pier. A lump rose in her throat, yet she plastered on a smile and looked forward toward her new life. Chilly breezes snatched at her skirts, but Sorcha breathed in the fresh air and huddled inside her wool cloak. Not wanting to miss this opportunity, she gazed at the passing land. On one side of the ship was New Jersey, and on the other was New York—two states she'd never seen until this trip. *What other first experiences lie ahead?*

Supper proved a lively affair, with conversations focusing on the excitement of starting the voyage. Afterwards, Sorcha and Blinne partnered for a game of whist in the lower salon against the Bermingham sisters. Their brother, an employee of the shipping company, read a newspaper nearby. Suddenly, cries sounded from above.

The purser, Mister Denbro, rushed into the room. "I apologize for the intrusion, but everyone needs to gather their tickets and return here for your name to be called."

Sorcha tossed down her cards and cast a worried glance toward Blinne. "The ship stopped moving. Can you feel it?"

Blinne shook her head and clasped Sorcha's hand. "What could be happening?"

Miss Bessie turned to her brother. "What a bother."

Captain Bermingham set aside his newspaper, stood, and buttoned his jacket. "Let me see what this upset is about. In the meantime, collect your tickets."

An hour later, the ship was underway again, but several passengers who hadn't paid their full fares were set off into a tugboat at Staten Island. Tired, Sorcha walked down the hallway to their stateroom with Blinne at her side. "Can you believe that coward Mercer actually hid in the coal bin and made Captain Bermingham handle the disagreeable affair?" She rubbed her gloved hands together against the cold air.

"Well, the captain is an agent for the shipping company. But I'm glad we're not among that group. How sad to have your hopes dashed in that way." Blinne clutched her reticule to her chest.

"Calm yourself." Sorcha paused and rested a hand on her cousin's shoulder. "Mister Mercer stamped our tickets paid in full before we boarded, so being cast off was never a possibility. He assured us both the one hundred dollars he excused from our ticket price came from the expedition fund. Now, let's get some rest."

The next morning, she rose at first light. All night long, the ship made creaking noises that she'd have to get used to. By seven, she and Blinne sat at the breakfast table. "Blinne, eat small portions until you know how your stomach handles the motion."

"My stomach didn't trouble me last night." She shrugged and speared another sausage from the platter.

Sorcha nibbled on a plain biscuit. Glancing around at the others eating a hearty meal, she hesitated to tell them the ship wasn't really at sea yet. Within hours, following the lifting of the anchor at nine, many of the ladies became seasick. Sorcha resigned herself to tending Blinne as she alternately vomited, then languished on the berth, begging for cool rags on her forehead. That night the seas were so rough Sorcha felt a bit queasy and stood near the porthole for brief breaths of fresh air. Long past midnight, she heard tromping feet in the hallway above and cries of "Mister Mercer!" Curious as to what now was afoot, she grabbed her cloak and eased open the stateroom door, hurrying to the stairs.

Pounding on a door echoed through the stairway opening. Several ladies demanded Mister Mercer rise and save them from drowning.

"Ladies, I am not your fathers. What do you think I can do about waves on the ocean? Cease this wailing and go back to your beds."

His gruff tone was proof they'd awakened him, and he wasn't too happy. *Not very sympathetic, but the man had a point.* Sorcha slipped into her room and eased into her berth.

For the next four days, Blinne was the patient and Sorcha served as the nurse. On the fifth day, she coaxed Blinne to sip broth. And on the next day, she assisted her to the deck for fresh air, where many of the others recuperated.

In celebration of their tenth day at sea, Mister Mercer carried crates with skeins of yarn and bolts of fabric into the lower salon. "Ladies, now that everyone has their sea legs, so to speak, you'll want to keep yourselves busy. Seattle is cold in the winter, and woolen socks are in great demand."

Setting a finger at her place in a borrowed mystery novel, Sorcha looked over the yarn of various colors and needles. Was this task mandatory?

Frowning, Widow Chase raised her chin and looked down her nose. "Whyever would we do so?"

The gentleman smoothed a hand over his hair. "I'll sell

them in a great fair in Seattle to recoup expenses from the trip."

Both Peebles sisters shot to their feet. Miss Anna jammed her hands on her hips. "My sister and I paid full fare. We did not come on this ship to do your bidding." They stormed out of the room.

Sorcha caught Mister Mercer's direct gaze, and her skin prickled. The novel would have to wait. "Blinne, grab a blue skein, and I'll help you roll it into a ball."

Mercer smiled. "For those of you who don't knit, I've delivered bolts of fabric to the sewing room, with the hopes many shirts will be made. Nothing too fancy. Just sew them in a variety of sizes, please." He nodded, then left the room.

Blinne gaped. "But I intended to have shirts to sell."

Leaning close, Sorcha pressed a hand on Blinne's leg. "Don't worry until you see how many others take on this task."

A happy event occurred on Tuesday, January 30, when a marriage took place in the upper salon. Albert Cunningham, the surgeon assisting Doctor Barnard, and nurse Cora Martin had become close while tending all the seasick ladies. Captain Winser presided over the ceremony, and Roger Conant, *The New York Times* reporter writing a journal of the expedition, stood as best man.

As the wedded couple kissed, Blinne turned to Sorcha with tears filling her eyes. "If only I can find a husband as easily in our new home."

Biting her tongue, Sorcha just smiled and nodded. Locating a husband was certainly not her goal.

Three

Ny Hoppas (New Hope) Logging Camp near Seattle
Early March

IN THE EARLY morning chill, Lang Ingemar scooted his chair closer to the potbellied stove. The heat didn't quite overcome the cold air seeping through crevices in the walls of the logging company office. He made a mental note to add mud-chinking the holes to his task list. Only pale sunlight filtered through the dirty window, so he angled the newspaper toward the oil lantern. He scanned the pages of the *Puget Sound Weekly*, hoping for an article about the progress of the *S.S. Continental*. The article from the ship's February 12 arrival in Rio de Janeiro was the last he'd seen.

His best guess put the ship near the Cape of Good Horn—still almost two months away from the expedition's arrival. He debated about when to broach the subject of building a small cabin for the teacher's use with his two foremen. The lumber required wouldn't be much, but Roald and Staffen needed to adjust their production levels to accommodate for the extra board feet.

After tossing aside the newspaper, he jumped to his feet

and paced. Waiting for a break in the heavy rain storms made sense. Unfortunately, the Pacific Northwest region experienced at least a daily light drizzle well into the spring months. All the crew could do was build the cabin and check back each week to daub the gaps created by the drying wood. Sometimes being the manager and having the weight of decision-making rest solely on his shoulders proved a lonely job. But he'd vowed to his father he could make this logging venture self-sustaining within four years, and he aimed to fulfill that promise.

Lang moved to the stove and refilled his tin cup with fragrant coffee from the metal pot. After blowing across the oily surface, he sipped the strong brew, then stood at the window. The sight of majestic evergreens surrounding the clearing always cheered him. Having been raised in a lumbering family in Nusnäs on the shores of Sjö Siljan, he craved the crisp, earthy scent. This area around Seattle didn't have his favorite lush spruces, but the pine trees were plentiful, as were the silvery lakes and the blue ocean.

Through the wavy glass, he spotted men emerging from the bunkhouse and heading toward the privies. Time to start the last work day of the week. He rubbed a hand over the tight-corded muscles of his neck.

The unknown issue of acquiring a teacher weighed heavy on his mind. Whenever he went into Seattle, Lang avoided being dragged into the frequent conversations about Asa Mercer's foolhardy trip of bringing women to the territory. Instead, he wanted to think he'd make the correct choice. Last spring, investing in the expedition by paying the full fare for a single passenger seemed like the only way Lang could obtain a teacher for his logging crews. Now, he wasn't so sure.

After two years of living in America, the native-born Swedes hadn't picked up enough English to keep them out of fistfights while spending time in saloons. Lang also suspected shopkeepers took advantage of the language barrier. Again, he murmured silent thanks for his mother being born in England so he and his siblings were raised speaking both Swedish and English.

Heavy boot scraping on the boards in front of the door announced someone's arrival.

Moving from the window, Lang tossed the newspaper on the stack next to his desk and dropped into the chair. Wood shavings dotted the desk surface, and he glanced at the unfinished horse he'd been carving yesterday.

The door opened, and sunlight beamed into the room, bringing a whiff of pine scent.

"*Hej, chef.*" Staffen closed the door, then shucked his wool jacket and hung it on a nearby peg.

Lang nodded, then waited for what his mill foreman had to say. Usually the standard greeting to the boss meant the subject was business related. Staffen Torburg stood about an inch taller than Lang's six feet and outweighed him by twenty pounds, much of the weight in his torso and arms. The man, who was one of his best friends, spent his days off riding into the nearest foothills and skiing. The sport was one Lang loved but rarely allowed himself the time to indulge in.

"Didn't see you at the bunkhouse." Staffen walked across the floor and extended his reddened hands close to the stove.

Has he lost yet another pair of gloves? "Woke early and wanted to catch up on a few tasks here in the office." Guilt attacked because although bookkeeping awaited, he hadn't even opened the ledger. Instead, he'd been obsessing about the arrival of a female he hoped would solve the company's most pressing problem.

"Need to know what to tell the crew about the prohibition on visiting town. Has it been lifted starting with their next days off?"

Nodding, he huffed out a long breath and scratched the stubble on his chin. Two weeks ago, three crew members returned from a boisterous Saturday night in town so bruised they missed several days of work. Similar incidents happened with too much regularity, and they impacted production. Frustrated, Lang put the entire camp on suspension—a decision that caused most of the men to avoid him for several days. "*Ja.* Starting tomorrow night, they're free to go."

"I know you wish they'd stay in camp." Staffen rubbed fingers over his clean-shaven chin. "But the men work hard and deserve to enjoy themselves."

"Let's don't have this argument again." Lang knew if the men were back in their hometowns in Sweden, family pressures would prevent them from spending the bulk of their pay on whiskey and gambling. He could set an example, but they were all adults and he couldn't make them act in a certain way. He also wasn't so blind as to ignore the few who indulged in spending time with the fancy ladies, too. "No one broke the prohibition, so they are released to visit town."

"Good to hear." Staffen grinned and gestured toward the door. "I'm starved. Let's see what Wikimak prepared today."

The native Chinook woman who appeared before they'd finished the clearing to establish camp had become an adequate cook. Lang grabbed his wool jacket and pulled a knit cap over his hair and ears. Today was not the day to mention the needed cabin. "I'll be the one to make the announcement about lifting the prohibition. At least then I'll receive everyone's smiles."

The next afternoon, the crew was back to grumbling, although nobody objected outright. Work always ended an hour early on the first Saturday of the month. As he'd promised his father before leaving Sweden, Lang required the workers to write home every month. He walked among the twenty-four men, who were spread throughout the bunkhouse bottom floor—some at tables and others sitting in blocky upholstered chairs. The company supplied the writing materials and paid the postage for a monthly letter to their Swedish hometowns surrounding the placid Sjö Siljan.

Once he'd determined they tended their task, he sat and faced his own half-filled piece of stationery. Last night, he'd completed Ny Hoppas's previous month's report—facts and figures were all his father cared about. Lang knew Rutger would share the details with Rikard and Hans, his older brothers.

Now, he wrote what he figured his mother, Levina, and younger sisters, Deana and Gleda, wanted to know. Each month, he did his best to include a new fact but probably wrote the same details, because his life was a well-established routine. He consulted with his two foremen regarding the activities of the business, he handled the correspondence with companies ordering lumber, and in the evenings, he read or carved wooden Dala horses. Once in a while, he strapped on metal spikes, grabbed an axe, and climbed to the top of a tree. Back home in the family business, he'd started as a tree topper, and he liked to keep his skills honed. Diversions from those tasks included trips away from the camp to buy supplies or accompany a lumber delivery to the Seattle docks and an occasional fishing trip.

Shifting through the details, he recognized how mundane his life had become. Maybe he should accept Staffen's open invitation and join him on a skiing trip before the snow melted. He needed more leisure time—a twenty-four-year old man should have some fun.

On a mild Monday morning six weeks later, Lang hunched over the *Puget Sound Weekly* spread across his desk. A report of a horrendous explosion at the Wells Fargo office in San Francisco held his complete attention. Last week's edition included only speculation as to the cause, but this article provided more details. An explosive material called nitroglycerine arrived in the office packaged with no special warning and was placed in unclaimed storage. He read a quote from a shipping company employee that bottles of the explosive were often transported on steamers, and a chill went through him. Hopefully, none was being carried on the *Continental.*

Two Wells Fargo freight clerks went to investigate, complete with hammer and chisel to open the wooden crate, which showed signs of leakage. Moments later, an explosion shot wood and glass into the air, demolished the building, and tore apart everything within a forty- to fifty-foot circle. Windows on California Street between Kearny and Montgomery and as far away as Third Street shattered. Doors shredded away from frames. The list of missing and dead totaled seventeen men, but additional casualties of tourists or itinerants would never be known.

With tightness in his chest, Lang slumped back in his chair, running a hand through his hair. The logging crew used black powder occasionally to blast out tree trunks, but he'd never heard of this liquid explosive and its incredible power. What if the Mercer expedition already arrived in the city and the women were housed in that area of town? Shoulders tense, he glanced at the masthead and read the issue's date—April 28.

On the next page, he found the news he'd been waiting for. Tension that he'd been carrying for three solid months released from his shoulders. The *S.S. Continental* had docked in San Francisco four days earlier. Folding the paper in quarters, he read on. The reporter mentioned swarms of men on the docks, all anxious to meet the "genus crinoline." Some hired boats so that a flotilla surrounded the ship, the occupants offering money to board. With nine men to a single woman in the western regions, the males were desperate to see and speak with the gentler sex. Police had to be called in to control the crowds and make the men desist.

The next paragraph brought back the tension tenfold. After the women moved to two hotels the next day, courtships started in earnest. A steady stream of beaus visited the "belles," as they were referred to. The reporter posed a question about how many would be wooed away from continuing the expedition and convinced to stay in San Francisco. "*Nej!*" He tossed down the paper in disgust. On his feet, he paced the small confines of the office, cursing in his native tongue. He needed a good number of women to come to Seattle to allow him the best teacher choice. Especially since Mercer hadn't procured hundreds of women as he promised.

That evening, Lang sat at his desk and looked at Roald and Staffen, who balanced a few feet away on the rear legs of their chairs. The time of holding back his news had ended. He needed to inform them what to expect, especially since he needed their support. "*Mina vanner.*"

Roald snorted and ran a hand over his full, reddish-brown beard. "When Lang starts a discussion with 'my friends,' he wants something. What is the favor this time?"

Do I do that? Lang inhaled deep. "In about a month, give or take a few days, Asa Mercer will return to Seattle with a number of respectable single women from the East Coast."

"*Ja,* the men heard talk in town about these Mercer's belles." Staffen linked his hands behind his neck. "Not everyone holds him in high esteem. Some say he's not thinking of the welfare of the area bachelors, but he made the trip solely to line his own pocket. You know how few he brought the last time. How does his arrival affect Ny Hoppas?"

Lang straightened. "I signed a contract and paid for an individual's passage. My goal was to secure one of those women as a teacher to bring to the camp."

Chair legs crashed to the plank floor, and the men gaped at each other before turning toward their boss.

"Why? We're all bachelors here." Frowning, Roald crossed a boot over the opposite knee.

"To teach you and the workers English." Lang did his best to hold a neutral expression.

"What?" Staffen shot to his feet and crossed both arms over his chest. "You want to send us to school? I completed my studies long ago back home."

Shoving back the chair, Lang mirrored his friend's confrontational stance. The only way to argue with Staffen was toe to toe. "Can you go to the mercantile or a saloon and know for sure you're being charged the correct price? Or at the shoemaker shop? What about ordering food at the hotel restaurant?"

Huffing out a breath, Staffen spun and stared out the window.

"What about you, Roald?" Lang turned his attention to his friend, who sat slumped with elbows on knees, staring at the floor. "You're a friendly guy. Don't you want to learn how to greet someone on the street?"

The big man shrugged, then after a moment, he looked up and jerked his chin in a quick nod.

"I'll expect you two to be the examples your crews will follow. You show an interest, and tell them how important learning to speak and read English is—"

"We have to read it, too?" Scowling, Staffen jammed hands on his hips.

"Reading is almost as important as speaking. The two skills go hand in hand." At the point his friend's stance relaxed, Lang shifted his gaze between his friends. "Now for the favor."

"Becoming a student again isn't a favor?" Staffen cocked a wheat-colored eyebrow.

"No. Building a cabin for the teacher is." Not wanting them to interrupt, he grabbed a sheet of paper from the desk's top drawer. In addition to a rough sketch of a simple log cabin, he'd drawn the floor plan. "I thought a design like this drawing. Not too big but adequate for the female to feel comfortable in her off hours." He pointed to the layout of three rooms—parlor, kitchen, and small bathing room—with an upper sleeping loft covering half the lower floor space. "Built-in cupboards on both levels will accommodate clothing and supplies."

Both men stepped close, gazes riveted on the drawing.

"Oskar, from my crew, has a skill with cupboards." Staffen nodded.

"Kristar comes from a family of shutter makers." Roald ran a finger around the squares in the walls indicating windows.

"Glad to hear you both agree." Not that they'd done so, but Lang wouldn't accept opposition. His plan had to work. "I'll entertain suggestions of where to build the cabin."

Several minutes passed as the pros and cons of multiple locations were discussed. Thankfully, they agreed a spot to the far side of the cookhouse, where the only other female in camp lived, made the most sense.

"I'll go to stay in town during the last week of next month and wait for the ship's arrival. I want to meet Mercer and arrange for an interview of the most experienced teacher in his group at once." His words might be confident, but what if the woman didn't want to leave Seattle? What would he do then?

Four

TUESDAY, MAY 29, Sorcha stood with Blinne on the deck of the *Maria*. Today marked the final leg of their long journey. After changing from the oceangoing *Huntsville* to this ship within Puget Sound, the rocking of the deck eased. All she could hope was that the reception in Seattle was nothing like what they'd experienced in San Francisco. Having to walk from the docks to the nearby hotels amidst crowds of gawking men had been the most uncomfortable experience of her life. Add in the fact that derogatory clippings about the character of women who would travel so far to snag a husband hung in shop windows along their path.

As the small ship chugged south, she reflected on the trip's high points—collecting shells at Sandy Point, a weeklong stay in the harbor at Lota, Chile, with visits to Doctor Silver of the American consulate and his wife, fresh fruits and vegetables bought in the marketplace, the April 1 lunar eclipse—and knew she'd never experience such events again. They just about negated the low points—several ladies' brazen refusal to stop consorting with the officers, which had caused the captain to personally escort each young lady to their staterooms one night, the arrest of second mate Lockwood prior to arriving in San Francisco for ignoring his duties to spend time with ladies, Mercer's attempts at setting curfews and his wish to keep the passengers from playing card games, a plan by Chilean officers to woo women off the ship to become teachers in their country.

Watching twenty ladies deserting the group in San Francisco was not a sad day. Not only would fewer women arriving in Seattle help her chances at obtaining a position, but some ladies were the reason for the upheaval on board. They treated the journey as an opportunity to flirt with every available male, which became tiresome to observe.

A gust of wind blew a tendril across her face, pulling Sorcha from her reverie. Straightening, she glanced toward the shore. Only an occasional cabin broke the line of dense pine trees almost to the water's edge. Trepidation danced along her spine, and she rose onto her toes, hoping for a better look. Where was evidence of civilization? She glanced at Blinne, who gawked at the surroundings, then placed a gloved hand over her cousin's on the railing. "Remember, I told you Seattle was very much smaller than Lowell."

Blinne swallowed and nodded. "I remember, but Sorcha, I don't see *any* houses."

"Don't worry. We haven't reached the town yet."

"Can we sit, please?" Blinne stepped away from the railing.

"Of course." Sorcha followed her to the benches along the pilot house and sat, nodding to Missus Pearson, who sat nearby with her two children. The poor woman had been separated from her husband since he'd traveled to Seattle with their two daughters on Mercer's first trip two years earlier. The Pearson family had been residents of Lowell, but in a town of thirty-eight thousand people, the two women hadn't claimed an acquaintance before sharing the trip. How excited the family must be to be reunited. At the idea of having someone special waiting, Sorcha let out a sigh.

"What if not enough people want the garments I sew?" Blinne twisted the strings of her reticule. "Oh, why did I agree to come?"

What a time to have such thoughts. Sorcha plastered on a bright smile. "Look at the long journey we've almost finished. Once we get settled in Seattle, we'll work hard to make our dreams happen. We'll be fine." She so wanted to believe the words she'd just said. Now that the ship voyage that had become her everyday life was ending, she'd have to figure out a new routine.

Hours later, running feet brought Sorcha alert from a light doze.

"I see houses. Mama, look." Young Flora Pearson leaned over the stern railing, pointing ahead.

Missus Pearson rushed by, escorted by her son, D.O., who had a hand on her elbow. "I'm coming, dear."

Sorcha followed with Blinne at her side, her excitement building as their destination came into view.

Other passengers converged on the forward deck, and conversations buzzed.

The *Maria* angled to the left and headed toward a pier jutting into the water.

Past the pier, a grouping of boxy one- and two-story clapboard buildings came into view. A few blocks back, a statuesque, two-story building with a cupola stood on a knoll. Probably the university, although it looked out of place with the other, less-refined structures.

Mister Mercer clapped his hands for attention. "Ladies and gentlemen, the end of our voyage has arrived." He swung an arm wide. "Here lies Seattle, your new home. I will guide you to the Occidental Hotel. The ship's crew will deliver the luggage. I've arranged lodging for three nights for those needing it. By June 1, the families offering to house you will make themselves known at the hotel, and then you'll move to your permanent homes."

Sorcha cast Blinne a skeptical look. "I'd forgotten that part." After living for the past four months without being accountable to elders, she didn't wish to relinquish the freedom. "Maybe if I sign a teaching contract quickly enough, we can rent a room in a boarding house." She'd worried about the timing of the arrival coinciding with the end of the school year. But between the two of them, they still had enough money to live frugally until the fall.

Before disembarking and facing the gathered crowd, Sorcha checked her brooch watch, wanting to include the exact arrival time in her next letter home. Five o'clock in the evening. Disembarking onto the dock didn't involve combating shaky legs like in San Francisco, because this part of the trip had only been seventeen days.

At another mooring not far away, men carried stacks of lumber from a wagon pulled by a team of large horses onto a ship named the *Scotland*.

As she walked along the dock's planks, Sorcha spotted a large crowd of people gathered at the end. A knot landed in the pit of her stomach. She steeled herself to withstand shouted innuendoes and jesting proposals like in San Francisco.

"Do you see them?" Blinne edged closer.

"I do, but we'll hold up our heads and ignore any rudeness." When she was within earshot, she heard only welcoming comments and relaxed her posture.

The crowd, comprised mostly of men of all ages, didn't surge forward but instead accompanied the Mercer group to town.

Sorcha smiled at the closest men, who called a pleasant greeting, but she didn't speak. She wasn't here to encourage gentlemen callers. Instead, she studied the location that was her new home. Sufficient sunlight remained to highlight the small settlement. About sixty buildings, a mixture of homes and businesses, filled a clearing surrounded by stands of pine trees. The structures were split among two main streets with sawdust covering muddy roads.

The Occidental Hotel sat at the corner of Second Avenue and Yesler Way. The white, two-story frame building would have garnered no special notice in her hometown, but Sorcha looked on the hotel as a sanctuary. Here, water wouldn't be rationed, so she could again immerse herself in a tub, like she had in San Francisco. Clothes could be laundered in fresh water, and undoubtedly the menu contained more variety.

Mister Mercer bounded up the steps to the hotel porch and spread his arms wide. "I've brought you all to the best hotel in town. Come inside to enjoy a wonderful meal, and the staff will get you settled into your rooms."

Sorcha scanned the crowd as the others climbed the steps. At the realization she hadn't seen a single child except for the ones she knew from the voyage, a chill went through her. How could a teaching position exist without children?

The next morning, Sorcha followed Blinne from their hotel room into the long, narrow hallway dotted with a multitude of doors. "I don't know what proved more enjoyable—the luxurious soak in the bathtub or the quietness of the room." She eased the pearl button on her glove into the thread loop.

"I say the hot bath." Blinne tucked a wayward strand of hair behind her ear.

"True, but without the creaking wooden decks or the ship's bells or the clanking engine machinery, I got a really good night's sleep." Sorcha rolled her shoulders. "So much time has passed since I felt so refreshed." She walked in step with her cousin down the plank hall, heading to the dining room for breakfast.

Around the corner strode a tall man, right into their path.

Sorcha collided with his muscled body. Strong hands grasped her elbows. A woody citrus scent emanated from the man's shirt and jacket. Without thinking, she closed her eyes and inhaled.

"Oh, miss, do you feel faint?" The man dipped his knees to connect with her gaze. "Please accept my apologies."

At his deep tone with the strange lilt, she popped open her eyes. Drawing in a breath, she looked into teal-colored eyes under arched, light eyebrows. "I'm sorry too, sir." Under his touch, her skin heated, and tingles inched along her arms. She frowned and eased away from his grasp. No man since Tully had incited such feelings.

"You're two of the ladies who traveled with Mercer, aren't you?" He looked between them, then chuckled. "Of course, you must be. I already know the few women who live in this town."

"Oh, yes." Blinne dipped a curtsy and smiled. "We arrived just yesterday evening."

Speaking with this man without a proper introduction was highly unusual. Sorcha glanced over her shoulder, hoping for a sighting of Mister Mercer. She wanted to learn the details about her position today. "As soon as I eat, I have business to discuss with Mister Mercer."

"Let me start over. My name is Lang Ingemar, and I believe Fate has brought us together." He grinned, displaying straight white teeth.

As if we haven't already met plenty of charmers in San Francisco. Sorcha rolled her eyes. "Look, Mister Ingemar, we know bachelors vastly outnumber women in the West. Believe me, we've been subjected to men inventing all sorts of ruses to meet us." She glanced toward Blinne, who just stared at the man with glassy eyes and a wide smile. *No help from that quarter.* "Now, if you'll excuse us, we wish to partake of a meal."

"Allow me to escort you, Miss . . ." Grinning, he turned to face away, then looked over his shoulder, both elbows crooked.

A mischievous glint filled his eyes, making ignoring his unspoken question impossible. "Miss Sorcha Geraghty from Massachusetts." She clasped her hands together at her waist. "But going anywhere with you is not proper." His speech had a cadence she couldn't identify.

"In the West, many social graces are relaxed." He faced them again and held up his hands, palms outward. "We'll be in a public restaurant, probably surrounded by many of your shipmates. And I would very much enjoy spending time with two lovely ladies such as yourselves."

Blinne giggled and raised a hand to her mouth.

Refreshing sincerity rang in his tone. So different from Mister Conant or the officers on the ship, who'd constantly schemed ways of spending time with the ladies. Mister Conant even went so far as to call them "virgins" and purport to want interviews for his articles.

"Oh, say yes, Sorcha." Blinne bumped her shoulder. "He's nothing like those men in San Francisco who gawked and leered." She turned to Mister Ingemar. "You should have seen those crass men waving money in the air to be allowed on board."

His brows lowered. "I couldn't miss the newspaper

account of those rude and ungentlemanly actions." The tall man again turned and crooked his elbows before glancing over a shoulder.

"Mister Ingemar, I'm so pleased to make your acquaintance." Blinne scurried forward and linked her arm through his. "I'm Blinne Geraghty, Sorcha's cousin."

Suppressing a sigh, Sorcha matched her cousin's move, glad she slipped her uninjured hand inside his elbow. She tucked the other hand into the folds of her skirt, her reticule dangling from her wrist.

"Two Miss Geraghtys? Might I address you with your given names to avoid confusion?"

Such familiarity so soon? Sorcha ran a response through her mind, but each one sounded much too prim.

"Of course, sir." Blinne giggled. "I don't mind at all."

Sorcha ground her teeth and seethed. As the older of the two, she felt a responsibility to watch out for her welfare. Marriage minded or not, Blinne should be more circumspect.

"Very well, Miss Blinne and Miss Sorcha. Allow me to welcome you to Seattle." He started forward. "I had every intention of meeting the ship yesterday, but business obligations kept me busy until almost dark."

As she walked, she stole quick glances at his profile. His blond hair was straight, and he wore it combed back, the length almost touching his jacket collar. His nose was straight, his face on the longish side, and his jaw had a blunt tip—together the characteristics created a handsome face.

"Oh, what business are you in?"

Blinne's voice trilled with sweetness, and Sorcha cringed inside at how obvious her cousin's flirting was. In truth, she wished she'd been quicker with a question, so he'd turn his attention on her like he did on Blinne now. The strangeness of the thought unnerved her.

"I manage the Ny, er, New Hope Logging Company." He guided them down the staircase and turned at the bottom.

Other people moved through the lower floor near the registration desk and in the foyer.

Scents of cooked meat and coffee wafted from the dining room, making Sorcha anticipate another meal as tasty as last night's supper. "Logging must be a good livelihood here. Seems all we saw our boat ride yesterday were miles and miles of conifers."

Mister Ingemar stopped and gazed at her, one eyebrow arched. "You recognize the type of tree?"

"I'm trained as a teacher, which is why I came on Mister Mercer's expedition."

A grin blossomed. "Then this meeting will prove fortuitous for us both, Miss Sorcha."

His direct look sent warm tingles through her chest. How she'd missed having a man's attention since Tully marched off to war. She shook away that thought. Once inside the dining room, Sorcha nodded at passengers she recognized as she eased her hand from Mister Ingemar's arm and followed the waiter to an empty table.

"Oh, Miss Stewart." Blinne hurried forward. "Good morning. How are you doing today? Isn't this hotel lovely?" She stopped to chat with a friend from the trip.

Mister Ingemar pulled out Sorcha's chair at a linen-clothed table. "Is this one all right?"

Smiling, Sorcha lowered herself and tucked her voluminous skirts as close as possible. She'd put on an extra petticoat this morning, knowing she wouldn't have to worry about narrow ship staircases. But in a restaurant with many tables, she struggled with the fullness. "Thank you." He was right that they were in a public place, but being together alone still felt strange.

Several minutes later, the three had ordered and sipped coffee while they waited.

Sorcha ran a finger along the rim of the porcelain saucer, such a treat after the thick crockery used aboard the *Continental.* From the corner of her eye, she spotted Blinne looking all around and waving at people she knew. Now that they'd arrived, they needed to secure their futures. "Tell me, sir, why did you state our meeting was fated?"

Smiling, he rested his forearms on the table and leaned forward. "Because I've been looking for a woman just like you."

She stiffened, her chin jerking upward. "I beg your pardon." Had her first thought been wrong? Was he like all those other brazen San Francisco men who thought they deserved audiences with the women?

"Oh, my word." Blinking fast, Blinne dropped her chin in her propped-up, open palm.

Frowning, Mister Ingemar glanced between the women and straightened, then his eyes widened, and he shook his head. "Accept my apologies. My conversational skills with cultured ladies like yourselves are a bit rusty. What I meant was I'm interested in the fact of you being a teacher."

Sorcha blew out a relieved breath. "Mister Mercer's appeal in the East was for women willing to accept available positions teaching children. I must find him today and get this matter settled."

His expression tightened before he raised his cup and took a long drink. All the while, his gaze moved around the room.

Blinne slid into her chair and glanced between them.

Although their acquaintance was brief, Sorcha recognized avoidance in his demeanor. She clenched both hands in her lap, creating a dull ache in her scar. "What aren't you saying, Mister Ingemar?"

"I was overseeing a lumber order at the docks yesterday and saw the reception. Just about everyone in town turned out to greet your group." He narrowed his gaze. "How many school-age children did you notice among the citizens?"

His words echoed her very same thought from the previous evening during the group's walk through town. But then she'd passed off the thought as being too suspicious. "I figured they were kept home with their mothers." Before she finished her sentence, she spotted his head shaking. Her chest tightened. "No?"

"No what?" Blinne glanced between them, her eyebrows arched. "Did I miss something?"

The waiter arrived with their food, refilled their coffee cups, and then moved on to seat new arrivals.

"I'm sorry to inform you, Miss Sorcha, but more people under voting age came off your ship than those living in town. Seattle residents are bachelors, widowers, and older married couples. The first settlers with families arrived in 1852 and 1853, and those children have grown well past school age."

A weight settled on her shoulders, and Sorcha slumped back in the chair. "I can't believe it. How could Mister Mercer promise jobs that don't exist?"

Blinne reached out and patted Sorcha's hand. "This situation is just plain awful, Sorcha. We'll hunt down that horrid man and learn his intentions." She angled toward Mister Ingemar and flashed a smile. "Do you know if this town has a seamstress shop?"

Sorcha snorted, then turned it into a cough and brought her napkin to her mouth.

"Don't judge me." Blinne shrugged. "One of us has to get a job."

"Teaching jobs could exist in surrounding areas that I'm not aware of. People are moving to Washington Territory all the time. A fact for which I'm glad, because my business is doing well." He cut off a slab of ham and slid it into his mouth, chewing hard. "Or possibly he intended teachers to be placed at the university."

Guilt attacked, and Sorcha exchanged glances with Blinne, who grimaced. A university would require proof of her credentials. She'd mailed her final coursework from San Francisco, so her teacher's certificate wouldn't be arriving for several weeks. "That advanced level of teaching wasn't discussed."

"Well, I'm sorry to say, ladies, but many people in town don't hold Mercer in the highest esteem." He bit into a biscuit and chewed, glancing between them.

"Not just in this town." Keeping scorn from her voice was difficult. Sorcha shook her head. "We've seen the newspapers." She scooped up a bite of fried egg. Even though she savored the fresh flavor, the food almost stuck in her throat. Had she been hasty in her decision to relocate? Could she have learned more about the man before signing onto the expedition?

After a sip of coffee to wash down the egg, she spread butter on her toast, contemplating how much to tell this almost-stranger with the kind eyes and open expression. "Do you know he called for private meetings and attempted to bully us into signing notes for additional transit monies? More than two months into the trip . . . as if we had another way to finish the voyage. He admonished us that our new husbands would be obligated for the payment." Irritation lingered over that unpleasant discussion. She tapped a clenched fist on the tabletop. "That strategy wasn't right."

"No, miss, it wasn't." His lips pinched into a tight line. "You didn't sign such a document, did you?"

What did the man take her for . . . a fool? She wrinkled her nose. "I most certainly did not."

"We sewed and knitted plenty of his garments to more than pay back the grant from the expedition fund." Blinne gave a sharp nod.

"Good to hear. I'll be happy to escort you to his family's house so the matter can be decided." Mister Ingemar ate in silence for several moments, then reached to an inside jacket pocket and pulled out a document. "To be completely honest, I should inform you that I hold a contract with Mister Mercer's expedition." He laid the folded paper in the center of the table.

Dreading what she'd learn, Sorcha dug her spectacles from her reticule, reached for the contract, and unfolded the thick paper.

It read, *I, Asa S. Mercer of Seattle, W.T., hereby agree to bring a suitable wife of good moral character and reputation, from the East to Seattle, on or about September, 1865, for each of the parties whose signatures are hereunto attached, they first paying me or my agent, the sum of three hundred dollars, with which to pay the passage of said ladies from the East and to compensate me for my trouble. (signed) A.S. Mercer, Seattle, W.T., March 1, 1865.*

Blood pounded in her ears. Gasping, she jumped to her feet, squaring her shoulders. "Do you mean to claim me as your wife?"

Five

AS SOON AS he laid the contract on the table, Lang wondered at the wisdom of sharing the document. Perhaps he should have provided more background on his reasoning for supporting Mercer's enterprise. He studied Miss Sorcha as she scanned the document. The spectacles didn't detract from her attractiveness. Her reddish-brown hair rolled away over her ears into a complicated twist. Short, curly wisps escaped the hairdo and framed her heart-shaped face. A becoming pink blush colored her cheeks, then deepened in color. He noted her tightening jaw and stilled, his cup raised halfway to his mouth. The paper crinkled in her tightening grasp, and he wanted to grab it back.

Her head lifted, and she connected with his gaze, eyes narrowed. She rose, her posture rigid. "Do you mean to claim me as your wife?"

All conversations at the closest tables quieted. Glancing around to confirm that his table was the focus of people's stares, he stood. Heat infused his neck. He stretched an arm toward her to urge her back to her chair but thought better of the action. "Miss Sorcha, please sit and let me explain." He really was woefully out of practice around women.

"I will not. Come along, Blinne." She tossed down the document and strode from the dining room.

The sights of her head held high and her stiff posture looked foreboding. A groan rose in his throat. He had to fix this misunderstanding. The success of Ny Hoppas depended on acquiring a teacher. He knew this fact as well as he knew which tree to cut and in which direction to drop it. After collecting the contract, Lang grabbed a few coins from his pocket and tossed them on the table, then hurried after the women. They could not disappear. He spotted them at the registration desk, stepped behind the chestnut-haired one, and spoke for her ears only. "Miss Sorcha, you don't have all the information."

"Really?" She shot a sideways glare. "The despicable contract was written in plain English, of which I'm perfectly capable of understanding."

Wincing at her injured tone, he reached out a hand to cup her elbow. For a reason he couldn't explain, he needed to relieve her hurt. The tingles running along his palm fractured his focus, and he dropped his hand. "But I don't want a wife. I want a teacher."

She stiffened and turned so fast the single peacock feather on her bonnet bobbed. Her eyes rounded. "You do?"

Aware of curious glances aimed in their direction, he swept a hand toward the door. He certainly didn't need townspeople knowing his private matters. "Could we perhaps continue the conversation on the porch?"

Shaking her head, she glanced at the door, then back, gaze narrowing. "You offered to take me to Mercer's house. We'll talk on the way."

At least he still had a chance. "Allow me to get the door." He stepped forward.

"I can open my own doors." Head held high, she marched across the foyer and onto the porch.

Miss Blinne followed but shot a smile over her shoulder.

Once outside, Lang followed the women down the stairs and then gestured toward which direction to walk. Tension radiated off this petite woman, from her stiff shoulders to her quick steps. He cast about for a subject to put the conversation back on neutral ground. "Mercer's older brother, Thomas, established one of the earliest claims here in Seattle, along with Yesler, who built a mill. After being a dairyman and a freighter, Thomas has become a prosperous farmer. He's also the area's probate judge."

The women remained silent, so he glanced around for a new topic. "On the knoll a couple blocks over is the Territorial University of Washington. Seattle citizens are quite proud of the two-story stone building with four columns in front. I'm sure you spotted the cupola from the docks." He sounded like he orated a tour of the city, but he wished to get himself back in Miss Sorcha's good graces. "The building, which is Seattle's most substantial so far, serves as a great landmark when arriving by land or by sea. When you get close, you can see the widow's walk all around the roof."

"Very nice." Sorcha angled her body to address him. "What's the rest of the explanation you mentioned earlier?"

The flash of her green eyes shot a stab to his chest. He disliked how his actions offended her. "Again, I apologize for how I presented the contract. I understand how its meaning could be misconstrued." He stepped close in order to match her gait. "What I should have said first was how, during the first year after I moved here, the men in town did nothing but lament the lack of women. The war in the states slowed the few arrivals Seattle received on the migrant trail. Most travelers go to Oregon for the rich farmlands. I'd heard about

Mercer's trip in 1864 that brought eleven women to the area, and he had such grandiose plans for this trip." Her expression was set, the feather still bobbed, and he couldn't tell if his words made much impact. "Turn right on this street."

Miss Sorcha glanced to her friend, then nodded. "We know he left New York with many fewer women than he'd hoped would pay passage to relocate. From what we later learned, financial problems kept delaying the departure date. A circumstance for which we're grateful, because we only saw the notice a couple weeks before Christmas."

Lang didn't fight his growing smile. Her tone no longer held censure, and her posture appeared more relaxed. "As someone who made a trans-Atlantic crossing not too long ago, I know conditions are not always the easiest. I neglected to inquire about your experience on the long voyage. Did you both fare well?"

"Sorcha's got the constitution of a bull. She handled the ship's rocking just fine." Miss Blinne leaned forward and shuddered. "I, on the other hand, languished for a dreadful week of being seasick. I have no wishes for another ship voyage in my near future."

After a sideways glare toward her cousin, Miss Sorcha nodded. "We fared well enough in a confined space when having no choice in traveling companions."

"Intriguing statement, Miss Sorcha. I suspect hearing about your travels would be interesting."

"The trip is too recent in my memory to do such a tale justice." A smile quirked the corner of her mouth. "Ask me again in a week's time." A blush colored her cheeks, and she looked ahead.

"I'll do that." He took a long stride forward and then swept an arm to the side. "Down this pathway is the Mercer place." The ladies' conversation turned to the naming of trees and shrubs, and he glanced around for a sight of the man they'd come to see.

Moments later, Miss Mary Jane, the eldest Mercer daughter, ushered them into a parlor. "I'll collect my uncle and return in a moment. Make yourselves comfortable, please."

Soon, footsteps sounded in the hallway. Mercer stepped into the room, pulling on a jacket. "Ladies, good to see you again. And Ingemar"—he brushed a hand through the wavy curls over his ears—"what business brings you here?"

By the way the man brushed at his shirtfront, Lang had the impression they'd interrupted him at his breakfast. "I defer to the ladies' business first." He lifted his chin in their direction.

Narrowing his gaze, Mercer glanced at the sofa where both ladies sat. "Yes?"

Miss Sorcha straightened, her hands in her lap. "I've come to inquire about the promised teaching position."

"So soon?" Mercer claimed a nearby upholstered chair. "Before you've become acclimated to life on land and been welcomed into one of the residents' homes? I believe your request is a bit premature." He smiled, then sat back. "Why not enjoy a couple more nights at the Occidental?"

Miss Sorcha's tightened jaw was subtle, but Lang had been staring, so he caught the movement. This woman did not like being told what to do—a fact he would do well to remember.

"I don't feel my request is out of line. After all, obtaining such a position was my purpose for boarding that sailing ship." Miss Sorcha leaned forward, her gaze narrowed. "Do you have a teaching position to offer or not, sir?"

Clearing his throat, Mercer tugged the lapels of his jacket tight. "Of course I do. The location, however, is not here in

Seattle. A teacher is needed for a small schoolhouse in Chambers Prairie, south of Olympia, the territorial capital."

From what he'd heard about the cousins' plans, Lang guessed that location would not be acceptable. Lang breathed a sigh of relief but didn't let his emotion show.

"Where's the capital located?" Frowning, she looked to her cousin, who sat wide-eyed.

"About sixty miles south."

"Oh." Her body slumped, then she angled her head.

Uncrossing his leg, Lang connected with her stricken gaze, hoping to relay the message that all was not lost. When she remained quiet for several moments, Lang stood. "Thank you for seeing us, Mercer. Miss Geraghty will give you her response in a few days." He bent enough to grasp Miss Sorcha's elbow and squeeze. "We'll be going now."

Shaking her head, she blinked and then rose.

Miss Blinne copied her movement and linked arms with her cousin before heading for the hallway.

When Lang was sure they were out of earshot, he looked at Mercer and hardened his expression. "I trust that no further requests for additional funds will be broached to these ladies. Between my contract"—he patted his breast pocket—"and their payments and onboard labors, their passages should be considered paid in full."

Mercer sucked a breath through his nose, then stood to his full height. "Certainly."

Lang gave a sharp nod and set his hat atop his head. "I'll see myself out." Knowing that obstacle had been cleared, he left the house with a spring in his step. Now the task was convincing Miss Sorcha of the advantages to the position he had to offer. As he approached the waiting ladies, he fought to keep his expression somber. He led the way to the street and then turned toward town.

Silence hovered over the group for the time walking several block lengths. The cloudless sky allowed the sun's strength to beat on his shoulders. A day without rain was a good day for a logger. His thoughts drifted to how the men fared at the camp and if production was on schedule.

"Mister Ingemar."

Lang shook from his reverie and glanced to his left. "Yes, Miss Sorcha?"

"You mentioned looking for a teacher. What are the details about the position?"

This time he allowed his optimism to show in his wide smile. "I have a crew of loggers from my homeland who need to learn English."

She stopped walking, and her eyes shot wide. "Adults? You want me to teach men who don't know English?" She glanced around and then cocked her head. "What language do they speak?"

"Swedish." He pressed a hand to his chest. "We're all from a region near Lake Slijan in Sweden."

"Hmm." Miss Sorcha crossed her arms and scratched fingers along her chin. "I don't know."

"How big is your crew?" Miss Blinne moved in front of him and looked up.

"Twenty-four men."

She giggled. "Really and truly?" Smiling, she glanced at her cousin. "I'll bet your crew will need new shirts or maybe warm knitted caps."

He remembered her inquiring about a seamstress shop. From the moment he'd come up with this teacher idea, he'd wondered how he would handle the issue of a chaperone. He thought Wikimak would fill the role, but after seeing these proper Eastern ladies, he doubted they'd consider an Indian woman sufficient. However, Miss Blinne provided the perfect solution. "I'm sure they do."

"Where is the school located, Mister Ingemar?" Miss Sorcha squinted against the bright sun.

Here's where my charm is needed. He fingered the brim of his hat toward Missus Gardner, who passed, her gaze moving between his two companions. "Morning, ma'am."

A team and wagon rumbled by with clanks from the harness, and the driver lifted his hat. "Good day, ladies."

Such interruptions would not do. "Our discussion needs privacy. May I treat you ladies to tea at the hotel?"

Miss Sorcha flashed a smile and started walking. "I appreciate the offer."

Ten minutes later, he sat near a hotel window and waited while the waiter placed steaming cups of tea before each of them. He reached for a sugar cookie from the heaping plate in the middle of the table. As soon as the server left, Lang looked at Miss Sorcha. "The camp doesn't have a separate schoolhouse. But the bunkhouse has a big open area downstairs with enough tables and chairs to seat everyone."

"Camp? How far away from town?" Miss Sorcha leaned back, rubbing fingers on her temples. "I have so many questions."

"Let me give you an overview. New Hope is a small settlement about four miles north of Seattle. My crew's first task on arriving was to cut a clearing in the forest and construct the buildings. The bunkhouse, cookhouse, *bastu*, and the company office are the original ones. Since that first year, we've added another set of privies, a smoke house, and storage sheds."

"So, we would have to live there?" Her brows wrinkled. "Out in the wilderness?"

Was he losing her interest? "Not really wilderness. But

traveling to and from town every day would not be practical, especially since classes would be taught in the evening." He kept from adding *especially in inclement weather*. They'd learn about that aspect of the Pacific Northwest soon enough. "The men built a cabin specifically for the new teacher this spring." He glanced at Miss Blinne and shrugged. "We planned on only one person, but I think the space is adequate for two. Plus we have the supplies to expand if either of you deem it is needed."

"I don't know." Miss Sorcha nibbled on a cookie.

He gazed at a pale cookie crumb stuck to her upper lip—such pink lips—then shook his head. "By accepting this position, Miss Sorcha, you wouldn't have to relocate every month and be fitted into the households of families sending children to the school." He clenched a fist on his thigh. He needed to keep his focus. "You'd have a house of your own."

Miss Blinne bounced in her chair. "Oh, Sorcha, wouldn't that be wonderful? We could fix it up however we want."

Lang studied Miss Sorcha's frown and wished he knew the exact words that would smooth her wrinkled forehead. He hadn't felt such a kinship with a female since he was thirteen years old and dancing around the mid-summer maypole with Birget Sigvard. Now, all he wanted was to obtain her agreement.

"What does the job pay?" She watched him over the brim of her tea cup, her green eyes intent.

Fördömma. He hadn't given this issue much thought. Plus whatever salary he offered came out of his earnings until he could convince his father the expense was essential. "Well, in addition to the cabin and meals, the wages are ten dollars a month."

"Only ten?" Her mouth crimped harder, and she locked her gaze on his. "For twenty-four students?"

He cocked an eyebrow. "For only two hours a day, not six."

"Sorcha." Miss Blinne leaned close. "A house of our own."

Shaking her head, Miss Sorcha held up a hand.

From her tone, he figured the amount didn't sound fair. "What did Mercer offer?" Not paying rent or buying food more than matched the cash sum.

"I don't know. I figured we'd discuss details when I was offered the job." She swallowed hard, then her eyes narrowed. "I was prepared to take less than what's offered on the East Coast, but . . ."

"Don't forget, Sorcha . . ." Miss Blinne pointed with the last bite of her cookie. "Depending on the location, you might have had to rent a boardinghouse room."

"Blinne, please." She tapped the table near her cousin. "The discussion is between myself and Mister Ingemar." Squaring her shoulders, she faced him. "Do you realize I'll have to restructure all my teaching materials?"

"True. But you won't have children who would rather be home with their mothers."

Miss Blinne stood and refilled the tea cups.

"Those recalcitrant students would at least know an English vocabulary of several hundred words."

A nod displayed his agreement. That fact couldn't be argued. He thought back to his years in school and how the teacher managed the classroom. "But you'd only have one set of lessons, because everyone will be at the same level." He quite enjoyed this bartering and watching the emotions run across her face as she worked through her decision.

"That's true." Brow crinkled, she munched on another cookie.

What other factor was a plus? "You won't be facing surly

youths taller than yourself who resent being there." As soon as he spoke, he thought again. Well, that statement might be a stretch of the truth. He could imagine one or two individuals who might fit that description.

"How do you know English and they don't?" She tilted her head.

The head tilt to her right was a most becoming look. "My mother was born and raised in England. So my siblings and I speak both languages."

"Oh, how fortunate. I always wished to learn a foreign language." She sipped her tea, then set down the cup. "What supplies are available?"

That question meant she was serious about accepting. Keeping his anticipation tight to his chest, he leaned forward. "None. Without a teacher, they would be meaningless. Tell me what you need."

Miss Sorcha turned toward her cousin and raised an eyebrow.

Smiling, Miss Blinne nodded.

"I will make no promise until I see the house and the location of the camp. Blinne's need to obtain sewing jobs has to be taken into consideration as well."

"*Ja.* Of course. We'll go right now." Glancing between the two women, he grinned. One-half of the deal was so close he could envision her signature on the contract. Now came the harder half—ensuring the men would be cooperative.

Six

THE WAGON BOUNCED over a rough spot in the road, rattled the trunks and valises in the bed. Sorcha did her best not to bump into Mister Ingemar, who sat to her left. But three bodies on a seat didn't leave much space. The longer the ride became, the less sure she was of her decision. How would they get to town often enough for Blinne to take in orders?

Tall trees created a thick border on both sides of the road, dotted with occasional puddles from a recent rain. The tangy scent of pine filled the air, and she filled her lungs with the freshness. Now, so different from when they'd walked to Mercer's house earlier, clouds obscured the sun. She was glad for the woolen shawl wrapping her shoulders.

Not only had he convinced her into bringing along all her possessions, he'd received agreement to use each other's first names. Once she expressed her willingness to consider the position, she'd been swept away by Lang's enthusiasm for how her skills could assist his crew.

Her first assessment had been correct—the teal-eyed man was a handsome charmer and an astute negotiator. Probably came from his experience with negotiating lumber contracts for his company.

Lang sat tall with the reins of the four-horse team held loosely in his hands. As he'd loaded the wagon, he'd identified each of the horses.

But the Swedish names felt uncomfortable on her tongue, so she hadn't repeated them. Although if she took the job, she'd have to get used to potentially mispronouncing a name or word now and then.

"Look." Blinne pointed. "I see smoke through those trees."

"Our cook keeps the fireplace and stoves going for most of the day." He angled his body so he met her gaze and smiled. "She's always got something in the oven or in the pots."

"She? Another woman lives at the camp?" Learning that fact eased her nervousness a bit.

His eyes widened, and he faced forward again. "That's right."

How odd. She was about to ask more about the cook but spotted Lang's raised hand.

"This path marks the cutoff to the camp. We're almost there."

The wagon rolled under a banner-type sign held high over the path by thick posts. Stylish carved letters painted yellow spelled a string of words—*Ny Hoppas Skogsavverkning Företag.* She probably mentally pronounced them wrong. The odd combinations of consonants confused her and made her quail at the thought of finding a way to introduce English terms. She thought of all the hours she'd spent during the voyage creating storybooks from Irish proverbs. New English learners wouldn't understand nuances or puns. Maybe she truly didn't have the training to take on such a monumental task.

"Oh, Sorcha, I see buildings." Blinne leaned forward. The seat jostled under her bouncing. "Lots of them."

Thankfully, Blinne didn't need much to be happy. Her positive outlook helped so many times on the trip when Sorcha struggled to deal with a few of the selfish ladies.

The first sight of a roof made Sorcha mimic her cousin's pose. Within moments, the wagon rolled into a clearing that wasn't much bigger than a square city block back in Lowell. Across the expanse stood a boxy, two-story building with a steep-pitched roof that must be the bunkhouse. Next to it was a single-story building with smoke curling from two chimneys. Other buildings dotted the grassy meadow, about equal distance from the biggest one. As she scanned the structures, she couldn't help but wonder which one was the newest cabin. Everything was much neater and more orderly than she'd envisioned.

"*Stanna.*" Pulling back on the reins, Lang stopped the wagon near the second biggest structure and set the brake. "Here's the logging camp. Barn in front of you, bunkhouse to the left, followed by the cookhouse and the new cabin on the end." As he talked, he swept an arm along the line. "I'll take you to the cabin and then bring in food." He hopped down, then braced a hand on the seat and looked up. "Until you make a decision, Sorcha, I don't feel the need for introductions to happen with the crew."

That arrangement didn't sound fair. "But how will I—"

"My decision stands." His gaze narrowed. "I don't need to disrupt the men until an agreement is in place." He nodded to the man who came from the barn and stopped at the first horse. "If I don't get your agreement, then I'll search out another new arrival to make an offer." He turned to the man and spoke while indicating the items in the wagon bed. Then he rounded the back of the wagon and held out his hand to Blinne.

Dismayed at the seriousness of his attitude, Sorcha barely

remembered to offer her uninjured hand for assistance. She walked in silence the thirty feet or so to the indicated building, listening to Blinne pepper Lang with questions. As she approached, she spotted the fresh cuts on the lumber. Yellow shutters adorned the large windows in the facing wall. A row of ivy leaves trailed across the heavy lintel above the door. From off in the distance, near the tree line, floated the drone of saws.

"Please come in and explore." Lang stood on the half-circle of stones at the entrance, holding open the door. "I'll be back in a few minutes with food."

Blinne stepped into the cabin and disappeared.

Sorcha paused on the stones and met his gaze. "I need to say thank you for the opportunity, no matter what I decide."

Lang tipped a finger to his hat brim and walked away.

Taking a deep breath, Sorcha stepped over the threshold and sucked in a breath. The space was divided not by walls like in her parents' house but by the arrangement of the furniture. In the left side stood a gleaming rectangular table with four chairs and a built-in hutch along the far wall. To her right, an upholstered settee faced a stone fireplace that covered a third of the wall. A dark-wood rocker sat to provide a good look out a front window. In the right corner sat a desk, and a bookcase stood to the left, abutted to a wall. Separating the dining room from the kitchen was a half wall. A wide counter atop the wall would be good for assembling items to be moved between the rooms.

"Isn't this cabin so cozy?" Blinne rushed up, her smile wide and her eyes flashing. "Don't you love it? I can already see the afghan your ma knitted spread on the back of the rocker. My mama's tablecloth and napkins would go on the table." She grabbed Sorcha's hand.

Sorcha stumbled forward at Blinne's hard pull, glancing

at details as she moved. Her feet thudded on thick floor planks. White paint covered the walls, reflecting the sunlight through numerous windows.

"The kitchen is already stocked with cutlery, plates, and cups. See the icebox on the far wall. And I spotted a full woodbox outside."

Her cousin's chattering and the weight of what was at stake rushed at her, and she stopped. "Let me take in the details on my own, Blinne. I agree the cabin is wonderful, but I can't think only of this place. I have to think of the work requirements." She cautioned herself not to get too excited, because the job still represented a huge challenge. The fact she'd been offered a teaching job was the point of being here in Seattle. Introducing foreigners to a language that would assist them to get along in their new home was truly a noble cause. Although her goal had been to provide learning for inquisitive minds, she just hadn't thought those minds would be accompanied by beards and moustaches.

"Oh, look. Sorcha, come see."

Sorcha followed Blinne's voice to an enclosure that held a long metal bathtub with one end higher than the other. A half-sized potbellied stove stood against the wall with a small woodbox. Two wall shelves held towels in different sizes and a wrapped bar of soap. She let out a sigh. This bathing room was twice bigger than the one in her entire family's house.

Blinne fingered carved pegs protruding from a board nailed to a wall. "Whoever designed this place thought of everything. Have you noticed how smooth and polished all the wood is?"

The open design esthetic of the cabin appealed to her senses, but she couldn't pick out one particular item. The smooth lines of the furniture cried out for cushions, but the light-colored wood looked fine without them.

A knock sounded, followed by a "*Hej.*" Lang stepped into the cabin carrying the bail of a pot in one hand, with a cloth-wrapped item tucked at his elbow and a jar of liquid.

Startled by the foreign word, Sorcha paused, then rushed forward and took possession of the cloth. Warmth penetrated her gloves. A yeasty scent filled the air.

"The meal is venison stew with wild onions and hot-out-of-the-oven rye bread." He walked to the kitchen and set the pot on the stove. "A crock of butter should be in the icebox." After a glance around, he headed toward the door.

"You're not staying?" Sorcha hated how plaintive her voice sounded.

"I've been away from camp for several days and need to check in with my foremen." He ran a hand over his hair. "You need time to evaluate your options, Sorcha."

"How will I find you?" Again, she sounded so helpless, a fact she abhorred. "I mean when my decision is made."

From nearby, a bell clanged, reminding her of the ship's call to meals.

He beckoned her forward, then pointed out the window. "See the building with the blue shutters across the clearing?"

She approached to see which one he meant, which brought her only inches from where he stood. Her heart rate kicked up. In such a short time, he'd captured her attention like none other. "I see."

"That building's the company office. Within an hour after the meal, I'll be there . . . waiting." He gazed into her eyes, then nodded and stepped around her to the door. A moment later, he was gone.

She stared until her eyes ached, then she blinked. Why had that single word, *waiting*, tied her tongue? She shook away such foolery and spun. "Let's eat."

Blinne stood at the stove with the lid raised and her other hand on her hip. "Did he say venison, as in deer meat?"

"We're not in a hotel with multiple choices on the menu, Blinne." Back home, Sorcha had been hesitant about eating new cuisine. But the foods and dishes they were served while in Lota, Chile, on the voyage—tamales, enchiladas, plantains, and mangoes—had all been enjoyable. She reached for a plate from a shelf. "Besides, if someone else cooked the food, it will taste wonderful."

"I don't know."

At the dining table, both chose chairs with a view out of the windows.

Sorcha savored her first bite of the solid texture of the bread softened by the creamy butter. The stew had a robust flavor, seasoned with herbs she didn't recognize.

"Oh . . . my . . . word."

"What?" Sorcha glanced at Blinne's plate, then at her awestruck face.

Blinne slowly rose and stepped to a window. Leaning close, she pressed her nose to the glass.

Through the window, Sorcha spotted a dozen men walking across the clearing. The men were of various heights and sizes, bearded and clean-shaven, but all were muscular and light-haired.

"You'll accept the job, won't you?" Blinne looked over her shoulder with a wide grin, then glanced back. "I want to stay."

Sorcha had the feeling that if her cousin sailed alone, she'd have been one of the giggling females flirting with the officers on the ship and in the ports. "Blinne, we haven't even talked about how the distance from town could hinder your business."

With a sigh, she left the window and returned to the table. "I don't care." She pushed around the meat on her plate before nibbling on an edge. "I'm not as interested in having a career like you are. I want a husband who'll take care of me and provide me with a home." Smiling, she scanned the room. "A cabin like this one would be perfect." She grasped Sorcha's hand. "I've been beholden to your parents for so many years."

"Ma and Da were happy to take in you, Rory, Conor, and Orla when—"

"And we so appreciate the fact." Blinne blinked away her gathering tears. "But as the oldest, I need to find a husband with a big enough heart to welcome my siblings into his family." She sniffled, then waved a hand in the direction of the bunkhouse. "Just imagine, that group that sauntered by was only half of the total crew."

Just imagine. Sorcha sucked in a breath. She's right. Lang said he managed two crews.

The rest of the meal passed in silence, then they washed the dishes and stowed the food in the icebox.

"Ready to look upstairs?"

"You go first." Blinne waved toward the stairs in the dining room corner. "I don't want to love this place any more than I already do until I know we're staying."

Although Blinne's heartfelt words about her wishes might have tipped the scales, Sorcha needed all the facts before she sought out Lang. Upstairs, she found a sleeping loft that measured half the floor space of the lower level. The furniture included a full-sized bed, a chest of drawers, an armoire, a vanity stand, and a framed mirror. The bed sat on a wood block containing storage drawers. Unfamiliar flowers with droopy bells painted in shades of white, pink, and violet blue decorated the outside armoire doors. Tucked inside the armoire were pull-out bins and several hooks for clothing. A single flower adorned each bin. Sorcha leaned a shoulder on the door and traced the outline of the flowers. Hot tears flooded her eyes. Someone added this feminine touch to help the newly hired teacher feel more at home.

Could this one tiny detail be the deciding factor? Walking to the loft's half wall, she glanced around, mentally arranging their belongings in the space. Ma's Irish Chain quilt on the bed. Da's lucky horseshoe over the front door. One of their trunks at the foot of the bed and the other downstairs. Her lap harp in the corner. Blinne's sewing machine under the window in the sitting room.

"Can I come up now?"

Closing her eyes, Sorcha searched her heart. Accepting felt right. Helping men learn English seemed honorable. The cabin provided security. With each other as chaperones, the living arrangement was respectable. "Yes, do."

Footsteps pounded up the steps, followed by a loud gasp. Blinne stood in the corner, eyes wide with clasped hands beneath her chin. "It's so cute." She bounced around the space, opening doors and pulling out drawers. "Of course, it needs a woman's touch."

"If you're sure, I'll search out Lang."

"I am." She touched the flowers on the armoire. "Did you see these? They're adorable."

"I did." Sorcha descended two steps before turning to look back at her cousin. "Promise me you'll stay inside until I return."

Blinne plopped stomach down on the bed, fist supporting her chin. "I promise, but hurry. I can't wait to put away our things in here."

Sorcha walked to the door and paused with a hand on the knob. A nagging thought emerged on top of the other ones racing through her mind. How would she explain to her mother about living in the wilderness with two dozen men?

Seven

THIRTY MINUTES HAD passed since the end of the meal. Lang paced the short length of the office between the stove and the desk. Did contemplating the offer and the cabin this long mean Sorcha was serious? Movement through the window caught his eye, and he watched Sorcha exit the cabin and start walking. He narrowed his eyes. Was her gait confident or hesitant? Even if he decided which, would he know how her stride indicated her acceptance?

About halfway across, she stopped and turned a full circle, her chin angled upward.

Impatience thrummed through his blood, but he restrained himself from galloping across the clearing to learn her answer. This teaching job was a solution where before she had none. But he couldn't pressure her. After a morning spent in her company, he knew he wanted her to accept it solely to give him the chance to become better acquainted. He timed opening the door to her approach. "Good afternoon, Sorcha. I hope you enjoyed your meal."

She lowered the hand she'd raised to knock. "We both did. I believe you and I have business to discuss. May I come inside?" She cast a glance over her shoulder.

Lang fought to keep a jubilant yell inside, and instead he stepped back to provide room. "Of course. Let's sit at the table." He kicked a block of wood toward the bottom of the door to keep it ajar.

She walked inside and then circled the room, gazing at the sketches pinned along the wall.

All aspects of the logging operation were on display—from tree topping, to felling, to branch chopping, to river transit, to sawing, to loading logs and lumber for transport. He used the drawings during safety meetings or when the cause of an accident was reviewed.

When she sat in a chair near the desk, she looked at him with a wide-eyed gaze. "I hadn't realized logging involved so many steps."

If he wasn't mistaken, she'd paled since entering the room. He scanned the sketches, but none displayed injuries or hazardous situations. Maybe she was nervous about the pending discussion. "Did you find the cabin to your liking?" He stood with an elbow resting on the top of his desk, waiting for her to broach the real subject.

"The cabin is a wonderful testament to the builders. We noticed all the places for storage, and the downstairs is so well lit." She clasped her hands on the tabletop and smiled. "Blinne and I will enjoy decorating it."

"Then you're accepting the job? I'm glad." Lang blew out a breath before grabbing the two sheets of parchment he'd prepared from his top desk drawer. He set the inkwell between them, then dropped into a chair. "I wrote out a contract that you should read through before we fill in the blanks." He slid one page within her reach and watched her scan the print after donning her spectacles. The day had warmed considerably from the morning, yet she still wore gloves. *Odd.*

Sorcha set down the paper. "I have two stipulations."

He expected she would. "Go ahead."

"Will you guarantee a weekly ride into town for Blinne?"

"Just for Blinne?"

"So she can get her seamstress business started."

"Ah." He pulled both sheets in front of him and added a sentence above the signature lines. "And the second?"

She cleared her throat, then straightened and met his gaze. "That if the situation isn't working, I want to be allowed time off to pursue other positions."

Frowning, he sat back and stroked a hand over his close-cropped beard. "I expected a minimum one-year commitment. The men must be taught enough English to handle purchases in town and to engage in simple conversations. I don't think those skills can be learned in a shorter time."

"I agree with your assessment. But I must think of my future. No less than two days off during both April and May, if a job search is needed." Green eyes flashing, she tapped a stiff finger on the table. "Each day at fifty percent wages."

Paying her wages to look for a different job? Not likely. He leaned forward, ready to make a counter offer, but he spotted a tremble in her fingers. Less than twenty-four hours ago, she stepped off a ship following a four-month sea journey. She was in a new town, knowing only her cousin. Of course she'd fight to protect her options, since this job was so different than what she'd anticipated. "Sounds fair." He wrote down the new contingency, filled in the starting date as June 1, and added the salary amount. Then he signed and added the date on both copies. "Please fill out your full name at the top and sign and date."

Her shoulders sagged, then she leaned forward and did as he'd directed. "Thank you for granting me tomorrow to settle in." She stood and extended her right hand.

Lang jumped to his feet and grasped her hand. "I look

forward to our association, Sorcha. I regret not taking this step for the men sooner." Only their hands touched, but he felt a connection circle in his chest. Gazing into her green eyes, he noticed flecks of gold. He admired how she stood up for herself, even though granting her demand bit into his bottom line. He covered the hand clasp with his second hand, wanting to make the connection stronger.

A pink blush flooded her cheeks.

"*Chef.*" Staffen barged through the doorway. "*Kom nu. Sågen är—*" The foreman gaped and glanced between them. After a few seconds, he dragged the broad-brimmed hat off his head and gave Sorcha a big smile.

Seeing the interested gleam in his friend's eyes, Lang stiffened. "Excuse the interruption, Sorcha." He released their handshake, then clamped a hand on his foreman's shoulder and steered him through the door. "*Tala.*" Within a few sentences, he learned what was needed and sent Staffen back to the mill.

When he turned, he spotted Sorcha lingering in the doorway. "I need to oversee an issue that shouldn't take too long. Then I'll have your luggage brought into the cabin."

She stepped close and tilted her head. "Thank you for entrusting me with this opportunity. I won't let you down."

Her expression was so earnest, with pinched brows and narrowed eyes, he had to smile. "I'll do anything needed to help you succeed."

A swishing sound of her skirts over the grass followed her departure. Lang couldn't stop himself from enjoying the sight of a woman—actually, this particular woman—in his world. Echoes of the lecture he gave to the men about not making fools of themselves over the expected teacher rumbled through his thoughts.

Sorcha opened the cabin door, looked over her shoulder, and waved.

Caught. He lifted a hand in farewell, then stomped toward the mill. He might have to ask Roald or Staffen to repeat the lecture on keeping a proper distance. On second thought, he acknowledged he wouldn't listen to a single word they'd say. His feelings for Sorcha were like when he swung at the top of a tree—a combination of giddiness and fear of falling.

Her first session would start in just five minutes, and butterflies danced in her stomach. Sorcha stood at the dining table and surveyed her supplies: twenty-four papers she'd neatly lined then written each letter of the alphabet down the left margin, her willow pointer—a handmade gift from Da when she entered the teaching academy—lead pencils, and four wood-framed slates. Two sticks of chalk rested in her skirt pocket.

For tonight, she'd enlisted Blinne's help—a request that was promptly agreed to. Blinne was responsible for writing a single letter on the slate for Sorcha to hold up and introduce to the men. With Blinne keeping the letters fresh, Sorcha could concentrate on circulating in front of the students, enunciating the sound and listening for any who needed correction. She'd seen the company sign on the camp's entry, and all the letters appeared the same as the alphabet she knew. The difference would be the pronunciation.

A knock sounded at the door.

Sorcha stepped into the sitting room so she could look up into the loft. "Blinne, are you ready?"

"Coming." Footsteps clattered on the stairs.

Pressing a hand to her stomach, Sorcha walked across the room and forced a smile into place before she opened the door. "Good evening."

"Evening, Sorcha." Lang grinned and jerked a thumb over his shoulder. "They're all corralled and waiting." He glanced into the room and nodded.

Seeing him always made her heart flutter, and she fought against allowing her reaction to show. "I need to gather my supplies. You're handling the introduction, right?"

He reached to cup her elbow. "Don't worry. I'll be close by."

Those words circled in her thoughts and settled close to her heart. She could handle this task. Three minutes later, as she listened to Lang's rapid-fire speech to the group, she wasn't so sure. She had never faced a group of this many men, with all their gazes on her every move. Some sat with rounded shoulders and gaped mouths, like they'd never seen a woman before.

Yesterday, in a panic, she'd rushed into Lang's office and asked for instruction in a few basic Swedish words. Then she stayed up late and reread the sheets from her teaching curriculum by the author of the popular *The Peep of Day*. The refresher helped Sorcha organize her thoughts on using phonetic sounds when presenting the vocabulary.

Lang stopped speaking and swung an arm in her direction as he stepped back.

Clearing her throat, she straightened and greeted the group, who sat in four rows of six chairs each. "*God kväll.*"

A booming "*God kväll*" echoed off the walls.

Well, they'd understood the way she pronounced good evening. Hopefully giving her name would be as easy. She pressed a hand to her chest. "*Jag heter fröken* Sorcha." She glanced at Lang to see if her pronunciation was right.

He nodded and leaned a shoulder against the wall.

"*Hej, fröken* Sorcha."

Communication occurred. She understood their greeting.

Confidence flooded her chest, then she pointed toward her cousin. "*Hennes heter fröken* Blinne."

Laughter broke out, and the men nudged one another.

Heat flushed her cheeks, and she turned to Lang, eyebrows raised.

"Not every sentence structure is the same." Lang shrugged and stepped forward, then turned to the group. "*Hennes namn är fröken* Blinne."

All gazes swung to where Blinne sat at the side of the room. "*Hej, fröken* Blinne."

Blinne giggled and gave a wiggly-finger wave. "Hello, all."

As Sorcha gazed at the group, she saw they all wore a wooden badge strung from their necks with a leather thong. Burned into the ovals were what she assumed were their names. Tilting her head, she glanced at Lang and tapped her chest.

He gave a single nod.

His thoughtful gesture tightened her throat and made her blink fast. Best get on with the lesson. Her plan was to have them say each letter in succession and then write it five times. Arranged as they were, the writing portion would have to come later. Instead, she reached for the top slate Blinne extended, held it over her head, and walked slowly along the front line of chairs. "This is the letter *a. Snälla säg bokstaven a.*"

They responded.

By the time she'd reached *e*, she shortened the "please say letter" phrase to "say" and the letter. More repetitions were needed on only two letters: *q*, which they kept saying as "coo," and *w*, which sounded like "double vee." Writing the letters took no time because they were just like the ones they already knew from Swedish. Lang explained the Swedish language had three additional vowels. Only an hour had elapsed, and the men looked to her for more instruction.

The next exercise she planned was to have them all stand and recite the alphabet, but they obviously knew it well enough. Thinking fast, she dashed over to Blinne. "Draw a cat, a rat, a house, and a tree, and write the names underneath."

"I'm no artist."

"I'm not either, but please do it." Sorcha grabbed a stick of chalk. "I'll draw the cat." Then she held up the slate and pronounced the name. When the men responded to each new word faster than Blinne could draw, Sorcha moved around the bunkhouse, touching and naming objects. The phonetic method would be used when she got them writing the words, and then she'd return to a more orderly way to introduce words. Now she didn't want to put a dent into their eager responses. By the time she'd made a circuit of the room, she had to fan her face. Perspiration trickled down the back of her neck. Undoubtedly, curls crimped along her hairline.

"Excuse me, Sorcha." Lang stepped forward, an open pocket watch in his hand. "Just a few minutes remain."

Wonderful. She blew out a breath. "I guess ask them if they have any questions."

Nodding, he turned to the group. "*Frågor?*"

Several voices talked over one another.

"*Nej.*" Lang stiffened. "*Nej.*" His hands curled into fists. "*Nej!*"

Men jumped to their feet and each yelled at the one next to him. Some shook fists in the air.

How could her methods have caused such upheaval? "What's happening?" Sorcha stepped close, aware she sought comfort from the confusion.

"Their questions have nothing to do with the class." His jaw clenched, then he stuck his curled fingers into his mouth and blew.

At the shrill whistle, she clapped both hands over her ears, unsure of what to expect next.

Lang shouted in Swedish.

The men straightened, shuffled their feet, and looked straight ahead.

At their change in posture, she dropped her hands.

"*Tack, fröken* Sorcha." The men spoke as one.

His posture relaxed, and Lang leaned close. "They thanked you. You could say *välkommen och god natt.* Welcome and good night."

His warm breath puffing on her cheek distracted her, as did the pine scent wafting from his clothing. But she caught his meaning. Nodding, she turned and smiled toward the group. "*Välkommen och god natt.*" The words were not so different from English.

Several returned the greeting, but most turned toward another man and started chatting, pulling off the name tags.

Tiredness pulled at her muscles, and she just wanted to sit and do nothing. But she moved to where Blinne waited and gathered the supplies.

A man with reddish-blond hair approached and smiled at Blinne. He reached his hands toward the slates and mimed lifting before patting his chest.

"Blinne, Torg would like to carry your slates the entire, incredibly short distance to your cabin." Lang stood with arms crossed, his face stiff.

Sorcha wondered if such a question had been one that Lang objected to in the shouting.

Blinne glanced toward Lang. "How do I say yes?"

"Just smile. He'll understand." He turned to Sorcha. "Ready? I'll escort you." He crooked his right elbow.

Pulse racing, she hesitated. No graceful way to switch sides existed, so she grasped his arm with her injured hand.

Would he feel the difference in the stiffness of her padded last fingers and ask? Worry gnawed at her stomach, and she needed to fill the silence. "I thought the class went well." She stepped over the threshold and into the cool air. The waning moon bathed the clearing and buildings in silvery light.

"I'm happy they minded the manners their mothers taught them."

Over the weekend, she'd have to work hard to prepare lots of flashcards. But with what materials? Maybe if each slate contained a simple sentence, and she broke the men into small groups—

"Sorcha."

She jerked and looked up. "Hm. What?"

"You're home." Lang tilted his head toward the cabin.

Blinking, Sorcha glanced around and spotted Torg ambling back toward the bunkhouse, whistling. Blinne's humming came from behind the front door. "Oh. I was lost in plans for the next class."

Smiling, he set his hands on her shoulders. "You did well tonight. I like how you adjusted your plan." He chuckled, then cocked an eyebrow. "Or maybe you planned to use the bunkhouse for vocabulary words."

At the intimate gesture, warmth invaded her chest, and she lifted a hand to squeeze his. "A spontaneous decision. But I relied on you interpreting, and we made a good team."

His head jerked back, and he jammed his hands into his pockets. "Sleep well, Sorcha."

What just happened? Did she offend him with her injury? She stared at his retreating back until he disappeared into the bunkhouse. Hot tears invaded her eyes, and she stumbled into the cabin, dazed over his obvious rejection.

Eight

ALMOST A MONTH later, Lang stomped into his office and slammed down his order book. The inventory of logs was down, and insufficient lumber filled the drying racks to ship the waiting order. Three men recuperated from injuries received in careless accidents, affecting the output. He'd filled in as best he could, but he couldn't perform three jobs... four, if he counted the manager duties. The men grumbled about having to work longer on Saturday to make up the shortfall. Roald reported more petty arguments than usual among the men. In the mill, Staffen struggled with preventing the boiler from overheating. Nobody was happy with Lang, and everywhere he turned, he couldn't meet expectations. He wished for someone on whom he could unburden his troubles.

He flopped into his desk chair and turned to gaze out the window. *Fördamma.* Had he positioned the teacher's cabin in his direct line of sight to torture himself? Maybe a troll whispered in his ear while he met with Roald and Staffen about the coming teacher and the cabin location. The presence of that mischief-making being in the camp could explain a lot.

His own turmoil had a personal basis. No getting around

how he'd overstepped proper boundaries the night of Sorcha's first class. Excitement over the success of the men's responses spurred him to touch her—in a way only a beau should touch a woman. The accusatory glares from his crew, who'd pressed their faces to the bunkhouse windows, caught him up short. The rules he'd laid down for the men about keeping their distance from the women had to apply to him as well. Even if his heart rebelled.

In the intervening time, he kept busy in the office each evening while she conducted the class. Occasionally, Blinne helped, but often she was too busy with sewing orders. Soon his entire crew would own new shirts. A wiser way to spend their wages than on whiskey. If the company duties were completed, he whiled away the time by carving Dalecarlian horses in the style he learned in his grandpa's shop. The brightly painted, stocky horses sold well at the mercantile for gifts. If asked the reason for wanting to see the small toys bought, he'd have to say national pride.

No matter what task occupied his evening, each night at five minutes before nine o'clock, he waited outside the bunkhouse door to carry a lantern to light her path home. On nights when enough moonlight shone, he still maintained the protective ritual. Only a simple good night or a few words about the men's progress were spoken between them. But every day, he looked forward to those two or three minutes more than he had a right to.

Maybe what he needed was a long sit in the *bastu*. Let the heated steam release his tension and relax his muscles. He shoved to his feet and moved the order book onto his desk. Sitting here musing hadn't presented a solution to his problem. Hopefully someone else had the same idea before him, and he wouldn't have to wait twenty or thirty minutes for the stones to heat.

When he arrived at the building situated near the tree line, he spotted other clothes hanging on pegs in the shed surrounding the cold-water tub. Steam would already fill the wood-paneled room. After stripping down and piling his clothes onto an anteroom shelf, he entered the *bastu,* laid a towel on a bench, and sat. This special hut held such a priority among the men that it had been completed before the bunkhouse roof received its final shingle.

Two figures, hunched forward with elbows on knees and a towel covering their heads, sat on the other side of the narrow space, several feet apart.

Perspiration popped out on his skin, and he sighed, then draped a small towel over his head. As the moist heat seeped into his muscles, Lang let his thoughts wander. Used to be he looked forward to receiving letters from home. After posting the one at the beginning of the month where he'd requested greetings to be forwarded to Olga, the girl on a neighboring farm, he dreaded his mother's reply. The day after he sent the letter, he regretted his statement, which only encouraged his mother's matchmaking. Although the original plan was to establish and run the company in America for four years, then return and take a Swedish wife, Lang knew his wishes weren't the same as when he left Sweden. The moment he first met Sorcha changed everything.

Someone poured a ladle of water on the hot stones in the middle, making them sizzle.

Lang mopped the sweat from his face, then reclined, resting elbows on the next higher bench. He watched the steam rise in clouds and crawl along the ceiling. At his movement, the towel dropped off. From somewhere close came sweet musical notes. Ones like he'd never heard before. He couldn't name the melody that pulled at him like one played by the legendary Pied Piper.

But compulsion to learn the source drove him to his feet.

He walked to the back shelter and eased down the steps into the pool, then ducked under the surface. When he shot upward, he sucked in a breath at the sudden cold. The resulting tingles along his skin pumped his heart faster, sending quickened blood throughout his body.

Moments later, he followed the musical sounds, wandering a distance into the forest. Water dripped from his hastily dried hair onto the shoulders of his shirt.

Sorcha sat on a tree stump, playing a small stringed instrument balanced in her lap. Her head was lowered, as if she was listening to the notes as she strummed.

The sweet and sad notes put an ache in his throat. He leaned a shoulder against a tree and closed his eyes. Notes of yearning sifted through the air and circled his head. How an instrument could make him feel wistful, he didn't know. A branch cracked behind him, and he glanced around. By his count, six other men stood in similar positions in a circle about thirty feet back from where she played.

Jealousy, hot and wild, ran through his body. He'd been a fool to remain silent about the connection he felt toward Sorcha. Had he risked her forming a similar attachment with another man in camp? The fact none of the others stepped forward to speak with her gave him hope. Direct, stern glares and a jerk of his thumb caused three of the men to leave. He'd had to hike around the outer perimeter until he convinced the remaining ones to find other diversions.

At least with those six, he'd made his claim known. After taking a deep breath, he stepped through the trees toward the musician who'd captured his soul. Now he could only hope for Sorcha to be as accepting after the coolness he'd displayed.

Sorcha plucked the last notes of "My Lady Greensleeves,"

then pressed a bare hand flat on the harp's metal strings to still their vibrations. Although normally she sought solitude to play, during the past month, she'd learned privacy was a hard state to achieve in a place filled with so many men.

She'd been grateful Lang granted her request for her and Blinne to take the midday and evening meals in the bunkhouse. The extra work Wikimak performed to keep two portions separate wasn't needed. Besides, eating with the men allowed for conversational practice. She only wished Lang wasn't so obvious in his aloofness. His sudden coldness the night of her first lesson hurt. Following his unexplained aloofness, she vowed that teaching must remain her true passion.

Crunching dirt announced the arrival of one from the many who had been listening.

She glanced around, and her traitorous heart fluttered faster. Over the past month, she told herself she had no right to expect his special attention. He'd provided a job when she needed one—nothing more. So why did the sight of the tall, handsome man heading her way set her atwitter? Facing forward, she reached for the harp's leather case and gasped at the sight of her bare hands.

"Don't put it away on my account."

"No?" She tucked her left hand under her leg. Had he noticed?

"*Nej.*" He dragged a fallen log a few feet closer and sat, facing her. "I miss hearing music. My papa and grandpa play the *nyckelharpa.*"

"I don't know that instrument." And she didn't care what he wanted to talk about, as long as the conversation continued. Her thoughts of the intervening time—that her feelings didn't amount to much and that she was better off with only her work—were all rubbish. A few moments in his proximity, and she knew Lang was a man she could truly care for.

"It's played with a bow like a fiddle, but finger keys stick out from the slender neck to change the tones." He demonstrated cradling an instrument across his forearm and in front of his body, mimicking the bow's movement.

"Interesting." She laid the harp across her thighs. To help calm her nervousness, she tapped her right fingers on the strings, producing a quiet hum.

"I apologize for my men disturbing you, Sorcha. If you're bothered by an audience, let me know. I can do better about keeping them away."

One look at his determined look—mouth set tight, brows furrowed—convinced her he'd do exactly that. What had happened to the smiling man she'd first bumped into? "I don't mind sharing my music." She tilted her head and smiled.

"I mind sharing you." In a slow move, he levered forward, positioning himself on his knees until their heads were only inches apart. "I've missed you. I was a fool to think I could deny my feelings."

Sucking in a surprised breath, she inhaled what little air existed between them. His words set her thoughts reeling. She reached out a hand to grasp his shirt front. "I wondered—"

Lang cut off her words with a brush of his lips over hers, then he eased back, eyebrows raised.

"Oh." Had he kissed her, or had she wished it? The touch was so light. Nodding, she tightened her hold, pulling more shirt fabric into her fist.

Smiling, he circled an arm around her shoulders and eased her close.

His chest was a muscled wall, and she relished its solidity. For too long, she'd ached to be enclosed in a strong embrace... Lang's secure embrace. Sorcha bent back her head and closed her eyes. His lips nuzzled her forehead, her cheeks, her chin, and finally the tip of her nose. The subtle seduction hammered her pulse, but the wayward touches left her mouth aching for a real kiss. A moan escaped, followed by heat flaming her cheeks at the expression of her need.

Then he pulled back and released his hold.

Wondering what stopped him, she popped open her eyes. At the sight of him setting the harp into its case, she couldn't stop a smile. She'd forgotten she held it. When she saw his outstretched hand, she let him pull her to a stand.

Lang wrapped one arm around her back and cupped her chin with his free hand, then gazed into her eyes. His breaths panted through opened lips.

Blood whooshed in her ears, and she returned the look, marveling at the various shades of blue in his eyes. Then he moved too close for her to focus, and she savored the sensation of his warm lips nibbling at hers, first from one direction—then he angled her chin higher and pressed harder. Sorcha slipped her arms around his waist and held tight as the kiss intensified, scrambling her senses. Her knees wobbled.

"Steady." Lang moved his other arm to support her and leaned back. "You all right?"

"I'm wonderful." She was glad to notice that his breathing was as quick and raspy as her own.

"How did the injury happen?"

"Oh, you saw that?" She shook her head. "I don't like to expose its ugliness to others." She let out a breath and lifted her left hand between their bodies. "It happened in a clothing factory where I worked several years ago. A piece of metal flew off a weaving loom and sliced my two fingers so badly, they had to be amputated."

He cupped her hand and grazed a thumb over the scar. "Must have hurt."

"It did, but the injury is also what made me decide I wanted to become a teacher." *Am I really sharing this personal story?* "I took a good look around and noticed I wasn't the only maimed worker, some being youngsters of seven or eight years. I knew then I wanted to bring education to children so they would not be forced to work in unsafe conditions."

"Such an admirable reason." Holding her gaze, he lifted her hand and brushed tiny kisses along her scar. "I'm so sorry you had to suffer. But if you hadn't, then you wouldn't have traveled west, and we'd never have met."

Seeing his lips touch the puckered skin clenched her stomach. In the next moment, his open acceptance rushed hot tears to her eyes, and she blinked them back. "I would have missed out on so much."

Lang rested a hand on her shoulder. "Speaking of missing out ... I want to be part of mealtime conversations where everyone around you and Blinne wears a smile as they eat. Tonight I request the honor of dining next to you."

"Consider the spot yours ... always." She hoped her words weren't too forward, but she no longer wished to hide her feelings.

With a nod, he gestured toward the camp. "We should return separately."

"Why?" Frowning, she stepped back. With a sharp exhale, she stooped to gather her gloves. Anger tightened her muscles, and she fumbled to unlatch the clasp. "Are you ashamed of me?"

Lang wrapped an arm around her waist and pulled her struggling body against his length. "Hey, stop." He pressed his cheek along her neck. "That's not what I meant."

Her resistance ceased, but she stood rigid within his hold, trembling. The warmth of his body seeping through her clothes strangely comforted her. "What did you mean?"

He turned her in his arms and cupped her cheeks then smiled. "Our feelings are too new. We need to become better acquainted, don't you agree?"

Part of her did, and the other part—the bigger part—enjoyed being swept away. "I suppose." She stepped back from his hold and brushed a hand over her skirt. "I'll go first." After grabbing her gloves, she pulled them on, then lifted her case. "See you at supper?"

He winked. "Count on it."

Each step she took proved harder than the last one. What she wanted was to return to his arms and soak in that feeling of security his strength offered. Ahead, the small hut behind her cabin came into view. Wanting one last look of Lang in their special spot, she drew in a quick breath and glanced over her shoulder. But all she saw was trees.

Nine

OVER THE NEXT week, as she went about her routine, Sorcha doubted her feet touched the ground. The men responded quicker than she expected to the lessons. Her idea of breaking them into groups facilitated spontaneous conversations. By rotating the slates, each with three sentences to copy, then practice reading, she exposed them to twelve new sentences a night. If a group finished early, they worked with flashcards she'd copied from Missus Mortimer's teaching sheets. Mister Morgan at the mercantile supplied her with scraps of torn paperboard from his deliveries, which served well for the cards.

Sitting near Lang at meals was a treat and allowed her to overhear his remarks to his crew. Although she didn't understand all the words, she recognized his caring or teasing tone, admiring his behavior. He also prompted the men to respond in English if they could.

But the walks following the class were her favorite times. With the warm evenings, they walked the perimeter of the clearing. If anyone crossed their path, she changed the topic to something about the curriculum. She never knew when he'd pull her into the shelter of the forest and sneak kisses during their walk. Each embrace grew longer and each kiss grew hotter, until heat flamed her cheeks. Thankfully, Blinne never said a word when Sorcha slipped into the cabin.

On Friday, she got an idea about using the next day's planned trip to the mercantile as a teaching experience for her best students. In her excitement, she dashed into the logging office without knocking. "Lang, listen to—"

"What the dickens, Sorcha?" Lang jumped to his feet and shoved a letter in a desk drawer before slamming it shut.

She stilled and clasped her hands at her waist. "I apologize. Did I startle you?"

"No. I was concentrating on ..." He jammed a hand through his hair and looked over her shoulder out the window. "Never mind. What do you want?"

The tone sounded like the same gruff one he used the first night of class, and she wasn't sure how to respond. "Well, I thought we might—"

"If this is about your class, can't you work out the problem yourself?" He jammed both hands on his hips. "Don't I pay you a salary to manage these issues?"

"Of course, Mister Ingemar. I'm so sorry I bothered you." Keeping her head high, she marched across the clearing. She vowed to dismiss class ten minutes early tonight so she could be gone by the time Lang showed up. Why risk being subjected again to his foul mood?

The next morning, Sorcha stepped outside at the appointed time for the weekly trip to Seattle for supplies.

Blinne closed the door. "I'm looking forward to an outing. As happy as I am with our life here, I enjoy going to town and seeing new people too." She retied the ribbons of her new straw hat. "Your blouse turned out well."

Sorcha glanced down at the tailored design, sewn in fabric with small yellow flowers that set off her hair color. "Thank you for the use of the pattern."

The rattle of harness chains and the heavy clumps of horses' hooves cut off further conversation.

Reaching into her skirt's side pocket, Sorcha pulled out a chunk of carrot and walked up to the first stocky horse with her hand extended flat. "Hello, *Kung*." She repeated the greeting to *Tvilling*, *Blixt*, and *Áska*, feeding each a treat. Then she strode past the driver's seat, where Lang sat. She'd decided to ride in the wagon bed with Sten and Nels for last-minute practice.

As he assisted her climb onto the dropped gate, Nels's grin kept spreading.

She settled herself opposite the two men and had them recite the script she'd written. With only part of her attention was she aware of Blinne's lively chatter and Lang's monosyllabic answers.

As soon as he set the brake on the wagon in front of Morgan's Mercantile, Lang jumped down and ran around to the back. "Please allow me to help you, Sorcha." He glared at Sten and Nels, who remained sitting before he lowered the gate.

Biting back a smile, Sorcha stood, then walked to the back of the wagon bed. "Of course."

Lang clasped his hands at her waist and swung her down to the packed dirt street. With a hand on her elbow, he took a breath. "I'm sorry for snapping at you yesterday, Sorcha, but you really didn't need to avoid me last night."

The scent of his citrus soap teased her nostrils, and she fought not to inhale. "The sun had barely set, and I am capable of walking the *incredibly short distance* in the twilight." She angled her head and glanced at him with a cocked eyebrow.

"I received . . . bothersome news from home that I had to deal with. And you caught me in the middle of my deliberations."

"I'm sorry." Now she felt awful for thinking he had an issue with her that caused his mood.

"*Tack*, er, thanks." He walked toward the front and scooped up a leather satchel from under the seat. "The matter has been dealt with."

Sten and Nels hopped down from the wagon, and Sten helped Blinne from the wagon seat.

Inside the store, Sorcha tagged along behind Blinne as she wandered the aisles, looking at practically everything as usual.

Lang went straight to the counter, where Mister Morgan stood, and handed over a list of needed supplies. He talked with the man as he pulled items to fill several crates.

When she suspected Mister Morgan had finished, she signaled to Sten and Nels to approach the counter.

Glancing at his crew, Lang creased his brow.

Sorcha hurried to the end of the closest aisle to listen.

"Meester Morgun." Sten cleared his throat. "I want candy."

"Sure. What would you like?" The storeowner waved a hand at the glass jars displayed on the back wall.

"I want candy, two sticks." Sten placed two copper pennies on the counter.

Her pulse pounded in her ears. Sorcha mouthed the words as Sten spoke, then glanced at Lang.

Lang's eyes widened, and a grin formed.

Mister Morgan turned to lift down the jar.

Nels stepped forward. "Yes, and *jag vill*—"

"I want," Sorcha whispered.

Without looking around, he nodded. "I want lemon drops ... um ... for nickel." He slapped down the silver coin.

Grinning, Sorcha clapped her hands, barely making a sound. But she shared a long look with Lang, accepting his wink as high praise. The first test of her teaching was a success.

The second jar landed on the counter, and the transaction finalized.

"Well done." Lang clapped each man on the shoulder. "You've learned well. Now help me load these into the wagon." The last he spoke in Swedish.

Sorcha glanced around for Blinne, who chatted with a dark-haired woman near the bolts of fabric.

"Sorcha, come." Blinne waved a beckoning hand.

She crossed the floor and offered the stranger a smile.

"Sorcha Geraghty, meet Missus Harriet Munns." Blinne waved a hand between the two women. "She arrived here with Mercer's first expedition two years ago. She traveled as Harriet Silverton, but she found a husband, Caleb, here in Seattle. Isn't that wonderful?"

"Blinne, let the woman speak." Sorcha bobbed her head. "A pleasure to meet you, Missus Munns." She glanced at the woman's thick middle, then back to her shiny blue eyes. "You appear to be thriving in your adopted city."

"Call me Harriet. I'm glad to meet more women. I was away when the ship arrived, and I've been busy catching up with my private tutoring." She rested a hand on her rounded stomach. "Actually, I recently visited Lizzie Ordway in her school on Whidbey Island."

Sorcha sucked in a breath. "Really? She was my Sunday School teacher back home in Lowell. How far away does she live?"

"Thirty miles to Everett, then a short ferry ride."

A distance that Sorcha heard others say was not considered far in Washington Territory. "You have private students?"

She nodded. "Since my pregnancy is advancing, the doctor recommended I give up teaching the children of the dock workers. So I arranged for a Miss Fleming from your group to take over the class."

On impulse, Sorcha reached out and clasped Harriet's hand. "I'm glad to hear of your success. I'm working at the logging company, teaching the loggers English, but my first love is schooling children."

The bell over the door rang.

"Miss Sorcha, Lang say we go." Nels stood in the doorway, his hat clamped in his hands.

The women said their goodbyes, and Sorcha and Blinne walked out to the wagon. This time, Sorcha claimed her usual place in the middle of the seat. On the return trip, everyone was in high spirits over Sten's and Nels's successful transaction.

"I don't like the looks of that." Lang raised a hand to provide more shade than his hat brim.

"What?" Sorcha followed Lang's squinted gaze and spotted a single rider heading their way fast. She'd never seen one of the big Finnhorses the camp used gallop. The flaxen mane and tail rippled with each step.

"What's wrong?" Lang stood in the wagon.

"*Stanna.*" Torg reined in the horse, then angled it until he stopped next to Lang. "Roald is hurt."

Lang dropped to the seat and slapped the reins on the team's backs. "Direct me."

Sorcha grabbed tight and held on as he raced the horses up the path, through the camp, and into the forest until she spotted a crowd of men, all looking upward.

Without saying a word, Lang handed Sorcha the reins and jumped out, shouting orders in Swedish. At the base of a tall tree, he strapped on climbing spikes, grabbed a thick belt with a rope attached, circled it around the tree, slipped it in a metal loop, and started climbing.

Two other men followed, keeping just below Lang's position.

"No." Her scream didn't turn a single head. Heart pounding against her ribs, Sorcha watched Lang lead the way up the trunk until her neck hurt from the awkward angle.

Blinne pressed close, a fist clamped against her mouth.

He reached the unconscious bearded man hanging upside down, his right leg clamped by a rope and the top of the tree swinging free. Lang kicked himself away from the trunk to jump around Roald's body. Next he tossed the end of the rope over an upper branch.

"I can't watch." Sorcha covered her face with her hands. Tully had been lost to her because of his dangerous choice, and she swallowed back a sob. Not again. "Is he all right?"

"They're strapping Roald onto some kind of litter."

Sorcha spread her fingers and watched through the spaces. Tense moments passed as the three men shared the weight of lowering the inert man to safety. Until Lang walked on the forest floor, she didn't take a full breath.

Someone jumped into the wagon and steered it in a circle.

At the moment she caught Lang's gaze, she charged forward. "You told me you worked as a manager. Someone who organizes and works from an office." She angled a stiff arm toward the tree. "What you just did looked so dangerous."

His head jerked back. "Not for me."

"What's that mean?"

"I do anything to protect my guys. Not everyone on the logging crew has my skill set. I spent years in Sweden as a tree topper, and I knew what had to be done."

Her lips quivered. "But you could have been hurt."

His gaze narrowed. "Life includes dangers, Sorcha—some we can control, and others we cannot. Look at you . . ." He jerked his chin toward her hand. "You were sitting at a loom inside a sturdy building, and you got hurt. An injury that's much worse than Roald's lump on his forehead."

"I can't be around such danger." What she wished she'd said was, *I can't love someone who runs toward danger.* Echoes of her pleas to Tully when he wanted to enlist sounded in her head. She'd sworn never again.

"That's part of being a logger." He leaned close and stared into her eyes. "If you don't like it, then maybe you shouldn't be here. Excuse me, I have to take Roald into town to see the doctor."

At his words, she staggered backward, her heart cracking. Then she turned toward the cabin. The walk was long enough to solidify her plan. A day and a half later, she stepped off the ferry onto Whidbey Island and asked directions to Miss Lizzie Ordway's house in Coupeville. A local farmer gave her a ride, and soon she knocked on the front door, using the pretext of satisfying a family obligation, or at least a Lowell, Massachusetts, one.

"Of course, I remember you, Sorcha. Always so inquisitive." Lizzie, a plain-looking woman, waved a hand inside. "I'm in the middle of a lesson, but we'll have tea when I'm done." Sorcha soaked up every tidbit of advice Lizzie offered during her short stay. Sure, Lizzie bestowed pats on the shoulders or backs and received smiling thanks from student and parent alike, which enlivened her features into a joyful look. But after the lesson ended, the children went home to their families, and the house became too quiet. Dedication to her profession, to the exclusion of having a man in her life, was Lizzie's choice.

Lang waited until Roald was back in his bunk and on the mend before he knocked on Sorcha's cabin door. He'd heard from the crew she'd cancelled a couple classes. By now she should be ready to hear his full explanation, and then she'd understand his actions.

The door opened.

"Hello, Blinne. I've come to see Sorcha."

"How's Roald?" Her brow wrinkled, and she clasped a hand at her throat.

"Something bigger than an eighteen-inch thick trunk is needed to hurt that guy."

"Sorry, Lang, but Sorcha left the day of the accident. Come inside." She walked to the desk and collected a note.

Dread balled in his stomach, but he accepted the envelope and ripped it open.

Dear Lang, I'm taking your advice and leaving the camp. You're probably correct that I need a different setting. Count my absence as the interview days in April and May I was promised. I'm sorry I disappointed you. Yours, S.

Pain ripped across his chest. He crumpled the note in his fist. "I had no idea she would react in this way."

Blinne's eyes shot wide. "She's coming back."

"You're sure? I've never seen her as angry as that day." He paced a few feet away and back.

"I'm sure." She smiled and nodded. "Sorcha would never leave me here for long."

He looked around the sitting room for evidence that Blinne spoke the truth. The harp case rested next to the desk. Relief unknotted his stomach. Nestled in the corner under a shelf were a stack of small books—the size that would fit into a child's hand. "What are those?"

Blinne walked to the desk and pulled out the stack. "On our long voyage, Sorcha wrote stories based on favorite Irish proverbs and blessings. She figured to supplement the children's reading." She shrugged. "So far, she hasn't used them, because the men aren't quite ready for some of the longer words."

An idea on how to structure his apology struck, but did he have enough time?

When Sorcha stepped into the passenger coach two days later, she'd made her choice, which included something—rather, someone—different. She wanted both to teach and to have a family of her own.

A thump sounded against the wheel, and a man climbed into the coach. He struggled to get inside with a crutch to compensate for his missing leg.

Once the coach was underway, she waited until he was settled. "Did you fight in the war, sir?"

"Naw. Not many from the territory did. Had no skin in the game." He patted his leg, which ended at the knee. "I own a Smithson's Dry Goods in Olympia. Last year, I was offloading a barrel of molasses that toppled off the ramp and crushed my leg. Doc Simms couldn't save it."

How unfortunate... and in his own shop. "I'm so sorry."

"Could be worse. I could be blind and not enjoy talking with a lovely lady like you." His wide grin exposed a missing eye tooth.

They chatted for several minutes, until he slept. Gazing out the side window, she pondered the rational reasons why she shouldn't be in love with Lang. Not a single one proved strong enough to counter the feelings of being alive when she was with Lang and lost when they were apart. Before she met him, he'd obviously done whatever task was needed at the top of the tree many times. Her fear over losing him to danger wasn't logical, especially when she learned that a "safe" profession had its dangers. Not when he had been supportive in so many other ways.

Doc Thompson was happy to give Sorcha a ride back to camp on his way to an outlying farm. "Too bad you're returning so late. You missed the town celebration."

"Right, today is the Fourth of July. Well, I'm sorry not to have seen it." She wondered what those at the camp had done. Had they come into town, or had Wikimak fixed a special meal?

By the time the buggy reached the clearing, the reddish sun shot its last rays through the stand of trees. The only building with lights brightening the windows was the biggest structure.

"Looks like everyone's in the bunkhouse." Doc tied off the reins and climbed to the ground. "I'd best have a look at those stitches in Roald's head." He helped her down before collecting her satchel from the luggage boot at the back.

She entered the bunkhouse, surprised to see the room set up for her class and all the men seated. Lang stood where she normally did, holding her pointer. All she saw was his profile, but the sight was enough to set her blood racing.

A grinning Blinne sat in a chair against the wall and waved.

"You're next, Torg."

Torg rose with a book held in his hand. "Bet-ter good man-ners than good looks."

Sten stood. "When the apple is ripe, it will fall."

Nels rose to his feet. "There is no fireside like your own fireside."

They read the titles from her proverbs stories. She glanced at Blinne, who must have provided the copies but couldn't catch her eye.

"May the sun shine ... all day long ... everything go

right . . . and nothing wrong. May those you love . . . bring love back to you . . . and may all the wishes . . . you wish come true" was recited by a row of men who said only three or four words each.

Her favorite Irish blessing. Blinne was definitely a participant. Pride swelled in her chest, and she swallowed hard against a dry throat. In her absence, someone coached her group. Their speaking cadence was smoother, and a few mastered new words.

After handing off the pointer to the nearest man, Lang turned, cradling a small book, but he didn't look at it. "*Jag älskar dig, puls i mitt hjärta.*"

A tingle ran over her skin. *Jag* meant "I" and *dig* meant "you," but she was lost about the other words. Sorcha pursed her lips and shrugged. A quick look around informed her that all her students wore wide smiles. *What is happening?*

Clearing his throat, Lang held up the opened book and glanced at it. "*Is tú mo ghrá—*"

He's speaking Gaelic. Sorcha gasped and smacked a hand over her mouth to keep from speaking.

"*Is tú mo ghrá, A chuisle mo chrá.*"

Tears welled in her eyes, and she swallowed against the hard lump in her throat.

Lang set down the book and walked across the bunkhouse, his smile growing. "In any language, Sorcha Geraghty, I love you, pulse of my heart. Will you marry me?" He reached for her hands and brought their handclasp tight against his chest.

"*Ja.*" She blinked hard, but a tear slid down her cheek as she gazed into his teal-blue eyes. "Many times *ja.*"

Lang flattened her left hand, reached into his trouser pocket, and then dropped something into her gloved palm.

Finally, she looked down and saw a silver ring with a chain of the same color bunched around it.

"Wearing the ring on a necklace is better, because it will rest closer to your heart." Lang lifted it from her hand and looped the chain over her head.

Speechless, she could only reach up to cup his jaw. "You're inside my heart."

"Let's set off these Roman candles and celebrate the ninetieth birthday of the United States." Staffen strode through the door, carrying a crate full of long cylinders.

Flashing lights and sparkly stars lit the night sky in long arches, accompanied by whizzing sounds.

Hand in hand, she and Lang walked outside to share in the celebration. But all Sorcha really cared about was the love shining in Lang's eyes as he drew her close for their most perfect kiss.

Linda Carroll-Bradd: As a young girl, I spent lots of my free time lying on my bed reading about fascinating characters having exciting adventures in places far away and in other time periods. In later years, I discovered and devoured family saga stories and romance novels. At a certain point, I grew cocky enough to think I could write one of these stories. Then I learned what a balancing act writing a novel is, but I wasn't deterred. Twelve years later, my first fiction sale was achieved--a confession story.

After reading Debra Holland's "Montana Sky" series and Caroline Fyffe's "Prairie Hearts" series, I wanted to try my hand at historicals. I was thrilled to be invited to contribute to Sweetwater Springs Christmas and continued writing in the Montana Sky world by developing my Entertainers of the West series.

Married with 4 adult children and 2 granddaughters, I now write heartwarming contemporary and historical stories with a touch of humor and a bit of sass from my home in the southern California mountains. Lots of my stories are set in Texas where I lived for a dozen years.

Visit Linda online:
Facebook: Linda Carroll-Bradd
Twitter: @lcarrollbradd

Dear Reader,

Thank you for reading *Mercer's Belles*. We hope you loved the sweet romance novellas! Each collection in the Timeless Western Collection contains three novellas. Sign up for our Timeless Romance newsletter and receive a free book: https://timelessromanceanthologies.blogspot.com

Your email will not be shared, and you may unsubscribe at any time. We always appreciate reviews but there is no obligation. Reviews and word-of-mouth are what help us continue this fun project.

If you're interested in becoming a regular reviewer of these collections and would like access to advance copies, please email Heather Moore: heather@hbmoore.com. We also have a blog where we post announcements as well as a Facebook page.

Thank you!
The Timeless Romance Authors

www.ingramcontent.com/pod-product-compliance
Lightning Source LLC
LaVergne TN
LVHW021801060526
838201LV00058B/3193